Christmas for the Bomber Girls

Vicki Beeby writes historical fiction about the friendships and loves of service women brought together by the Second World War.

Her first job was as a civil engineer on a sewage treatment project, so things could only improve from there. Since then, she has worked as a maths teacher and education consultant before turning freelance to give herself more time to write.

In her free time, when she can drag herself away from reading, she enjoys walking and travelling to far-off places by train. She lives in Shropshire in a house that doesn't contain nearly enough bookshelves.

GW00701687

Also by Vicki Beeby

The Women's Auxiliary Air Force

The Ops Room Girls
Christmas with the Ops Room Girls
Victory for the Ops Room Girls

The Wrens

A New Start for the Wrens
A Wrens' Wartime Christmas
Hopeful Hearts for the Wrens

Bomber Command Girls

The Girls of Bomber Command
A Wedding for the Bomber Girls
Christmas for the Bomber Girls

VICKI BEEBY

Christmas
for the
Bomber Girls

🔟CANELO

First published in the United Kingdom in 2024 by

Canelo
Unit 9, 5th Floor
Cargo Works, 1–2 Hatfields
London SE1 9PG
United Kingdom

A CIP catalogue record for this book is available from the British Library.

Print ISBN 978 1 80436 686 8
Ebook ISBN 978 1 80436 687 5

Cover design by Becky Glibbery

Cover images © Arcangel, Shutterstock

Look for more great books at www.canelo.co

Printed and bound in Great Britain by Clays Ltd, Elcograf S.p.A.

As always, to my family:

Mum

Duncan, Jana & Emma

Chris, Katka & Elena

Chapter One

November 1944

Pearl walked into the cosy breakfast room of the Teme Guest House, hand in hand with Greg. She caught his eye as they took their places at a table in the window and felt the heat of a blush rise to her cheeks. Taking a moment to compose herself, she gazed through the rain-spattered panes at Ludlow Castle. After eighteen months of marriage, one glance from him could still make her feel like a bride on her honeymoon.

Once the blush had subsided she met his gaze again and instantly regretted it. 'Don't look at me like that,' she murmured.

'Like what?'

Like he wanted to eat *her* for breakfast. It wouldn't have been a problem had they been alone, but the room was busy and they were attracting more than a few curious stares. She couldn't think why, unless it was because Greg looked so dashing in his Royal Australian Air Force uniform. Personally, the sight of it gave her a twinge of sadness, because it was a sign that his leave was ending and they only had another two hours together before he needed to begin the journey back to his unit.

Before she could say anything, a waitress who looked no more than fourteen or fifteen approached. 'Good morning, Mr and Mrs Tallis. Are you ready to order?' She pulled a pencil from her pocket and seemed to be having trouble controlling a tic at the corner of her mouth while she said, 'Our hens are laying well, so we can offer you an egg each, and we've also got some tasty sausages in fresh and a lovely lot of mushrooms.'

Once the girl had taken their order and returned to the kitchen, Pearl asked, 'Have I grown an extra nose? Only she was giving me some very strange looks.'

Greg's eyes twinkled. 'Nothing wrong with your nose. But possibly she'd noticed that your blouse is buttoned up all wrong.'

'What?' Pearl glanced down in horror only to see Greg was right: the pretty green and white polka-dot blouse was, indeed, buttoned askew. 'Why didn't you say something?' The blush that had only just started to recede flared again as she buttoned up her cardigan to the neck. Before leaving their room, Greg had pressed her against the door and treated her to a passionate kiss that her pulse had yet to recover from. She really should have checked her appearance in the mirror after that, but, understandably, she hadn't been thinking clearly.

'I didn't notice until now,' Greg said, looking smug. 'I was too busy admiring your messy hair.'

Pearl shot him an exasperated look and surreptitiously glanced at her reflection in her spoon. Even in the distorted image she could see that, while the left side of her hair was arranged in the same shoulder-length waves that she'd brushed it into before Greg had waylaid her at the door, the other side was looking distinctly mussed. She didn't have the heart to tell Greg off, though. Instead she simply tidied it as best she could with her fingers, the reason for their kiss uppermost in her mind. Who knew when they would see each other again?

Worse, now they were coming to the end of their five days together, she was painfully aware of all the things she had intended to discuss yet had put off, not wishing to spoil their rare time together with any conflict. But with the time ticking down to the moment they would have to part, the unspoken questions burned in her chest. They were important matters that needed to be talked over, and, as Allied troops were making their way across Europe, liberating areas that had been under Axis control for years, Pearl was feeling under increasing pressure to reach an understanding with Greg before the war ended. Questions like where they would live once they were free of their service: Australia or Britain? Would Greg object to her continuing to work after she left the WAAF, and was it time to start a family? Pearl had definite ideas about the last two questions at least, and maybe that was why she hadn't dared broach the subject.

As they tucked into their breakfasts, she considered introducing the question of where they should live. However, before she could say anything, Greg said, 'I might be able to get a forty-eight-hour pass next month. How would you feel about spending Christmas together?'

Pearl gratefully seized upon the excuse to avoid a difficult subject a while longer. 'Do you have to ask? It would be wonderful! Can you get the Saturday before Christmas off? Or at least arrive that evening. RAF Fenthorpe is having a party at Fenthorpe Hall.' Even though she was no longer attached to RAF Fenthorpe, and was now billeted in Lincoln, she maintained close links to her

3

former station, as her sister Thea and friend Jenny still lived and worked there.

'Sounds good. I'll see what I can do. It'll be fun to catch up with everyone.'

And the conversation turned to the latest doings at Fenthorpe. Pearl couldn't seem to find an opening to turn the conversation to more important matters, not that she tried too hard. All the while she was aware of their precious time together slipping away, and she was reluctant to introduce a subject that might cause friction.

It was only when they were on the train, having managed to secure a compartment all to themselves, that they addressed a more serious issue, and it was Greg who brought it up. Pearl had been staring out of the window, fighting tears, as the train drew away from the picturesque town of Ludlow and came ever closer to Shrewsbury, where they would part ways. Greg, who was at the end of his week's leave, was going on to the Operational Training Unit at Market Harborough, where he had been based ever since 28 OTU near Loughborough had been disbanded; Pearl was staying with her grandmother in Shrewsbury for the final two days of her leave.

'I've been thinking of volunteering for a second tour.'

It was as though an icy wind had torn through the carriage, leaching away all the warmth. Pearl stared at him in shock. 'You can't be serious.' Painful memories flooded her mind, of long, dark hours, standing in the cold, waiting as the Lancasters sent out on operations limped home. Of hearing reports of Lancasters going down in flames and praying that none of them were Greg's.

'I'm deadly serious. You know I wouldn't joke about this.'

Deadly. She wished Greg had used a different word. 'Why bring this up now? We've had five days together. You could have mentioned this at any time. Why wait until we've only got' – she glanced at her watch – 'half an hour left?'

Greg ran a finger under his collar. 'I knew you'd be upset. I didn't want to spoil our holiday.'

She could hardly blame him. Hadn't she done the same – avoided serious conversations because their precious time together was far too sweet to spoil by letting the war and real-life concerns come between them? All the same, it was too important a subject to be left to the last possible moment.

'So you decided to wait until there was no time left to discuss it properly? Why do I get the feeling you don't want to discuss it at all, but are simply letting me know what you've decided?'

'That's not true. I'm telling you now, aren't I? I wouldn't dream of making this decision without seeing how you felt.'

'Fine. Well, I should think my feelings are obvious. You've done your bit and survived when many others didn't, and now you want to do it all over again? You want *me* to go through that all over again? It's not as if you're doing nothing now. You're training new crews. Isn't that enough?'

Greg leaned forward and took her chilled hands between his. 'That's just it. I thought it would be. But the war's grinding on, and we need more and more crews to support our advance. I know what I'm doing now is contributing, but if I volunteered for another tour, I could be making a real difference. It could help shorten the war in Europe.'

Pearl clutched his hands as she struggled to find an answer that didn't sound selfish. After all, what gave her the right to forbid her husband from doing what he considered to be his duty when wives, mothers, sisters and aunts all across the world had no choice in the matter? Before she could think of anything, the train came to a juddering halt at the next station.

'Church Stretton!' the guard called. 'This is Church Stretton.'

The door to their compartment opened and a chilly gust of wind blew raindrops onto Pearl's face. Pearl and Greg were forced to stop holding hands to allow two women burdened with cases climb aboard. Greg sprang up and helped place their baggage on the overhead rack, and, by the time he took his seat again, the train was already moving, the two women discussing knitting patterns in carrying voices.

All Pearl could do was gaze at Greg helplessly, not wishing to say what was on her heart with an audience. 'I'll think about it,' she said finally. Then, aware that their time was running out, she said, 'Promise you'll write as soon as you get back.'

'Of course I will. I'm going to miss you.'

Their last minutes together sped by, no matter how much Pearl wished she could slow time. All too soon the train was crossing the Severn with a screech of brakes before coming to a standstill at the platform. She didn't need the guard to tell her they had arrived at Shrewsbury. They climbed down, and Pearl stood with their bags while

Greg went to enquire about the train to Birmingham, the next stop on his journey.

'Birmingham?' she heard the guard reply. He pointed at a train standing on the next platform. 'Better hurry, it leaves in one minute.'

Greg dashed back, and she melted into his arms.

'I have to go,' he said into her hair.

'I know.' She kissed him and, when she broke their embrace, it felt as though she was tearing herself in half. Then she spoke in a rush. 'Take care of yourself. Promise you won't make any decisions until we've had a chance to talk properly.'

'I will, and I promise. See you at Christmas!' Then Greg was sprinting across the platform. He swung himself on board the train just as the guard's shrill whistle cut through the clamour of the crowded platform. For a brief time she saw him waving to her through the window, then the train gave a jolt as its brakes were released, and a swirling cloud of steam billowed between them, obscuring her view and overwhelming her with the smells of hot metal, coal and oil. Slowly, the train chugged away from the station. Pearl waved until it could no longer be seen. Then she picked up her case with a heavy heart, already counting down the days to Christmas.

—

When Deedee heard the knock at the door, she flew to answer, still clutching the duster she was using to give Pearl's room a last-minute clean. Knowing that her granddaughter would have recently said goodbye to Greg, she was fully prepared for the red-rimmed eyes and blotchy face that greeted her and guessed that Pearl must have been weeping all the way from the station.

'There now, dear. Come on in and warm yourself by the fire.' She relieved Pearl of her bags, setting them at the foot of the stairs, then helped her out of her coat, damp from the steady drizzle.

Pearl sniffed, dabbing her eyes with a damp handkerchief. 'I'm sorry to be such a misery. I *have* been looking forward to seeing you. I thought the walk would help, but...' Her face crumpled, and the remainder of her words were unintelligible through sobs.

Deedee wrapped a comforting arm round Pearl's heaving shoulders and steered her into the parlour. She had lit a fire before going to put the finishing touches to Pearl's room, and it needed no more than a fresh shovel of coal to bring it to a roaring blaze. 'Settle down here while I make us a pot of tea, then you can tell me all about it.'

A short while later, Pearl sat in Deedee's most comfortable armchair cradling a cup of tea while she poured out her story. 'I can't believe he waited until the very last minute to break the news,' she said in the end.

Examining Pearl by the glow of the firelight, Deedee observed the fine lines of strain around her granddaughter's mouth and eyes and wondered if there was more to the tears than Greg's abrupt announcement. 'I expect he was reluctant to spoil your time together,' she said carefully.

Pearl nodded. She seemed to have got the tears under control now and was able to speak without her voice wobbling. 'That's what he said.'

'And he did promise not to make a final decision until you'd had a chance to talk it over properly,' Deedee reminded her.

Pearl nodded again, gazing into her teacup, but didn't reply.

'You don't think he was lying, do you?' Deedee felt a jolt of alarm. She had always considered Greg to be the perfect match for Pearl. It had warmed Deedee's heart to see how her granddaughter had gradually opened up under Greg's encouragement, and started to explore who she was, free from the weight of obligation she seemed to feel over Thea's upbringing. Where Deedee had tried and failed to persuade Pearl to enjoy her freedom, Greg had succeeded, although Deedee doubted Pearl would ever completely let go of her need to care for her younger sister.

Deedee's fear seemed to rouse Pearl from her distraction. 'Oh, no. I do trust him.' She sighed a deep sigh that seemed to emanate from the depths of her soul. 'The thing is, do I really want to be the kind of wife who holds her husband back from doing what he believes to be right?'

There was nothing Deedee could say in response, because the fact that Pearl could put the question in those terms was an answer in itself.

Pearl gave a humourless chuckle. 'You've brought me up to be free-thinking, and I've always appreciated that, although' – here a glint of genuine humour lit her eyes – 'I do wonder if you didn't go a bit too far in that respect with Thea.'

Deedee joined in the laughter, glad to see that Pearl could still see humour in dark situations. 'You leave Thea out of this. She's not the one who turned up on my doorstep in tears.'

'I know.' Pearl gave another sigh. 'I suppose it hit me today that I don't feel as though my relationship with Greg has grown. I mean, I love him, but I'd have thought things would have moved on after eighteen months of marriage. Every time we meet, I feel like we're no different from being newly-weds.'

Deedee couldn't help herself. 'Must be fun, though.'

Pearl glared at her, faint spots of red glowing on her cheeks. 'Honestly, Deedee, there are times I wonder which of us is the elder.'

'I'm sorry,' Deedee said, not feeling at all repentant. 'But in a way you are still newly-weds. How much time have you actually spent together since the wedding? You haven't even lived together.'

Pearl frowned and appeared to do some complicated calculations on her fingers. 'About seven weeks,' she said, eventually.

'There you are, then. You can't expect to be acting like an old married couple after less than two months of actual time spent together.'

Pearl's brow cleared. 'What about you and... Grand-father?' As ever, when speaking of the man who had been gone long before Pearl's arrival in the world, Pearl hesitated as though not knowing how to refer to him. 'How long did it take before you got used to each other's ways?'

'A while,' Deedee said, deliberately vague. 'But times were different then, of course. You mustn't be too hard on yourself.'

'But you don't think I got married too soon?'

Ah. So this was what Pearl was really worried about. 'What do you think?'

'I didn't have any doubts at the time.'

'Then it was the right thing to do.'

'But there's so much we haven't discussed,' Pearl persisted. 'At the time, all I cared about was being with Greg and having as much time together in case… in case the worst happened.'

Deedee nodded. 'And now Greg's survived the last eighteen months, you're having second thoughts?'

'Of course not. How can you—? Oh, you're pulling my leg.' Pearl glared at Deedee. 'I see what you're doing.' She drained her tea and placed the cup on the tea tray before continuing. 'Of course I don't regret marrying Greg when I did. But I'm beginning to see that we got married so quickly we never sat down and talked about the things we should probably have worked out before we got married.'

'Like?'

'Like where we're going to live after the war. Will he want to go back to Australia? I never even considered it. And does he want children? I'd like to start a family eventually, but right now I want to carry on working. What will he think about that?'

Deedee nodded. 'You're right, these are all very important questions, and in normal times you would have had time to discuss it all and reach an understanding. But even though you've not had much time together, surely you've not spent every moment in bed. You must have paused for breath occasionally.'

'Deedee!'

Pearl looked so outraged that Deedee couldn't hold back her laughter. 'I know, I know. Apparently an old woman like me isn't supposed to know how it feels to be young and in love. Well, I've got news for you. The only difference between now and my young days is that it took a lot longer to get out of one's clothes. Be thankful for the advances in women's fashion, my girl.'

Pearl's face was glowing beetroot red, but she was smiling. 'Honestly, you're worse than Thea. But seriously, what do you think I should do?'

'You need to work out what's held you back. You had time to talk, so why have you avoided the big subjects?'

From the way Pearl bit her lip and lowered her gaze, Deedee could tell this question had hit home. Eventually Pearl looked up, the blush fading. 'You're right.' She gave a twisted smile. 'I suppose every moment together has been so precious I haven't wanted to introduce any subject that might start an argument. I must be braver next time we meet.'

She rose, picking up the tea tray. 'Anyway, it's lovely to see you again, Deedee, and not just because you always give me good advice. When I come back, you'll have to tell me all your news.'

Deedee rose too. 'If you're volunteering to do the washing up, I'll tell you in the kitchen. I've been saving my rations to make a lamb hotpot. There's a recipe in one of the Ministry of Food leaflets I've been wanting to try. The trouble is, the recipes are all for four people. As it is, we'll have to eat the same thing tomorrow, but at least we can try it.'

'Sounds wonderful. Anything will be better than the food we get at my digs in Lincoln. Mrs Dale does her best to eke out the rations, but she's not the best of cooks.'

'Then let's hope this recipe lives up to expectations.'

A few hours later, Pearl mopped up the last of the gravy from her plate with a piece of bread and popped it into her mouth. Then she leaned back in her chair with a contented smile. 'Now that's a meal I don't mind repeating. Far better than anything I get in Lincoln. Thea's going to be green with envy when I tell her.'

'Talking of Thea, I had a letter from her yesterday.'

'Oh? It's been a couple of weeks since I've seen her. Does she have any particular news? I hope she's managed to avoid jankers without me being around.'

Deedee drew the letter from her pocket. Not that she needed to read it again, having already committed just about every word to memory, but it always gave her a warm glow to handle the letters her granddaughters sent her, and she usually kept one or two on her person. Pearl always wrote letters full of detail about life in Lincoln, enough to make Deedee feel as though she were there, witnessing the incidents Pearl described. Thea's letters were short on detail, but she more than made up for that with her breezy, informal style that never failed to make Deedee smile and feel as though Thea was there beside her, reading the letter aloud. 'She's full of news about a Christmas party being held in the officers' quarters.' She hesitated before adding, 'Most of the letter is spent trying to persuade me to come.'

'Oh, you should. We haven't been all together at Christmas since before the war.'

13

Deedee pursed her lips. 'I don't think this is about a family reunion. I think it's another effort of Thea's to get me and Thomas Haughton together.' In the letter, Thea had mentioned, apparently in passing, that Fenthorpe Hall, the large house currently being used as officers' quarters, just happened to be owned by Thomas Haughton.

'Ah.' A speculative gleam lit Pearl's eyes. 'Well, I'm sure Mr Haughton would love to see you again. I get the impression he's been quite lonely since his wife died.'

'Honestly, you girls are as bad as each other. Tom and I were different people when we knew each other. What happened is over fifty years in the past, and it's too late to reopen old wounds.' She immediately regretted mentioning wounds, knowing Pearl would be unlikely to let that lie.

She was right.

'Yet you've just advised me to talk to Greg about what's bothering me.'

'Yes, because you and Greg are married, and if you can't communicate with one another, your marriage is headed for trouble. Tom and I never married.' Even now, all these years later, Deedee felt a stab of pain at the memory. She hurried on, reminding herself sternly that she was no longer the young, naive girl who had thought she and Tom could overcome all their problems because they were in love. 'What's in the past should stay in the past. No good can come from meeting him again.' She had worked hard to rebuild her life and was contented here in Shrewsbury, knowing she had the love of her two granddaughters and her garden and volunteer work to keep her busy. She had no desire for change.

Pearl threw up her hands. 'You're right. I'm sorry.' Then she grinned. 'You can't blame me for being curious, though. And as for Thea, you only have yourself to blame, encouraging her to ask questions instead of staying quiet and doing as she was told like a good girl.'

Deedee snorted. 'In my experience, women have stayed quiet and done what they were told for far too long.' Then she saw Pearl's grin and shook her head. 'If you think you're going to get me that way, you've got another think coming. All you need to know about what happened between me and Tom is what I told Thea at your wedding. I'm sure Thea didn't waste any time in telling you.' Deedee had been unable to hide her shock that day when the man giving Pearl away had turned out to be none other than the man who had broken her heart fifty years earlier. When Thea had asked her about it, Deedee had been economical with the truth, telling Thea she had let Tom go because she had mistakenly believed it the best thing for them both. However, she had really said that to persuade a heartbroken Thea to mend her shattered relationship with Fitz, as Thea had been under the misguided impression that Fitz would be better off without her. Deedee had been so determined to see Thea happy that she had ruthlessly changed the facts to suit.

Pearl gave a rueful smile. 'She made sure to tell me before Greg and I left for our honeymoon. Are you sure there's nothing more you want to tell us? I still can't get used to you referring to him as Tom. No matter how many times he's asked me to call him Thomas, I can never think of him as anything other than Mr Haughton.'

'Quite sure. Now, do you want some ginger pudding? I made it especially.' Deedee felt a wistful pang, remembering someone else who had always enjoyed her cooking. 'It was your mother's favourite, too.'

As hoped, the mention of pudding proved a strong enough distraction, saving Deedee from having to field any more questions regarding Tom. She hoped and prayed neither Pearl nor Thea would ever discover the truth of her past, because she didn't think she could ever look them in the eye again if they knew what she had done.

Chapter Two

It was an evening three weeks later when Thea breezed into Pearl's office in Lincoln. Pearl was working on the dummy sheets for the next edition of the *Bombshell* with Jenny for company. Jenny had made a space for herself on Pearl's desk and was putting the finishing touches to an article on a day in the life of a parachute packer. Thea waved a letter in Pearl's face. 'Deedee says she won't come for Christmas.'

Pearl, knowing she wouldn't get any more work done that evening, put down her pencil. 'I told you she wouldn't. What else does she say?'

'Oh, just some stuff about the Shrewsbury Spitfire fund. Apparently she's volunteered to help with the fundraising. But why doesn't she want to come?'

'I don't know. Perhaps because she knows you're going to spend her whole visit trying to throw her together with Mr Haughton.' Pearl had already seen Thea, the week after her return from Shrewsbury, and explained what Deedee had told her about her reluctance to meet Thomas Haughton again, but Thea merely seemed to have taken it as a challenge.

'So what if I do? Deedee definitely seemed to regret losing him when she told me about him at your wedding.'

'She can't regret it too much. Don't forget she must have met our grandfather afterwards.'

Thea shrugged. 'Only he wasn't around for long, was he? And don't you think it strange Deedee doesn't often speak of him? Maybe he made her unhappy, in which case it's probably a good thing he died so young.'

Pearl gave Thea a sharp look. 'That's a horrible thing to say. You can't possibly know they were unhappy.'

'I've got a pretty good idea. I mean, look at Thomas. It's obvious he loved his wife – he often speaks of her, and you can tell he's sad she's no longer around. Don't you think Deedee would want to tell us all about our grandfather if he was someone she'd loved?'

Pearl hadn't looked at it that way before. 'I suppose you've got a point. I always thought it was because it hurt too much to speak of someone she still misses.' But now Thea had planted the idea in her head, she had to admit Deedee would have been more likely to want to tell her granddaughters all about their grandfather.

'She misses Mother, but she often talks about *her*.'

Pearl couldn't deny that, either.

Thea must have sensed her wavering, for she gave a triumphant grin. 'And you call yourself a journalist. Where's your curiosity, your investigative skills?'

Pearl was willing to concede that Thea had a point. 'I'll see if I can bring the subject round to Grandfather next time I see her. But promise you won't try and force her and Thomas together. She told me that seeing him would only reopen old wounds, and I think we should respect that. I don't want either of them getting hurt.'

Thea gave a glum nod. 'I won't get a chance, anyway, considering Deedee's determined not to set foot in Lincolnshire again.'

Although she seemed resigned, Pearl couldn't resist making sure. 'Promise me. Whatever happened in the past, it must have been a very long time ago, and they both seem content with their lot now. Please don't do anything to upset them.'

Whatever Thea might have said in response, Pearl would never know, for Mr Haughton's secretary put her head round the door, looking unusually grave. 'Excuse me, Corporal Tallis.'

Pearl beckoned her in and said with a wry smile, 'How many times do I have to ask you to call me Pearl? I always—'

The words died on her lips as she noticed first Mrs Norris's strained expression and then the envelope in her hand. It was thin and brown and bore the words: *POST OFFICE TELEGRAM*. She swallowed, her mouth suddenly dry. When she spoke, her voice was hoarse, and she had the strange feeling she wasn't speaking at all but was listening to someone else. 'For me?'

Mrs Norris nodded. A heavy silence descended over the room as Pearl took the envelope and opened it with hands that trembled so violently she could barely hold the paperknife. She was dimly aware of Thea and Jenny moving to stand on either side of her, although her whole attention was focused on the slip of paper she pulled from the envelope. The typed letters on the telegram form danced in front of her eyes, and it took a moment for the message to sink in.

REGRET TO INFORM YOU YOUR HUSBAND FLYING OFFICER GREGORY TALLIS IS MISSING AS A RESULT OF AIR OPERATIONS ON NIGHT OF 27/28 NOV STOP LETTER FOLLOWS STOP ANY FURTHER INFORMATION WILL BE IMMEDIATELY COMMUNICATED TO YOU

Pearl shook her head. 'No. They must have made a mistake.' She looked wildly from Thea to Jenny, willing them to agree. 'I know he was thinking of volunteering for another tour, but he would never actually do it without telling me.'

She belatedly became aware that Thea held her arm in a painful grip. With her free hand, her sister snatched the telegram and scanned it. 'It's from 14 OTU.'

This was the Operational Training Unit in Market Harborough where both Greg and Fitz were now stationed. Not a mistake, then. The communication was definitely about her Greg and not an error involving some other poor pilot with the same name.

Now Jenny spoke. 'I'm so sorry, Pearl. Something must have gone wrong on a training flight.'

But that made no sense either. 'Then why is he missing? Surely if there was an accident during a training flight, someone would have seen what happened. There would be…'

Bodies. She couldn't bring herself to say the word, but it didn't stop images flooding her mind. When she had first met Greg, she had been serving as a radio telephone operator at Fenthorpe and had talked a pilot down to land who had been struggling to maintain control of an aircraft on fire. Moments after he had escaped, the plane had been consumed by an uncontrollable blaze. The pilot had been Greg. And now she remembered Thea telling her of the time she had witnessed a trapped gunner burning to death. Had that happened to Greg? But then he would be reported as dead, not missing. Still, it didn't stop her thinking of burning bodies and praying that hadn't happened to Greg.

The pain in her arm brought her back to the present. She could feel every one of Thea's fingers digging into the flesh of her upper arm. She grasped her sister's wrist. 'Let go. That hurts.' Then she saw Thea's face, white and strained.

Thea released her grip and met Pearl's gaze. 'Sometimes they take more experienced crews on leaflet-dropping missions across the Channel,' she said in an agonised voice. 'If he went down over France or the Netherlands, say, that would explain why no one knows for sure what's happened.'

'Oh God, you're right.' Now it was Pearl's time to clutch her sister's arm. 'Fitz would know. You have to call him.'

She turned to Mr Haughton's secretary, who still hadn't left but stood in the doorway, twisting her hands together. 'Can you put a call through to 14 OTU for my sister?'

Mrs Norris, looking relieved to have a reason to escape the heavy atmosphere, said, 'Of course. I'll see what I can do.' She scurried away.

It was only then that Thea's anguished expression seeped into her consciousness. 'What if Fitz isn't there?'

her sister said. 'What if he was on the flight too? They wouldn't tell me. The telegram would go to his mother.'

It was the need to support Thea that brought Pearl fully back to her senses. 'I never thought of that.'

The wait for the call seemed interminable. Pearl sat at her desk, gazing unseeingly at the papers spread in front of her. Jenny sat beside her, looking as stunned as Pearl felt, and Pearl supposed she was thinking about Edwin Holland, another member of Greg's old crew, who was also now serving at 14 OTU. Jenny had been friends with Edwin when he had been at RAF Fenthorpe, and Pearl had suspected that they had feelings for one another, although Jenny usually protested that they were no more than friends. Even so, Jenny must be wondering if Edwin was safe.

Thea paced around the small office, saying nothing but jumping every time the sound of a ringing telephone echoed down the corridor.

When the telephone on Pearl's desk shrilled, Pearl's heart constricted, and she gazed at it, frozen, unable to force her muscles to obey her will and answer it.

In two strides, Thea reached the desk and snatched up the receiver. 'Hello? Yes, thank you.' There was a pause in which Pearl knew the secretary was putting through the call to RAF Market Harborough. Then Thea spoke again. 'Hello. I'm trying to reach Flying Officer James Fitzgerald, or his CO if that's easier.' She gave the name of Fitz and Greg's commanding officer. There followed another pause that stretched out for an age. Then Pearl heard the sound of a tinny voice coming through the receiver, although she couldn't make out any words.

Thea stood up straighter. 'Hello, yes. This is LACW Thea Cooper.' She started to gabble. 'I'm Fitz's girlfriend, but I'm really ringing on behalf of my sister, Flying Officer Tallis's wife.' She paused, obviously listening to whoever was speaking on the other end of the line. The colour flooded back into her cheeks, and the tension seemed to drain from her body. 'He is? Oh, thank God.'

Pearl felt a surge of hope and had to restrain herself from snatching the receiver from Thea's hands. She waited in tense silence while Thea spoke again, although it was hard to hear through the pulsing blood in her ears. She was dimly aware of Jenny's arm round her shoulder. Her hearing gradually came back in time to hear Thea say, 'Yes, I'll tell her,' before replacing the receiver.

'Who did you speak to? What did he say?' Pearl demanded.

'That was Squadron Leader Cole. It's as we thought. Greg was taking a crew on a leaflet drop and they didn't return. That's all he knows at the moment, but—'

'But you sounded relieved. I thought that meant he was safe.'

Thea crouched beside Pearl's chair, biting her lip. 'I'm so sorry. I wasn't thinking. Cole said Fitz was on his way up here to report to you in person, and I was so relieved he wasn't missing too I didn't think.'

Pearl knew she couldn't blame her. She would feel the same were their situations reversed. Nevertheless, she couldn't help feeling a stab of jealousy. It was so unfair for Greg to be missing while Thea, who always got what she wanted, was happy because Fitz was safe. No matter that she hated herself for feeling that way, she couldn't help it. Praying that her feelings didn't show, she forced a smile.

'Fitz is coming? That's kind of him.' And it was. Fitz was a lovely man and perfect for Thea.

Thea nodded. 'He's got a forty-eight-hour pass. He's been holding off on applying for it, waiting until I can get one too, but he must have badgered Cole into giving him leave the moment Greg was reported missing. Cole said he's coming up to explain what he knows. He had to finish up some paperwork before leaving, but he's on the way now. No idea what time he'll get here, but I should go to the station to wait for him. You should wait here with Jenny. Is there anything else I can do before I leave?'

There was no mistaking Thea's concern and love. It brought tears to Pearl's eyes, and suddenly she couldn't stem the flood. Cold reality crashed down upon her, and she felt like a terrified child trapped in a nightmare. And just as she had when she was a child, she wanted the only person who always made her feel better. 'Deedee,' she said. 'I want Deedee.'

–

Deedee was just pulling on her coat, getting ready to go to a Women's Voluntary Service meeting, when the rattle of the door knocker made her jump. Answering the door, she saw a messenger boy, his bicycle propped on the path behind him.

'Telegram for Mrs Pritchard.'

Her head in a spin, Deedee took the telegram, and the lad had mounted his bike and was sailing down the lane before it fully dawned on her what had just happened. She stepped back into the hall and opened the envelope. Her first thought was that something had happened to Thea. Pearl she was less concerned about now she mostly worked in Lincoln, but, ever since Thea had told her of the accident that had killed her fellow instrument repairer the previous year, she had worried about Thea's safety.

It was a relief to see that the message was from Thea, but the relief was short-lived.

GREG MISSING STOP PEARL NEEDS YOU STOP WILL CALL SHOP 5PM THEA

Greg! Deedee's heart went out to Pearl as she remembered how worried she had been during her recent visit. It seemed her fears had been justified. She glanced into the parlour, at the clock on the mantelpiece. There was still an hour before Thea's call, but she wouldn't be able to attend the meeting. First she hurried a few doors down to ask Mrs Harris to give her apologies, then she settled in the parlour to wait until it was time for Thea's call.

The telephone at Jones' Newsagents was treated like a public phone by Deedee and her neighbours. Not that Mr Jones complained, for it increased his custom. Accordingly, at five to five, Deedee hurried down the road to the shop and bought a copy of *Woman's Own*, as always feeling she had to buy something if she was using the phone.

'Anything else I can help you with, Mrs Pritchard?' Mr Jones asked as he handed over her change.

'I'm expecting a call from my granddaughter,' Deedee replied. 'She arranged to call at five.'

'No problem. Go on through.' Mr Jones raised the counter to allow her to access the door at the back of the shop. 'We're not expecting any other calls, so take your time.'

'Thank you.' Deedee squeezed into the passageway that connected the shop to the little office and Mr Jones' living quarters. The telephone was on a shelf at the foot of the stairs, and Mr Jones had thoughtfully placed a chair beside it so his customers could sit while waiting for calls to be put through. Deedee took a seat, knowing that Thea could be delayed by any number of hold-ups. The magazine lay unread on her lap; her mind was far too occupied by worries over Pearl and Greg. She was painfully aware that 'missing' all too often meant 'dead', but, with the countries involved being in turmoil, it could take weeks or months before information filtered through. Sometimes it never arrived. If an aircraft went down over the sea, for example, it would usually be lost for ever. Deedee's heart had always gone out to families with loved ones reported missing, but she had never imagined being in the same position.

The shrill telephone bell made her jump. She sprang up and answered, and a moment later heard Thea's voice.

'Deedee? Oh, it's so good to speak to you.'

'What do you know?' Deedee's heart sank as she listened to Thea's tale, hope dwindling.

'That's all we know for now, which is precious little,' Thea concluded. 'Fitz is on his way, but I don't know what else he can tell us.'

Deedee was glad that Thea had Fitz in her life. Thea had settled down considerably since being involved with him – mostly, Deedee suspected, because she didn't want to end up being confined to camp when Fitz got leave. 'That's good of him. I'm sure Pearl will be grateful for any information. How is she?'

'Pretty cut up. It doesn't help that she used to work in Flying Control, so she knows exactly how unlikely it is for a missing crew to turn up safe and well.' The sound of Thea drawing a deep breath echoed down the line. 'The thing is, Pearl asked for you almost straight away. Can you come, Deedee? Jenny and I will be there for her as much as we can, of course, but neither of us gets much free time.'

From Thea's apologetic tone, Deedee knew she must be thinking of the letter she had sent in response to her Christmas invitation. She had been regretful but firm, saying that, although she would have loved to spend Christmas with her granddaughters, she could see through Thea's plan to reunite her with Tom Haughton, and had asked Thea to put all such nonsense from her mind. She now hastened to put Thea at ease. 'Of course I'll come. There's no reason why I can't pack up and catch a train first thing in the morning.' In her mind she was already running through the list she would need to pack. Ration book, gas mask, identity card and money being top of the list.

'Thank goodness. I can't bear to think of Pearl going through this alone.'

Nor could Deedee. Once they'd made what arrangements they could, not knowing what time she would arrive, Deedee returned home, her head full of Pearl and what she must be suffering. Her heart was heavy as she scurried around her house, gathering up her belongings and cramming them all into as tiny a case as possible. She knew what a leap of faith it had been for Pearl to give her heart to Greg. If either of her granddaughters was going to enter a hasty marriage, Deedee would have bet good money on it being Thea. Therefore she had been both shocked and delighted when Pearl had announced her engagement to Greg and their determination to marry as soon as their separate duties allowed. On the rare occasions when she had seen the couple together, it had filled her with joy to see how she had blossomed under Greg's influence and seized love with both hands in a most un-Pearl-like manner. She couldn't bear to think of how she might regress should Greg be lost. No matter that there was a high chance of running into Tom once she was in Lincoln, she had to risk it.

Chapter Three

The evening was wearing on. Thea had telephoned Deedee and then walked to the station, saying she would wait for Fitz. Jenny had declared that she would stay with Pearl, however long it took. Pearl did the only thing she could do – she got on with her work. She had dummy sheets to lay out, and she was the only person who could do it. Jenny retook her place at the side of the desk, saying she would finish her article.

Pearl wished in vain that her work would occupy her mind enough to drive out all other thoughts, for the notes on the page frequently blurred, and haunting images of Greg would drift before her eyes. Greg lying in twisted wreckage. Greg in a burning aircraft. Greg freezing to death in an icy sea.

Finally she flung down her pencil with a sob.

Jenny was instantly at her side. 'Why don't we go back to your digs? No one expects you to work at a time like this.'

Pearl shook her head. 'Thea said she'd bring Fitz here. I have to see him, Jenny. I need to know what else he knows.'

'Then at least let's have a drink. A building this big must have somewhere to make tea.'

'You go. There's a little kitchenette at the end of the corridor. I need to finish this.'

Jenny didn't budge. 'I'm not going anywhere without you. What's the problem with the sheet?'

Pearl sighed. 'It's this report about the concert at RAF Scampton. It needs about two hundred and fifty words cutting if it's to fit in the space set aside, but I can't see anything I can remove without ruining the piece.'

'Let me look.' Jenny leaned over the pages. 'No problem. You've set aside more space for my "Day In The Life" article than I need, so all you have to do is swap them round.'

Pearl stared, then rubbed her eyes. 'Why didn't I see that?'

'Because you've got more important things on your mind. Anyway, with that sorted, it's ready for typesetting. Let's get a drink.'

But at that moment hurrying footsteps could be heard in the corridor outside and then the door was flung open and Thea strode in with Fitz close behind. Pearl sprang to her feet and, the next thing she knew, she was being pulled into a hug, the scent of tobacco, coal tar soap and engine oil engulfing her and reminding her so strongly of Greg it made her dizzy with longing. She stepped back, blinking tears from her eyes, her throat so tight she was unable to speak.

'I'm so sorry, Pearl,' Fitz said. 'I wanted to get here ahead of the telegram, but it was impossible. I hate that you had to learn the news like that.'

Pearl swallowed and managed to speak. 'It's good of you to come at all. What can you tell me?'

Fitz hesitated, glancing around the office. 'Is there somewhere more comfortable you'd rather go?'

Pearl shook her head. 'Please. I need to hear what you know.' Only then did it sink in that Fitz had dark shadows under his eyes and his uniform looked rumpled, as though he'd slept in it. 'I'm sorry. You must be tired and hungry. We can go back to my digs for a hot drink if you don't mind cocoa or Ovaltine.'

Fitz shook his head. 'I can wait. I suppose I was trying to put off saying what I know, because' – he took off his cap and ran his fingers through his hair, looking suddenly lost and very young – 'there's not much hope, I'm afraid.'

Pearl sank onto a chair, gripping the arms. 'Tell me.'

Fitz perched on the corner of the desk, but immediately sprang back up and started pacing. 'I saw it happen, you see.' He paused as though waiting for her to comment, but Pearl could only gaze at him, feeling strangely disconnected.

'It was supposed to be a straightforward training run with a couple of crews who were nearly ready to join operational squadrons. It was a leaflet drop over the Netherlands. I think the point was to persuade the German troops to give themselves up. Anyway, I'm rambling. Sorry. You want to know what happened to Greg. Well, we were in a group of three Lancs. He was observing one Lancaster crew while I was in one of the others. He had Edwin with him, too.'

There was a sharp indrawn breath from Jenny. 'Edwin? Edwin Holland?'

Fitz shot Jenny a sympathetic look. 'Yes. Sorry. I forgot you two were friends.'

Now it was Jenny's turn to sink onto her chair as though her knees had given out. Oddly, the sight of Jenny's distress shook Pearl from her torpor, and she gave Jenny's hand a squeeze. 'Go on,' she urged Fitz.

'Okay. Well, the drop itself was as straightforward as we'd expected, and we were soon approaching Allied territory.' He looked at her as though to ensure she understood, and she nodded. Since the D-Day landings in June, Allied forces had gained a foothold in parts of the Netherlands, but they still struggled to gain more territory. 'But then we were attacked by two enemy fighters. We had a fighter escort, and they soon saw them off, but Greg's Lanc had been hit and he must have had engine damage, because it started to lose height.'

Pearl clung to Jenny's hand, unsure who was comforting who, as Fitz continued his tale. 'It was awful, not being able to do anything.' He swallowed. 'Anyway, most of the crew managed to bale out – we counted seven parachutes in all, and the crew consisted of seven trainees plus Greg and Edwin as observers. The last I saw, it was going down over woodland.'

Pearl leaned forward, aware of Jenny's fingers digging into her palm. 'But he might have landed safely.'

Fitz shook his head. 'There was no clear space where they could have landed. They must have crashed into the trees.'

'But they could still be alive. You should have gone back to look.'

An expression of such pain crossed Fitz's face that Pearl instantly regretted her outburst. 'We couldn't. We had to get away because more fighters were on their way. Our escort planes were getting low on fuel and wouldn't have been able to defend us.'

'You did the right thing. I didn't mean—'

'I know. You were only saying what I've been telling myself ever since we left them behind.'

'You had to keep your crew safe.' Pearl glanced at Jenny, who had released her hand and was now dabbing away tears with a handkerchief. 'What about the men who baled out? Any news of them?'

'Not yet. They must have landed in enemy territory, so we can only hope they manage to evade capture.'

'Any chance Edwin was among them?'

Fitz addressed his reply to Jenny even though Pearl had asked it. 'Greg and Edwin were there as observers, in addition to the crew of seven, so there were still two men in the Lancaster when it went down. I can't see either Greg or Edwin leaving a trainee crew to fend for themselves, can you?'

'No.' Jenny gave a watery smile. Pearl agreed.

'And I'm sure Greg would have taken over the controls at the first sign of danger.'

'Me too. He's been itching to get back into an operational unit.' Pearl refused to speak of Greg in the past tense. After a pause she asked, 'What now?'

Fitz didn't pretend to misunderstand her. 'We'll know more if any of the parachutists make it back so they can be debriefed. As for Greg and Edwin' – he stopped pacing and picked up a pencil from the desk before continuing – 'there are three possibilities.' He paused again, biting his lip.

Pearl saved him the trouble by saying in as matter-of-fact a tone as she could muster, 'If they survived, they'll either be captured or they'll make it back to Allied territory.' She refused to say the third option aloud: that they had not survived the crash.

'Precisely. And where they went down – near Blerick – isn't too far from Allied territory, so there's a good chance of them reaching safety, assuming they're unhurt. If they were… killed… well, the Lancaster will have been spotted going down, so the authorities will identify any… remains. Whatever happens, we'll find out in due course.'

Pearl pulled herself straighter. 'I'm going to assume the best until I hear otherwise. From what you say, Greg had control of the Lanc, so it would only have crashed when it reached the trees. They might have survived.'

'They might.'

Whatever Fitz might have said next was interrupted by a tap at the door, and Mr Haughton walked in.

'My dear,' he said to Pearl, 'I've just heard. I'm so very sorry. Is there anything I can do to help?'

Pearl fought the sudden urge to run to him, like a crying child seeking comfort from her father. She had only vague memories of her own father and was painfully aware that she was perhaps starting to regard Mr Haughton as a parental figure. She had to remind herself that he was the owner of the newspaper group and was offering practical help, not a shoulder to cry on.

'That's very kind of you, but there's nothing to do, bar waiting.'

'At least take tomorrow off.'

Pearl was horrified. 'I couldn't do that. The latest edition is going to press tomorrow, and I need to be around in case of last-minute emergencies.'

'I'd be happy to take over.'

Pearl shook her head. 'It's very kind, but I need to keep myself busy.' And the day the *Bombshell* went to press was always busy, with last-minute adjustments having to be made before the deadline. It was exactly what Pearl needed. Mr Haughton looked like he was about to object, so Pearl met his gaze. 'It could be weeks or months before we hear anything. I need to remain occupied and optimistic, and I can't do that if I'm sitting around doing nothing. Besides, my grandmother arrives tomorrow, and she's going to come here if I can't get away to meet her, although I really don't like to think of her all alone in a strange place, especially with the latest news.' Her gaze drifted to a newspaper on her desk with a prominent headline proclaiming: *Foul Play Suspected in Case of Missing Cambridge Girl*. Although Cambridge was miles away and she knew she was overreacting, she couldn't seem to help herself.

Mr Haughton placed a comforting hand on her shoulder. 'Let me meet her. It's one less thing for you to worry about.'

'Now that's a good idea. What do you think, Pearl?' Thea had retreated to the far corner of the office with Fitz once Thomas had arrived and had been having a murmured conversation with him. She must have been keeping half an ear on what Mr Haughton had been saying, though, for now she met Pearl's gaze with a positively wicked smile.

'Oh, I couldn't let you do that. I wouldn't like to ask Deedee to meet a complete stranger.' Pearl crossed her fingers behind her back as she said this, and studiously avoided glancing in Thea's direction. Deedee would usually be not at all bothered by meeting a stranger; in fact she would revel in it. However, there was enough going on in her life at the moment without the added complication of her grandmother coming face to face with her long-lost love. As far as she knew, Mr Haughton had not seen Deedee at the wedding, having needed to leave as soon as the ceremony had ended, and so had no idea of her identity. As Deedee was determined to keep him in ignorance, Pearl had to respect that and do her best to keep them apart, no matter what Thea thought.

Fitz stepped forward. 'I'll meet her. Deedee knows me, and I'll be at a loose end with Thea being on duty. I might as well make myself useful.'

That settled, Mr Haughton turned to leave, then paused in the doorway. 'By the way, where will your grandmother be staying?'

Pearl stared at him, flummoxed. 'I never even thought.' She glanced at Thea. 'Did you sort a room out for her?'

Thea's aghast expression was her answer. 'I thought… can't you put her up in your digs?'

Pearl shook her head. 'Mrs Dale has a strict no overnight guests rule. She won't even let Greg—' She broke off as pain tore through her heart. For that one instant she had forgotten Greg was missing.

Thea looked contrite. 'I'm sorry. You did mention that before and I completely forgot. I'll sort something out.' But she looked worried, and Pearl knew it was because she would be on duty all the following day with no time to get away to find a room. 'I suppose I could drop into the White Horse on the way back to the Waafery and see if Norah can give her a room.'

Fitz looked apologetic. 'I already booked it. I rang her before I left for the train. But Deedee can have it.'

Mr Haughton stepped back inside the office. 'No need. I think I can offer a solution. I have a small apartment at the top of this building where I stay when I need to work late. It's no trouble for me to move in here for a while, and your grandmother would be more than welcome to stay at the Gatehouse. I'm sure Mrs Stockwell would welcome some female company.'

Pearl exchanged glances with Thea, who was looking very smug, and she realised with a sinking heart that, much as she dreaded telling Deedee where she would be staying, this was the only option. Even so, she tried. 'I hate to think of you turned out of your own house.'

'Nonsense. It's the least I can do. And she'll have company when you're all at work.'

Pearl wished she could think of an alternative, but that would mean finding Deedee a room in Lincoln. And finding a suitable place would be difficult when the town was full to bursting with servicemen and women already occupying most available accommodation.

Mr Haughton looked pleased. 'Good. Then that's settled,' he said when Pearl had nodded in acceptance. 'I'll let Mrs Stockwell know tonight.'

Pearl could imagine Deedee's face when she told her where she would be staying. She was not going to be happy.

Chapter Four

'Mrs Pritchard?'

Deedee turned, unsure if she had really heard someone call her name or if her ears had been fooled by the din of the busy station. Then she saw Fitz jogging along the platform, dodging the crowds, waving to her as he closed the distance between them.

She hastened to him. 'Have you come to meet me? How kind.'

Fitz took her suitcase and offered her his free arm. 'It's a pleasure. Pearl's asked me to bring you to her office. It's not far.'

As they walked, Fitz explained all he knew about Greg's fate. Deedee listened with a growing dread, finding it hard to believe her grandson-in-law, as she liked to call him, could have survived a crash into trees. From Fitz's haggard expression, she could tell he felt the same way. 'You don't think there's much hope, do you,' she said when he finished.

Fitz sighed. 'I suppose I've seen too many deaths and it's hard to stay optimistic. But it's possible he survived, and I'm trying to be positive around Pearl.'

'How's she holding up?'

'Thea thinks she's trying to bury her feelings in work. But it might be for the best. It could be weeks or even months before we hear anything, especially if he was captured.'

This was something that hadn't occurred to Deedee, and she listened in growing dismay. How long would Pearl have to live in agonising suspense, not knowing if her husband was alive or dead? Memories from the Great War sprang to mind unbidden, of families who never learned the fate of missing loved ones. But no, that was unlikely to happen in Greg's case. He had crashed not far from a populated area and someone on the ground must have seen his Lancaster go down. The authorities would be bound to investigate. Sooner or later Pearl would hear, and Deedee would be there for her when she did.

In her worry for Pearl, it had slipped Deedee's mind that the man who owned the newspaper group where Pearl had her office was the man she had loved and lost so many years ago. But she received a rude reminder when Fitz delivered her to the reception desk, for on the wall was a portrait of a stern-looking man with full Victorian whiskers. Tom's father. The sight made her feel sick, and she turned away. 'Pearl must be busy,' she muttered to Fitz. 'Maybe I should wait elsewhere.'

Fitz gave her an all too understanding look. Speaking in a low voice, he said, 'Mr Haughton's not in the office. An unexpected meeting cropped up, and he's out for the rest of the day.'

So Thea had told him about the conversation they'd had at Pearl's wedding. She wasn't surprised. She had brought up her granddaughters to be open in their relationships, hypocrite that she was, and she hadn't really expected Thea to keep such huge news to herself. Some of the knots in Deedee's stomach eased, although she couldn't relax fully, not under the glare of the Victorian gentleman in the portrait. 'Even so, I think it would be better if I wait in my lodgings. Do you know where I'm staying?'

If Deedee hadn't known Fitz better, she'd have described the expression that crossed his face as distinctly shifty. 'It's a bit complicated. You really need to speak to Pearl. She's expecting you.'

'Oh, very well.' She marched up to the desk. 'Mrs Pritchard to see Corporal Tallis.'

While she waited for Pearl to come and meet her, Fitz took his leave, saying he was heading for Fenthorpe. 'Thea's on duty all day, worse luck, but if I can get into the station I'll wait for her in the NAAFI.'

She patted his arm. 'They're saying it's only a matter of time before this war ends. It won't be long before you'll be together properly.'

'I hope so.' Fitz gave a wan smile. 'Anyway, I must dash if I'm to catch the bus. We might see you later.'

'Why, are the two of you coming to Lincoln this evening?'

There it was again. She wasn't imagining it. Fitz looked distinctly awkward. She would have said something, but at that moment the lift doors opened with a clatter and Pearl walked out. Her first sight of her granddaughter drove all suspicion from her mind, for the tight line of Pearl's mouth revealed that she was struggling to hold back the tears. Saying a hasty goodbye to Fitz, she enveloped Pearl in a tight hug.

Up in Pearl's office, two drenched handkerchiefs later, Pearl finally dabbed her eyes and said, 'I'm so glad you're here. I thought keeping myself busy would help, but it really doesn't.'

Deedee cast an eye over the empty in-tray on Pearl's desk and the teetering pile of papers in the out-tray. 'Not for want of trying, I see.'

Pearl huffed a laugh. 'I dealt with eight last-minute changes before we finally went to press, edited five items for next week and wrote two articles myself.' She glanced at her watch. 'And now I'm finished for the day.'

'Then perhaps you can show me where I'm staying. Fitz was surprisingly cagey on the subject. But I've left my case at reception and I'm sure the poor receptionist doesn't want it cluttering up her space for much longer.'

'Poor? That's the first time I've heard her called that. Most people in the office call her the Gorgon.'

'No wonder she looks so sour. Anyway, stop trying to change the subject. Where am I sleeping tonight? Please don't tell me it's in the cathedral crypt.'

'Promise you won't fly off the handle?'

'Why, what have you done?'

'The thing is' – Pearl picked up a pencil and twisted it between her fingers – 'last night we were wondering where you could stay, because none of us really had time to go out looking. Anyway, to cut a long story short, Mr Haughton made us an offer we couldn't refuse.'

'Tom? Why, what's he got to do with this?' Although Deedee had a sinking feeling he had everything to do with it.

'He said you could stay at his house.'

'Absolutely not! This is Thea's idea, isn't it? I told her not to meddle.'

'It really isn't. Please just listen, Deedee.'

'I can't stay with him.'

'You won't. He's moving into the apartment here at the office. Please let me explain.'

'Fine.' Deedee subsided, hating to make Pearl's life any more difficult.

'You see, even if we did find you a place in Lincoln at this short notice, it would be cold and uncomfortable, and Thea and I hated to think of you stuck somewhere so depressing. Well, Mr Haughton came in while we were discussing it – he was desperately sorry about Greg, and he really wanted to help. When he mentioned about putting you up in the Gatehouse, I knew you wouldn't like it, but it's a lovely house, with a housekeeper who'll only be too delighted to look after you. Mr Haughton says you can stay there for as long as you need, and the trouble is we have no idea how long it will be before I hear anything.' Here Pearl's eyes filled with fresh tears.

Although Deedee could see this was an argument she was going to lose, she had to try. 'Pearl, I promise to be here for you, however long it takes. But is there really no other option? Things… didn't end well between Tom and myself.' That was an understatement and a half. 'It would feel wrong to stay in his house. I dare say he would be horrified if he knew who I really am, and he's bound to find out.'

Pearl, who had been hunched over her desk, dabbing her eyes, suddenly sat up straighter. 'And who are you really?'

'What on earth do you mean?'

'I know who you are now, but I've no idea who you were back then. From what you've told me and Thea, you've always been Edith Pritchard of Shrewsbury. Then

42

out of the blue you announce to Thea that you used to know Thomas Haughton. That you and he were in love. Yet when we were making the wedding arrangements, he asked me your name and he didn't recognise it. And where did you meet? He's told me something of his life, and he's never mentioned any time spent in Shropshire. As far as I know, he's only ever lived here or in London.'

Deedee saw she was going to have to own up to some of the truth, although certainly not all of it. 'That's where we met. London.'

'I never knew you'd been there.'

'My dear, I didn't just appear out of thin air the day you were born. I had a life – a long life – before you came along.'

'I know, but you tell us everything. More than I want to hear half the time.' Pearl gave a wry smile, and it did Deedee's heart good to see her sense of humour still survived. 'A life in London sounds glamorous and exciting. I don't understand why you wouldn't have told us about it.'

Because, although it had been glamorous and exciting at first, she had left broken-hearted and ashamed and had never wanted to remember that time. Furthermore, she hadn't wanted any scandal from her past to cling to her daughter or granddaughters, so had kept her past hidden. Her granddaughters, however, deserved an explanation. 'I suppose it's time you learned the truth. I know Thea's been bursting to know more ever since I dropped that bombshell on her at your wedding. But if you don't mind, I'd prefer to tell you together. I'd rather you both hear it first hand, and I don't want to repeat myself.'

She glanced out of the window and saw the sun was sinking low, casting a golden light on the cathedral at the top of the hill.

Pearl followed her gaze and rose to fix the blackout. 'I'm sorry we agreed to Mr Haughton's offer without checking with you first. I knew you wouldn't like it, but I didn't stop to think how awkward it would feel. I suppose we could do a tour of the guest houses in Lincoln before it gets dark.'

She looked so despondent that Deedee's heart went out to her. She must be tired after her long day, not to mention emotionally wrung out. Traipsing around Lincoln on a cold and gloomy November night would be the last thing she wanted. She reluctantly made up her mind. 'Tell you what. I'll stay in Mr Haughton's house until the weekend. Then, assuming you still need me, we can hunt for an alternative.'

Pearl's face brightened. 'Really? Oh, thank you. That'll be such a help. I'll do my best to keep Mr Haughton away.'

–

It was nearly dark by the time the bus arrived in Fenthorpe. Deedee moved to get out, but Pearl stopped her. 'The bus carries on, and there's a stop right outside the Gatehouse.'

'Is this the last bus?' Deedee asked.

Pearl shook her head. 'They're quite frequent.'

Deedee pointed to a young couple strolling down the high street, and Pearl saw it was Thea and Fitz. 'If I must tell you and Thea my story, let's go to the White Horse. I'd rather not be under Tom's roof while I say what I've got to say.'

44

As they climbed off the bus, Pearl reflected that Deedee had a point. While Mrs Stockwell was not one to listen at doors, there was a real risk of the housekeeper inadvertently overhearing any conversation they might have at the Gatehouse. She didn't know why Deedee was so adamant she didn't want Mr Haughton knowing her identity, but Pearl had to respect that and not risk him finding out through his housekeeper.

Thea and Fitz made a lovely couple, walking in the twilight, hands entwined and so absorbed in one another that they didn't immediately notice Pearl and Deedee's arrival. The sight gave Pearl a pang of loss, reminding her all too clearly of evening walks with Greg, and she wanted to lash out at the unfairness of it all. How come Fitz was safe when Greg might even now be cold and hungry, seeking to evade unfriendly eyes. Or even— No. She cut off that train of thought before it could form. Nevertheless, the comfort she had gained from Deedee's presence dissolved.

'Have you seen Jenny today?' she asked her sister the moment Thea and Fitz joined them. 'I'm worried about her.'

Thea's guilty look was its own answer, and Pearl's temper flared. 'Honestly, call yourself a friend? She must be worried sick about Edwin, yet you're too busy gallivanting with your boyfriend to see how she is.'

Deedee put a hand on her shoulder. 'That was unfair, Pearl,' she murmured, too quietly for her words to carry to Thea and Fitz. Then, before Pearl could reply, Deedee moved to Fitz's side. 'I didn't thank you properly for meeting me earlier.' She accompanied him into the pub, talking nineteen to the dozen. Leaving Pearl alone with Thea.

'Sorry, Thea,' Pearl muttered, feeling like a five-year-old being forced to apologise for a misdeed.

Thea sighed. 'No, you're right. I was so relieved Fitz was all right I didn't stop to think about Jenny. I'll be sure to check up on her when I get back to the Waafery.' She turned to follow Deedee and Fitz into the pub, then paused, frowning. 'Anyway, what are you doing here? I thought you'd be taking Deedee to the Gatehouse. She didn't refuse to go, did she?'

'She came close but no, she's agreed to stay until the weekend, and then I'm going to help her find somewhere else.' She indicated Deedee's suitcase. 'Which means I'll be lugging this around again. But listen' – Pearl lowered her voice even though there was no one within earshot – 'when we were talking about the reasons why she didn't want to stay in the Gatehouse, she let slip that she'd met Mr Haughton while she was living in London.' As she focused on the mystery surrounding Deedee, she forgot her jealousy. 'I mean, she's got this whole past she's kept hidden from us. I wanted to know more, but she insisted on waiting until you could hear her story too. Which brings us here.'

Thea's face lit up. 'She's going to tell us about her secret past? What are we waiting for?' She grabbed Pearl's hand and pulled her into the White Horse.

Deedee must have said something to Fitz, for he offered to put Deedee's case in his room and muttered something about needing to write to his mother and that he would join them in half an hour.

'Come on, then,' Thea said when the three women were huddled in a corner with their drinks, 'Pearl says you've got something to tell us.'

Deedee sipped her whisky and soda, taking her time before finally saying, 'Pearl pointed out that apparently Thomas Haughton asked what I was called, and didn't seem to recognise my name. Well, the truth is that I used to go under a different name.'

Thea leaned forward, her eyes shining. 'You had a secret identity!'

Pearl rolled her eyes. She should have known Thea would think it terribly exciting instead of being upset that their grandmother had a part of her life she had never spoken about.

'In a way.' Deedee's lips twitched. 'Although not for any nefarious reasons. I'm sorry if that disappoints you, Thea. You see, I was an actress and went by my stage name: Hope Burnell.'

'An actress? I can't believe we never knew that. Were you famous?' Thea clasped her hands. 'Hope Burnell's the perfect name for a West End actress.'

Deedee's lips curved into a soft smile, and her eyes took on a faraway look. Maybe it was the golden light from the snug's electric lamps, but her skin seemed to take on a youthful sheen, and Pearl could almost see her grandmother as the young girl she had once been. 'I didn't do badly. I came from a theatrical family, you see, so I was on stage from a very early age. Then in the Nineties, when I was just twenty, I got my big break with a leading role at the Gaiety Theatre. I was a huge hit and got invited to lots of society events.'

'And that's where you met Mr Haughton?' Pearl was agog. Then she was struck by a memory of one of the first times she had met Thomas, when he had shown her around his rose garden and spoken of his favourite rose. 'Wait, your stage name was Hope? Thomas has a rose called Heart of Hope. He told me it was cultivated in honour of an actress. That was you?' In her mind's eye, she saw the rose as it had been on that June day, its yellow petals streaked with a fiery orange. An apt colour for the vibrant Deedee.

Deedee's eyes widened. 'He still has it?' Then, in a low voice full of wonder, she murmured, 'After all these years.' For a while her focus seemed fixed on something in the far distance, then, visibly pulling herself together, she continued her story in brisk tones. 'Yes, that was where I met Tom. He had got himself a junior role with one of the Fleet Street papers, and he interviewed me before the opening night of *The Milliner's Girl*. No one knew it was going to be such a huge hit, of course, or the paper would have sent a more senior reporter. Well, we got on like a house on fire, and the rest is history.'

Thea, however, was looking thoughtful. 'But why did you move to Shrewsbury? At the wedding you said you split up through a misunderstanding. What happened?'

Deedee looked slightly ashamed. 'I might have exaggerated my heartbreak, to persuade you to make up with Fitz.'

Thea's face cleared. 'In that case, all is forgiven, because I don't know where I would be without Fitz. So I suppose you just met our grandfather and moved to Shrewsbury to be with him.'

Pearl didn't pay much attention to Deedee's reply, for she was suddenly overwhelmed by a stomach-curdling mixture of grief and jealousy. When Thea had spoken of Fitz, her face had glowed as though she had a light shining behind her eyes. She had always felt like that when she was with Greg, and seeing Thea so happy was too sharp a reminder of what she might have lost.

Therefore it was only a few minutes later, when Deedee made a trip to the ladies' room, that the inconsistencies in Deedee's story dawned on her. 'Thea, when Deedee first told you about her and Mr Haughton, did you think she was making it up?'

Thea, looking thoughtful, took a sip of her shandy before replying. 'Well, she *was* an actress, so I suppose... but no. I'll never forget her face when she first saw Mr Haughton at the church. She looked really shocked and upset. And she didn't know anyone was watching her, so there would have been no reason to put it on. Why – do you think she's just made all that up?'

'I don't think it was made up, but I do think she was skirting around the truth when it came to her break-up. You didn't see her when she heard she was staying at the Gatehouse. She was genuinely distressed at the thought of running into Mr Haughton. Yet if they simply had a light flirtation in their younger days that came to a natural end, why would she be so upset at the prospect of seeing him again? I mean, they both married other people. I'd have thought they'd enjoy meeting again and talking about old times.'

Thea was nodding. 'Yes, exactly. I wonder what really happened?'

But any speculation was prevented by Jenny's arrival.

'Jenny, I didn't think you were coming!' Thea moved around the table to make room for their friend. Jenny's mouth was set in a determined line – an expression Pearl had often seen when she was absorbed in an exciting new textbook. Exciting to her, anyway. The last book Pearl had seen her poring over was *An Introduction to Vector Geometry*.

Jenny looked at her friends in turn. 'I've had an idea. Something to keep us occupied while we're waiting for news.'

'Jenny, you're a Met WAAF. You're out taking readings at all hours and in all weather. Isn't that occupation enough?'

'Not when I'm off duty. I was trying to work on vector diagrams this evening – and I *love* vectors – but I just couldn't concentrate.'

Pearl knew what she meant. While she had been rushing to meet her deadline that day she had been able to maintain focus, but as soon as the pressure was off her thoughts had drifted more and more to that wood in the Netherlands and the wreckage of Greg's Lancaster. 'What do you suggest?'

'You know the Christmas dance at Fenthorpe Hall?'

Pearl nodded. 'What about it?'

'Well, they're asking for volunteers to help organise it, and I've signed up for the decorations committee.'

Thea's lip curled. 'That sounds fun.'

Clearly Jenny hadn't picked up on Thea's sarcasm, for she breathed a sigh of relief. 'Oh, good, because I put your name down too. I thought it would be fun. You know, collecting pine cones and holly, making wreaths. It'll take our mind off things.'

Thea's expression softened as Jenny rattled on, and she said, 'You're right. That *does* sound like fun. Count me in.'

Jenny turned to Pearl. 'What about you? I know you're not at RAF Fenthorpe any more, but you're still one of us. And it would do you good to have something to work on in the evenings. They're holding all the meetings at Fenthorpe Hall, so you'd be going there anyway to see Deedee.'

Pearl chewed her lip. She had to admit Jenny had a point. On the one hand, it would mean bus rides in the dark to and from Fenthorpe, but on the other hand, as Jenny pointed out, she would be going that way anyway, at least as long as Deedee was staying at the Gatehouse. 'I suppose I could join in for the first couple of meetings, although Deedee's only agreed to stay there until the weekend, so whether I can carry on afterwards depends on her.'

'I feel my ears burning.' Deedee had returned to the table. She sat down and, after greeting Jenny, demanded to know what they had been talking about.

Pearl filled her in on the decorations committee.

'I think that's a wonderful idea.'

'But it would mean leaving you alone some evenings. It doesn't feel right when you came all this way for me.' Then Pearl added hastily, before Deedee got the idea she wasn't wanted when Pearl desperately needed her, 'I really do want you to stay.'

'I'm sure I can find ways to occupy myself.'

'Why don't you help us with the decorations?' Jenny asked. 'I'm sure no one would mind.'

Deedee brightened. 'I am a dab hand at making wreaths. I'd love to join in if no one objects.'

And so it was agreed that they would all attend the meeting at Fenthorpe Hall the next evening. With Jenny and Thea working shifts, they wouldn't be able to attend every meeting, but Jenny assured them that the work would not involve many meetings and they would be working on their separate projects when time permitted. 'We're using the ballroom,' Jenny told them. 'It's going to look amazing when it's finished.'

'A ballroom will need an awful lot of decorations,' Pearl cautioned.

'I don't care what it looks like, as long as there's plenty of mistletoe,' Thea said. Then she grinned. 'I'm inviting Fitz, and I want to make the most of the occasion.'

And there was the stab of jealousy again.

Jenny must have noticed Pearl's expression, for she said, 'I'm going to work on the principle that Greg and Edwin will be there too. We'll make it the perfect occasion to welcome them back.'

That was a good way of looking at it, Pearl decided. Since she had no idea what had happened to Greg, she would imagine him making his way home. And after all he'd been through, he deserved the best welcome they could give him.

Chapter Five

The rattle of pots and pans drew Deedee downstairs at eight the following morning. She arrived in the hall just in time to see Mrs Stockwell emerge from the kitchen.

'Good morning, Mrs Pritchard. I do hope I didn't disturb you.'

'Oh no, I'm usually up long before this. Yesterday's journey must have tired me out. And please call me Deedee – everyone else does.'

'Are you ready for breakfast? There's porridge on the stove, but I could also do you some toast. I don't have any eggs today, I'm afraid. My sister lives nearby, and she keeps hens and often brings us some, but they've not been laying recently.'

'Porridge will be lovely, especially on a day like today.' For although it was still too dark to see out, the chill in the air told her there must have been a hard frost overnight. 'That reminds me.' She fished in her handbag and pulled out her ration book. 'I suppose I ought to leave this with you.'

When a most satisfying breakfast had been finished and Deedee had washed up, insisting she didn't expect to be waited on, Mrs Stockwell – or Izzy, as she had insisted Deedee call her – asked how Deedee intended to spend her day.

'I'm going to meet Pearl in Lincoln for lunch, and I'd enjoy looking around the shops in the afternoon.'

Izzy offered to show her where to catch the bus when she was ready to leave, then disappeared into the kitchen. Deedee went to fetch her knitting and retired to a comfortable armchair in the living room to work. One of the many voluntary jobs she had become involved in was knitting socks for sailors, and she might as well make what progress she could before it was time to catch the bus.

It still being dark outside, the curtains were closed, so she worked by the light of a standard lamp. She had been so tired when she had arrived the night before that she had barely taken in the rooms when Izzy had shown her around, only registering that the house was large for a gatehouse and had two bedrooms – one of which Izzy occupied – and that the downstairs consisted of the living room and kitchen, plus a tiny room set aside as a study. She had gone straight to bed and fallen straight into a deep sleep. Now, however, Deedee could see Thomas's hand in the decor, and the realisation that she was staying in his house weighed heavily on her. Despite Pearl's assurance that he wouldn't enter the house while she was there, Deedee couldn't help jumping at every creak of the house, wondering if it heralded his arrival. She did her best to concentrate on her work, but the trouble was, years of knitting socks had made her so proficient that she didn't need her full concentration, and she found herself gazing around the room, at the items lit by the pools of light cast by the various lamps.

A set of framed photographs occupied a prominent position on the mantelpiece, and, unable to restrain her curiosity, she set down her knitting and rose to inspect them. One was a sepia-tinted picture of a young man and woman. Both were stiffly posed, the woman's hand on the man's arm, looking very serious. It was clearly a wedding photograph, for the woman wore a white gown and a flowing veil held off her face by a pearl circlet. At first Deedee avoided looking at the man's features, but when she did she felt a jolt of recognition. Any lingering doubt faded away. Pearl's Mr Haughton was most definitely her Tom. This was Tom as she remembered him – young and heart-stoppingly handsome. The photo gave no hint of his character, but Deedee hadn't expected that, remembering as she did how long you had to stand still for a portrait photograph in those days. But she could imagine him turning to his bride once the photographer had given him permission to move, smiling the loving smile he had always directed at Deedee.

Her heart clenched, and she deliberately studied the bride. She appeared to be everything Deedee was not, nor had ever been – demure, conventional and very beautiful. Not even the brownish tint of the photograph could conceal the glory of her golden hair and flawless skin. So this was the woman Tom had chosen over her.

She turned to the other photographs, surprised to find herself blinking away tears. It had been over fifty years since she had left Tom, yet the memories were as vivid as ever. The next photograph looked almost as old and showed Mr and Mrs Haughton in another stiff, unsmiling pose. This time the young Mrs Haughton carried a bundle of lace that draped across her lap. A tiny face could be seen peeping out from the elaborate clothing, a dimpled fist curled beside one ear. So Thomas had a child. She turned hurriedly to the third and final picture. Judging from the fashions, it must have been taken in the early Thirties, and it showed a more relaxed side of Thomas and his wife. They were clearly at ease and happy in one another's company. Although they smiled at the camera, their heads were tilted towards each other, and their hands were clasped. Both faces showed lines of age, although their eyes had a youthful light.

A light step sounded behind her, and she spun round to see Izzy regarding the pictures with a soft smile. 'I think that's my favourite picture of Mr Haughton and his wife,' she said. 'I'd just started working for them when that was taken, and I'd never seen a couple so in love.' She moved to the windows and pulled back the heavy blackout curtains, allowing pale winter sunlight to filter through the French windows. She paused to straighten another photograph that stood alone on a low table. 'Such a pity about their son, though.'

Deedee, who had hurried to switch off the various electric lamps, paused and looked at the picture. She saw a young man in the Royal Flying Corps uniform from the Great War. 'Oh dear, was he killed in the last war? Now I think about it, Pearl did mention something about that.' She hadn't paid it a great deal of attention, not knowing at the time that Pearl's benefactor was her very own Tom. She sighed. 'That war took so many young people from us. My son-in-law was killed not long before the Armistice, and then my daughter Clara died of the Spanish flu that followed.' Meaning both she and Tom had lost their children at around the same time. Although, whereas she had Pearl and Thea to keep Clara's memory alive, there was no sign of any grandchildren in the family photographs.

Izzy nodded. 'Indeed. I lost my husband to the Great War and, do you know, I'm almost glad we never had children, because I'd hate to see them caught up in this one.'

Deedee tried to remember anything else Pearl had told her about Mr Haughton but could only recall that she'd said he was a widower.

Izzy was still speaking. 'It was a lonely existence, though. No one seemed to want us widows after the war. I'd got a job in a munitions factory and was told I was doing vital work, but as soon as the war ended I was expected to make way for the returning men, with no thought as to how I was going to make a living on a meagre widow's pension.'

It was a tale Deedee had heard all too many times, and it never failed to give her a stab of guilt, as she had been left well-provided for. 'I know, it's shameful. I hope the country does better for our women at the end of this war.'

'Of course, you've got two granddaughters, haven't you? I've met them a few times. You must be so proud of them. I was terribly sorry to hear about Greg Tallis. He's a lovely man. I do hope he's safe and sound. Has there been any more news?'

Deedee shook her head. 'Pearl would be the first to hear, of course. That's why I want to be there for her.' On reflection, this was the perfect lead-in to the question of her finding alternative accommodation. 'It's very kind of Mr Haughton to give up his house to a complete stranger,' she said, 'but I've no idea how long I'll need to stay, and he must want his house back soon. I was thinking of looking for somewhere in Lincoln. Do you have any suggestions of somewhere suitable?'

Izzy looked horrified. 'Mr Haughton gave strict instructions that you were to stay as long as you need. Besides, he's been using the apartment at his office more and more, what with it being impossible for him to get petrol for his car now. You'd be doing both him and me a real favour by staying here.'

Deedee could see she wasn't going to get anywhere, so graciously thanked Izzy, then asked, 'Is there a garden? I wouldn't mind stretching my legs.'

'Of course. You can go out through the French windows. There's only a small garden here, but Mr Haughton told me to say you would be free to walk in the grounds of Haughton Hall, too. The officers there have been very good about letting him and any guests use the grounds, although most of the gardens have been dug up for vegetable plots. They left the rose garden, but it's too late in the year for roses, and the bushes have been pruned right back. You should see them in the summer, though. They're a wonderful sight, and the smell...' Izzy closed her eyes in ecstasy as though the scent of roses had drifted into the room.

Deedee couldn't deny a great curiosity to see Tom's real home, and so hurried to put on her coat and outdoor shoes and let herself out. She quickly saw that, as Izzy had said, there was only a tiny plot attached to the gatehouse, and that had all been turned over to growing vegetables. However, a path led through a gap in the hedge, and she followed it out into the grounds of Haughton Hall. Her eye was immediately drawn to the imposing brick hall at the end of a long, gravelled driveway. There were several military trucks parked outside, but they were dwarfed by the sheer size of the late-Elizabethan manor. Pale sunlight shone across the frosty grass and lit the red brick in a mellow glow. Deedee tried to imagine what it must have been like to live in a house that size. In its heyday the number of staff needed to keep it running must have been enough to fill a small village.

No wonder he had never considered her good enough to marry.

Pushing that intrusive thought from her mind, she hurried along a path that branched out from the driveway and seemed to lead towards a secluded orchard. The fruit was long gone, apart from a few rotten windfalls that had been left to lie among the gnarled roots, but it was pleasant to wander under the boughs and imagine how breathtaking the orchard must look in the spring when the blossom was out.

A towering yew hedge bordered the orchard, and she followed its line for a while, stamping her feet to fight the chill. She was on the point of turning back when she spied an archway in the hedge, and she couldn't resist peering through. She had found the rose garden and could understand why it had inspired Izzy to wax lyrical. Narrow gravel paths criss-crossed the garden and each plot held carefully pruned rose bushes. Deedee, who was a keen gardener herself, wished she could have seen them in bloom, for they must be a magnificent sight. She was glad one patch of beauty had been allowed to remain despite the need for growing vegetables elsewhere in the grounds. Even though the garden was a mere shadow of what it would be in the summer, she couldn't resist stepping through the archway and strolling along the path that led around the perimeter. If nothing else, it would do her good to have a proper walk after spending the day before on cramped and crowded trains.

Set at intervals into the deep hedge were benches, and she reflected on how pleasant it would be to sit there on a warm day, listening to the hum of insects while breathing in the heady scent of roses. On a day like today, however, she would have to keep moving unless she wanted to lose all feeling in her feet.

Yet, when she walked past one of the benches, she was surprised to see a gentleman sitting there. He was swathed in a thick coat, the brim of his hat obscuring his face, and her first thought was that he was connected with Bomber Command and resident at the Hall. 'Excuse me,' she said, stepping away, not wishing to disturb him. But then thinking she ought to explain her presence in a place that was, after all, in the hands of the RAF, she added, 'I was told I was allowed to walk here, but I'll leave you in peace.'

She turned round, but the man said one word that caused her to freeze. 'Hope?'

Chapter Six

She closed her eyes. It was him!

Breathe. Stay calm. He hadn't laid eyes on her for over fifty years, so she could try to brazen it out. Summoning her best acting skills, she put on an enquiring smile and turned to face him. 'I'm sorry – were you speaking to me?' She could have kicked herself the moment the words were out of her mouth. Who else would he have been addressing – the roses? 'My name isn't Hope, though. I'm Mrs Pritchard. Edith Pritchard.'

Until that point, she hadn't dared look him in the eye but instead had been speaking to his chin. A good chin. As strong as she remembered. The passing years had refined his features, made him, if possible, better looking than she remembered. How unfair that many men only seemed to grow more handsome with age, whereas she was suddenly conscious of the wrinkles on her forehead and around her mouth that stubbornly persisted despite the frequent application of rosewater. She also tried to remember when she had last hennaed her hair. Were her roots showing? Now, however, she dared to meet his gaze, giving him what she intended to be a polite smile that somehow conveyed she was needed elsewhere.

It was a mistake. Those blue eyes. She had spent hours contemplating them when she had been foolish enough to believe him in love with her. They were unchanged, deep blue windows into his agile mind. She could read his puzzlement. 'No. You *are* Hope. Hope Burnell. I'd know that voice anywhere. I'd know *you* anywhere. You haven't changed a bit.'

Any further lies would be pointless and leave her looking foolish. She sighed. 'Yes, although no one calls me that now. Hope was my stage name. I don't have to ask who you are. You haven't aged a day, Tom.'

'I haven't been called *that* in a while, either.' He frowned. 'Wait. Edith Pritchard – you're Pearl and Thea's grandmother?' When she nodded, he said, 'Who'd have believed it? All this time they've been telling me about their grandmother, and it was you? I offered my house to Hope Burnell!' Then, 'Why did you never tell me your real name?'

She shrugged, relieved he was sticking with the easy questions. 'I'd got so used to it by the time I met you that it felt more real than my true name. It never occurred to me to correct you.' Which had been convenient, considering she had been able to use her real name in Shrewsbury, secure in the knowledge no one would connect her to Hope Burnell.

She felt a hysterical laugh bubbling up from deep inside her and threatening to burst forth. They'd been lovers. They'd been everything to each other. Or so she'd thought. Yet here they were, conversing like casual acquaintances who'd happened to meet in the street. Any minute now, they'd start commenting on the weather.

Or maybe not. In Tom's expressive eyes she could see a hesitancy, and she guessed he was building up to asking the question she didn't want to answer. In an attempt to discourage him, she said in a dismissive tone, 'Well, it must be at least fifty years since we last saw each other. A lot's happened in our lives since then,' trying to imply that the episode with Tom had been a passing whim rather than the axis her life had revolved around. But then, because she didn't want him to think her completely heartless, she said in a softer voice, 'Pearl told me you lost your wife and son. Of course, I had no idea at the time exactly who you were, but I'm very sorry.'

He gave a stiff nod. 'Thank you. And I'm sorry for your losses too.' He rose. 'If you'll excuse me, I must get on. I just wanted to introduce myself, but, as it turns out, there was no need. I'm sure you don't want to be disturbed any longer, so I'll return to the office. Please stay for as long as Pearl needs you.'

With that he lifted his hat and then walked away. Deedee gazed after him, partly relieved and partly indignant that *he* was acting like the injured party. And if he could leave like that, he wasn't the Tom she had known and loved. Her Tom had been loving and kind, and some people had mistakenly taken it as a sign of weakness. But at heart he was passionate and stood up for his principles. If he could walk away now, then she had been right to believe he had never truly loved her.

Five paces down the path, Tom stopped, then turned to face her. 'Fifty-one.'

'I beg your pardon?'

'Fifty-one years. That's how long since we last saw one another.'

'Oh. I—'

But he wasn't finished. 'I've had a question for fifty-one years, and if I don't find the answer now, I never will.

For all that time I've longed to know why you left without a word. Without so much as a letter. Why did you leave?'

'Why did I leave?' Deedee's voice was high with indignation. How dare he pretend he wasn't to blame? 'I only left because you'd made it quite clear you didn't love me. Now, if you'll excuse me, I've got a bus to catch.' Then she realised with dawning horror that the only way out was past him. There was nothing for it. Stiffening her spine, she marched towards him. Why didn't he move? Surely he could have nothing more to add to this painful conversation. She certainly had nothing more to say. Not anything she wanted to make known, anyway. However, seeing he remained stock-still on the path, and unwilling to let him have the last word, she pulled herself up to her full height and when she had drawn level with him said, 'No doubt you regret allowing me the use of your house, now you know who I really am. Rest assured, I've already told Pearl it's quite impossible for me to stay in your home for longer than strictly necessary. We'll be looking for alternative accommodation tomorrow, so I'll be out of your hair very soon.' She could only pray Tom didn't turn her out of the house right away, or she really would be sleeping in the cathedral crypt.

She walked past, but Tom's voice stopped her. 'You already knew this was my house? *Pearl* knows?'

Blast and buggery, now she'd dropped Pearl in it. Why couldn't she think before she spoke? 'I recognised you at the wedding,' she said with a sigh. 'I told Thea at the time, because she noticed my shock, but I only mentioned that we had been involved in the past – no details. Thea told Pearl later on and she wanted to tell you, but I begged her not to. Neither of them liked keeping it secret from you, but they did what I asked. So if you want to blame anyone, blame me, but please keep Pearl out of it, especially now.'

Now Deedee was shaking, desperate to get away. She set off down the path again, braced for Tom to call her back at any moment, but he said nothing more.

When they had got off the bus the night before, Pearl had pointed out where to wait for the Lincoln one, and she headed in that direction until she remembered that Tom had said he needed to return to his office. He would surely need to catch the bus too, and the thought of sitting in the same space as him for fifteen minutes was too horrible to contemplate. Instead she returned to the house and retreated to her room. She was able to see the bus stop from her window, and it wasn't until she had seen Tom depart that she allowed herself to relax. Then she remembered she was sleeping in *his* room and got upset all over again. Really, what was Pearl thinking, agreeing to such an outrageous arrangement!

Of course, Pearl didn't know the whole truth. Only two people in the world had ever known that, and one of them – Tom's father, the man whose portrait hung in the foyer of the Haughton Newspaper Group – was dead. That left only her, and she would make sure it remained that way. Because she didn't think either of her granddaughters would look at her in the same way if they ever found out what she'd done.

–

Pearl's telephone rang, causing her heart to thump against her ribs. She picked up the receiver with hands that shook. 'Corporal Tallis.'

But the person on the other end was a representative from an advertising firm they dealt with, wanting to buy space in the next four editions. Her heart rate eased as she dealt with the call, trying to steady her hands enough to write legible notes. It wasn't Greg's CO with news, nor was it anyone informing her she had a telegram waiting for her. Just as none of the other fifteen calls she'd taken that morning had been.

When she finally replaced the receiver, she blew out a breath. Although she knew she'd done the right thing by refusing to take any time off, it was proving harder than she'd anticipated to stay focused. On a whim, she opened a drawer and pulled out the invitation she'd been sent from RAF Fenthorpe.

> The officers of RAF Fenthorpe cordially
> invite you to their Mistletoe and Merriment
> Christmas Dance. Come and celebrate like
> it's the last Christmas of the war.

And surely that had to be true. The Allies were marching for Berlin. Everyone said it was only a matter of time. Even if it was too late for Greg, it was something worth celebrating. Jenny had been right; decorating the ballroom would be a good way of taking her mind off this interminable waiting.

A tap at her open door made her glance up, and she saw Mr Haughton. She smiled and invited him in, glad of the interruption. But when he sat down, she noticed that he appeared agitated, not a state she usually associated with him. 'Is everything all right?'

Her curiosity turned to concern when he pulled out a handkerchief and mopped his brow.

'Not really, no.'

Convinced he was ill, she hastily said, 'I'll ask Mrs Norris to call a doctor.'

She half rose, but he waved her back into her chair. 'No, no. There's no need. I'm quite well.' He put away his hanky, then looked her squarely in the eye. 'I met your grandmother this morning.'

Well, that would certainly explain why he was so flustered; Deedee tended to have that effect on people. 'Oh?' she replied, her thoughts churning, wondering how to discover if he'd recognised Deedee without giving her away if he remained ignorant. 'How was she this morning?'

'Full of vim and looking remarkably like an actress I used to know in my youth.'

'Ah.' Then he must also know that she and Thea had been aware of his role in their grandmother's past. 'Look, I'm sorry—'

'No, I'm sorry. I don't want you to think I blame you or Thea for keeping your grandmother's identity secret. She told me she'd made you promise against your better judgement.'

'Well, against Thea's better judgement, really. She had this notion that it would be fun if the two of you met.'

'It was certainly *not* fun.' He raked his hands through his hair, and Pearl had a sudden glimpse of the handsome young man he must have been when he had captured Deedee's heart.

'I am sorry you had to find out that way. If you don't mind her staying in your house a while longer, we've already arranged to look for other lodgings tomorrow.'

'No, that's why I've come to see you. I said the same thing to her but, in the circumstances, she might not have believed me. She's free to stay as long as she needs. I don't like to think of her in an uncomfortable boarding house, and I'm sure that's all she'll find at short notice. Besides, with no fuel for the foreseeable future, I should have made the move to the apartment months ago. It makes much more sense for me to stay here until I can use my car again, and I don't like to think of Mrs Stockwell all alone. Your grandmother would be doing me a favour if she stayed.' His eyes shadowed. 'Although after this morning, I'm not sure if she'd want to do me a favour.'

At lunchtime, Pearl met Deedee at the bus stop as arranged and they went to get lunch. A British Restaurant had been set up not far from the newspaper office, so she took Deedee there. Now Pearl was lodging in Rosebery Avenue, she had been issued with a ration book, which she had handed to her landlady Mrs Dale. Although she was sure she was getting her fair share, the food never seemed to go far. The British Restaurant – a fancy name for a community-run canteen serving nourishing if unimaginative fare – was a convenient place for Pearl to eat a filling meal at lunchtime without having to use her precious rations.

It was based in a church hall a five-minute walk from the bus stop. They spoke of nothing more than the cold weather and the likelihood of snow during the walk, and Pearl was grateful that her grandmother didn't ask her how she was feeling, because she didn't think she could speak of Greg without crying, and she had struggled all morning to keep her emotions in check. When they arrived in the busy hall, Pearl and Deedee handed over nine pence each

– another reason why Pearl chose to eat here whenever possible – and joined the queue. There was no choice of menu, but Pearl always found the food tasty. Today there was carrot and parsnip soup with a slice of bread, followed by mutton stew and a bowl of jam sponge with custard. Plus a cup of tea so strong it stained the inside of the mug a peaty brown. She and Deedee carried their laden tray to a table close to the stove at the back of the hall.

Deedee picked up her cutlery, only to fumble. Her knife, fork and spoons dropped onto the wooden floor with a ringing clatter, adding to the already noisy hall. 'Bugger!' Her exclamation burst out just as there was a lull in the scraping of chairs and clashing of cutlery around the room, and several heads turned.

Pearl stared at her in surprise. While she was used to Deedee muttering the occasional oath in the privacy of her own home, she had never known her grandmother say anything coarse in public. Not without severe provocation, at any rate. To her shock, she saw that Deedee's eyes brimmed with tears.

'It's no problem.' Pearl handed over her own cutlery, then rose and helped Deedee retrieve what had fallen. 'Here, you use mine, and I'll fetch some more.'

When she returned, she found Deedee slipping her compact back into her handbag and looking more composed. Yet the fresh layer of powder couldn't completely conceal the unusually red cheeks, and Pearl studied her grandmother in growing concern. 'Has something happened? You don't look yourself.' Then she remembered her earlier conversation with Mr Haughton and put two and two together. 'Ah. Mr Haughton told me you'd met.'

Deedee picked up her bread and shot Pearl a glare. 'Did you put him up to it?'

'Of course not!'

'Hmmm.' Deedee started to tear her bread into shreds. 'Are you sure you didn't drop even the tiniest hint for him to visit his new tenant?'

'Positive. You told me you didn't want to see him, and I respect that. He must have made that decision all by himself. Not unless Thea—' She shook her head. While she didn't put it past her sister to try to bring the two together, Thea hadn't seen Mr Haughton since the day she'd received the telegram. 'Forget that. Thea hasn't been out of Fenthorpe since you arrived.'

Deedee sighed. 'I suppose he must have thought it was the proper thing to welcome me to his home.' Her lips twisted in a wry smile. 'I don't know who got the bigger shock, him or me.'

Pearl finished her soup, then picked up her fork and prodded a lump of cabbage. She was starting to wish she had considered the choice of eatery more carefully. Swallowing the soup with a stomach knotted with anxiety was bad enough. She had no idea how she was going to manage the stew. But wasting food was unforgivable. Although she sensed Deedee's reluctance to say more about her encounter, Pearl desperately needed a distraction. What would Thea do? She had her answer in the time it took her to skewer a lump of meat with her fork. 'So are you going to tell me exactly what happened, or should I ask Mr Haughton?'

'Don't you dare!'

Pearl simply grinned and raised her eyebrows expectantly.

Deedee subsided, muttering, 'I knew it was a bad idea for you to serve in the same place as Thea.' She stared at the pieces of bread on her plate as though not understanding how it could have got into such a mess, then tipped the lot into the remains of her soup and stirred. 'Fine. I'll tell you, but let me finish my soup before it gets cold.'

When Deedee finally took up her tale, Pearl put down her knife and fork and gave it her full attention. She felt no surprise at hearing how awkward the meeting had been, but when she heard how Thomas had demanded to know why Deedee had left London she fixed her grandmother with a narrowed gaze. 'Wait. The story you told me and Thea last night implied that the relationship died a natural death and ended with no hard feelings. It doesn't sound like that now.' She also remembered Thea's recollection of the shock on Deedee's face when she had seen Mr Haughton at the wedding.

'It all happened over fifty years ago. You can't expect me to remember everything perfectly.'

Pearl said nothing but continued to regard Deedee with an unwavering gaze.

Finally Deedee flung down her spoon. 'Oh, very well. I suppose I did leave abruptly, and Tom had reason to be upset at the time, but how could I have known he'd still want answers all these years later?'

'What did you tell him?'

'That I left because it was obvious he didn't love me. I mean, he married not long after and was happy with his wife, so he can't have been upset with me for long.'

Pearl thought about this as she finished the last of her stew. 'It's true, he always speaks with fondness of his wife. I'm sure he genuinely loved her.'

'There you go. So he can't have felt too bad. Anyway, I told him we would start looking for new lodgings tomorrow, so he won't have to put up with my presence in the house for much longer.'

'Well, that's what I need to speak to you about. Mr Haughton came to see me this morning – he must have just got in from seeing you – and insisted that you remain at the Gatehouse for as long as you need. He said that, although he had been shocked to see you, it didn't change his mind.'

Deedee snorted. 'Always was too chivalrous for his own good.'

Pearl thought Deedee looked more wistful than contemptuous, though. 'Well?' she prompted. 'Are you going to stay? You'd be far more comfortable there.'

Deedee scraped the last of her stew onto her fork before replying. 'It's tempting – it really is a lovely house, and I like Mrs Stockwell.' She appeared to hesitate before giving her head a shake. 'It's no good. It wouldn't feel right.'

Pearl supposed she couldn't blame her. She tried to imagine how she would have felt if she and Greg hadn't got back together after their break-up and she'd discovered some years later that she was staying in a house that belonged to him. But thoughts of Greg brought the tightness back to her throat. She gave Deedee a tight smile. 'Fine. We'll look for somewhere else on Saturday.' At least it would be something to keep her occupied when she wasn't at work. 'And it's the decorations meeting tonight, so we'll be in Fenthorpe Hall most of the evening.'

'I was thinking about that,' Deedee said as she tucked into her jam sponge. 'I'd feel awkward going into an RAF house when no one knows who I am. I think it's best if I stay in the Gatehouse while you go into the meeting this time. You can ask everyone if they don't mind me joining in next time.'

Pearl agreed and turned the conversation to the latest news from Shrewsbury. It was only after lunch, when she and Deedee had gone their separate ways, that it struck her how Deedee's tale still didn't explain Thomas's agitation that morning. She could have sworn her grandmother was telling the truth when she had claimed she'd fled London because Thomas had never loved her, yet in that case why had their meeting put Thomas in such a state? Surely it was nothing less than the agony of lost love.

Chapter Seven

True to her word, Deedee stayed behind when Pearl, Thea and Jenny left for Fenthorpe Hall later that evening. The three friends had popped in to the Gatehouse to see her and promised to return to tell her how the meeting had gone.

'Are you sure you won't come with us?' Pearl asked as she pulled on her greatcoat to protect her from the icy wind.

Deedee shook her head. 'I don't want to create any awkwardness if any others aren't happy for me to join in. They could hardly say so to my face, could they?'

'I don't know,' Thea said with a grin. 'You never seemed to have a problem creating awkwardness before. I'll never forget you marching into school to tell off Miss Oldhurst for giving me a D for my essay on Dickens.'

'That woman had no right to mark you down simply because you didn't share her opinions. And Dickens' heroines *are* insipid. It made me so cross that those women were being held up as examples to all the girls at that school.'

'I rest my case,' Thea said, wrapping a scarf round her neck.

Deedee shooed them away, then retired to the living room fireside and picked up her knitting. The truth was that the prospect of setting foot in Fenthorpe Hall gave her uncomfortable, prickly sensations down her spine. It was, after all, Tom's true residence, home to generations of his ancestors. It had been bad enough seeing the portrait of Tom's father in the Haughton Newspaper Group foyer; no matter that all the family portraits at Fenthorpe Hall would have been packed away for the duration of the RAF occupation, Deedee felt that the very walls would have absorbed centuries of contempt of 'her sort'. She couldn't summon the courage to cross the threshold. Not yet.

The tinkle of a bell roused her from her musings; too faint to be the front door, so Deedee guessed it was a visitor at the back door. Probably a friend of Mrs Stockwell. The low murmur of voices in the kitchen confirmed her suspicion, so she set her concentration to the sock she was knitting. She had managed to drop a stitch somewhere and was so busy trying to correct it that it took a while for the insistent knocking on the living room door to filter through her consciousness. Strange. It could only be Mrs Stockwell, and she had never bothered to knock before.

'Come in,' she called without turning to the door, then looked down at her knitting. 'Can you help me with this? I've dropped a stitch, but I can't for the life of me see where.'

A masculine hand took the half-completed sock. A hand that was definitely not Mrs Stockwell's. 'I'll see what I can do.'

Her heart pounding, Deedee turned her head and found herself looking at Tom. She sprang to her feet. 'What are you doing here?'

'I know I said I would leave you in peace, but I wanted to come and apologise.' He sank into the armchair opposite Deedee's and gestured for her to sit, hampered slightly by the ball of yarn he held in that hand. 'Please will you hear me out?'

Deedee sank back into the chair, eying him warily. 'Very well.' She pulled another knitting needle from the workbag she had placed at the foot of her chair and waved it at him as though it was a rapier and she was Errol Flynn. 'Although I can't be responsible for my actions if I don't like what I hear.'

Tom chuckled. 'Still the same fiery Hope.'

'And don't think you can get around me with flattery. Say what you have to say then leave me in peace. Unless you really can correct my knitting.'

'If only everything in life was as easy. You've clearly picked up two stitches just here.' He pointed out the place. 'I can put it right in a jiffy.'

And under Deedee's amazed gaze he did just that, deftly unravelling the work until he undid the mistake, then took up the needles and completed the row with nimble fingers.

'Where did you learn that?' Deedee asked, forgetting in her admiration that she was supposed to be annoyed with him.

Tom set down the knitting on the table beside his chair before replying. 'Not long after I was married, I made the mistake of implying that my work was far more demanding and difficult than Ursula's.' He cleared his throat, looking awkward. 'Ursula was my wife.'

Of course she was. Ursula sounded like the name a genteel Victorian family would give their daughter. Ursula's family wouldn't have encouraged their daughter to go on the stage. The only singing Ursula would have done would have been in drawing rooms. And possibly she had learned the pianoforte or the harp. The correct accomplishments for a well-brought-up young lady.

However, Deedee was burning with curiosity to hear Tom's tale, to get a glimpse into the life he had led after Deedee had done the right thing and left him to lead the life he could never have had with her. She leaned forward, looking him in the eye for the first time that evening. 'Go on.'

Tom's expression softened as he clearly lost himself in recollections of happier times. 'Well, Ursula was having none of that. She was rather like you in that respect. She insisted on teaching me to knit and darn, saying I had no right to pass judgement until I had tried it for myself. And she was right, of course. I didn't find it easy.'

'But you obviously stuck with it,' Deedee said, with a nod towards the knitting.

At that Tom grinned, and the years fell away until she was looking at the man she had fallen in love with. The breath caught in her throat. 'I couldn't give up, could I? I'm proud to say I became a dab hand, thanks to the expert tuition I received, of course.'

For a moment, Deedee found herself regretting that she had never met his wife. She sounded like the strong-minded kind of woman she would have liked. Only for a moment, though. It hurt more than she cared to admit that Tom had not married a simpering miss that she could have held in contempt but a woman who sounded suspiciously like Deedee herself.

She swallowed. 'What a charming tale,' she said, hating herself for the bitterness lacing her tone. 'Now perhaps you could explain why you decided to disturb me. I thought you said you owed me an apology.' She knew she was being unfair. She was the one who had wanted to hear the story, after all.

If her tone annoyed him, Tom didn't show it. Instead he nodded. 'I do. I shouldn't have brought up the past. That can only lead to ill feeling. I have no excuse. It was ungentlemanly of me, especially when you are my guest. I don't want you to feel uncomfortable about staying here.'

'That's… good of you.' Deedee wasn't usually one to lack words, but she found herself floundering now.

'That's not really what I came here to say, though,' Tom went on. He gripped the arms of his chair. 'Look, I admit I was shocked when I saw you earlier. You were the last person I expected to find at my house. But Pearl tells me you intend to leave.'

'I think it best, in the circumstances. Don't you?'

'No. I invited you to stay for as long as you need. As long as *Pearl* needs. I'm not going to throw you out just because we… knew each other years ago.'

There was a slight pause, and Deedee wondered if he, like her, was recalling the same vivid memories of exactly how well they had known each other. Mrs Stockwell must have got hold of better-quality coal because Deedee could swear the fire was burning hotter than before. 'Even so, I wouldn't feel comfortable staying.'

Tom nodded. 'Because of me. The thing is, however you feel about me, I know you think the world of Pearl and would do anything for her. While I haven't known her as long, I think the world of her too. I want to give her all the help I can through this terrible time, and that means I won't stay away from her, even if that means running into you from time to time.'

'I refuse to let you drag Pearl into this. Doesn't the poor girl have enough to deal with?'

Tom spread his hands in apology. 'That's not what I meant. Of course I don't want to give her any more trouble. Please hear me out.'

'Go on.' Deedee didn't trust herself to say any more.

'Thank you.' He pulled out an antique pocket watch and twisted it between his fingers. The sight made Deedee's heart swell, for, when she had known him, he had always done it when he was agitated. She remained silent, waiting for him to resume, which he did shortly afterwards. 'The last thing I want is to cause Pearl any more distress. That's why I'd like to clear the air between us. Not by raking up the past,' he added, throwing up his hands again as though to ward off Deedee's objections. 'I just mean that, as we're inevitably going to bump into each other during the course of your visit, it would be best if we could do so without there being any bad feelings between us. I can't deny that the way you left without a word hurt a great deal at the time, but it was a long time ago, and I'm willing to forget it, if you're willing to forgive me for whatever it was that caused you to leave.'

Deedee drew a sharp breath. Of course she had left without a word. She couldn't have stayed a minute longer after discovering that he had never meant to marry her. But common sense took over before she could blurt out the protest on the tip of her tongue. Tom was right about one thing: if they couldn't meet without sparks flying, Pearl wouldn't get the support she needed. 'Fine,' she said. 'You have my word that I'll be polite if we meet again, and we'll leave the past in the past.' Easier said than done, though, when seeing him caress his watch with long, agile fingers brought back memories that, while they were over fifty years in the past, could still make her cheeks burn. Thankfully, he didn't appear to notice the effect he was having on her, and some of his tension seemed to drain from him with her words. 'Anyway,' she added, 'we won't be so likely to run into each other once I find accommodation in Lincoln.'

'And that's the other thing I needed to say. Please don't feel you have to leave. I have a comfortable flat in Lincoln, and it makes sense for me to stay there rather than have to catch the bus every day.'

'It still doesn't feel right.'

'But my house is available and convenient. And consider this. You and Pearl will have to spend Saturday seeking a room, and I can guarantee you'll only get a very basic room at this short notice. And knowing Pearl, she'll be worried about you, worried that you're cold and uncomfortable. Whereas if you stay here, you would at least be putting her mind at rest on that score.'

Deedee could have argued with him for hours on any of his other points, but this last one struck home. 'I'd hate to cause her any more worry,' she conceded.

'Then you'll stay?'

Deedee considered it. She did genuinely feel uncomfortable staying in Tom's house, yet she couldn't deny that moving elsewhere would be an added burden for Pearl, and it was this that decided her. 'Very well. I'll stay for now and see how it goes.'

Tom's face cleared. 'Good. And you have my word that I'll leave you in peace here and won't visit unannounced again. And should we meet in Lincoln, neither of us will give Pearl any cause to think we're not friends.'

Maybe not, Deedee reflected when Tom left soon after, but she couldn't imagine ever seeing him without feeling a stab of betrayal. Or a lurch of guilt when she remembered what she had done. She could only pray Tom never found out, because she couldn't imagine him allowing her to stay in his house if he knew.

–

Stepping into the imposing hallway of Fenthorpe Hall, Pearl was struck by a fresh wave of misery. She was taken back to the day Greg had proposed and she'd cast caution to the wind and agreed to marry him as soon as possible, deciding to seize whatever happiness was possible when each day brought the very real possibility that it could be his last. Greg had received his commission at the same time, and they had imagined that they would start their married life here, at RAF Fenthorpe's officers' quarters. It felt cruel that the first time she was seeing the inside of the place she didn't know if she was a wife or a widow.

A WAAF with a clipboard addressed them. 'Here for the decorations committee? Names, please.'

Once their names had been ticked off on the list, the WAAF directed them to the ballroom.

'Trust the RAF to turn something fun into a boring committee meeting,' Thea muttered as they headed towards a huge set of double doors.

Pearl shot her a sharp look. 'Are you always this grumpy or is it just because Fitz left this afternoon?' Then she winced; she'd been aiming for a jokey tone but had ended up sounding bitter and shrewish.

Thea glared back and opened her mouth, then subsided when Jenny gave her an unsubtle nudge. That only made

Pearl feel worse. She hated having her sister and friend tiptoeing around her as though she was so fragile she might shatter at the slightest upset. She grabbed Thea's hand before she could push open one of the doors. 'I'm sorry. That came out wrong. Of course you're going to be upset you've said goodbye to Fitz.'

Thea's expression softened. 'It's fine. Really. I under-stand.'

That only made Pearl feel worse, though. She wanted to lash out at someone, and Thea, whose boyfriend had returned when Greg hadn't, was the perfect target.

However, some of her bitterness seeped away when she saw the magnificent ballroom. Even in its wartime state, with windows boarded up and chandeliers removed, the pillared walls and polished oak floor retained the grandeur of its heyday.

Jenny was looking around in awe. 'Look at the size of this place. We'll have our work cut out decorating it for Christmas next year!' Although she had spoken in a hushed voice, as though she were in a library or church, the high ceiling magnified her words. A huddle of uniformed men and women who were gathered at the far end of the room beckoned them over.

A woman with a single thin ring on her sleeves denoting the rank of assistant section officer smiled at Jenny and said, 'I know we've taken on a huge job, but I'm sure we're up to the task.'

Once everyone had sat in the chairs arranged in a semicircle at one end of the long room, the WAAF officer cleared her throat and introduced herself as Assistant Section Officer Annie Brown. 'I know there are only nine of us and this is a huge room,' she said with a small smile at Jenny, 'but I'm confident we can make this place look spectacular for the party. We've been allocated a small budget' – here she named a modest amount – 'but, as that won't stretch far, I'd like us to make as much as we can, including collecting greenery for garlands and wreaths. What I'd like to do this meeting is hear your ideas and then allocate tasks to you in pairs. We all work different shifts, so be sure to partner up with someone on the same watch.'

There was a short break while everyone organised themselves into pairs. Thea and Jenny immediately paired up as, although they worked in different sections, their hours roughly coincided. At the end, Pearl was the only one left without a partner.

'My grandmother is staying at the moment,' she said to Brown, 'and says she'd like to help. Would that be all right?'

Brown looked relieved. 'Of course. Give me her name and I'll make sure she's allowed entry.' She made a note. 'Now you've all had time to look around the ballroom, let's hear your ideas.'

A young aircraftwoman's hand shot up. 'We've got to have a tree. It wouldn't be a proper Christmas dance without one.'

There was a murmur of agreement, but Brown looked doubtful. 'I agree it would be lovely, but does anyone know how much one would cost? I've got a feeling that would be our whole budget gone right there.'

Then Pearl remembered the day Mr Haughton had shown her and the rest of the *Bombshell* team around the Fenthorpe Hall grounds, back in the days when the newspaper had been for RAF Fenthorpe alone and not distributed to the whole of 5 Group, as it was now. 'You know, I think there's a patch of woodland in these grounds that has some suitable trees. We should probably ask Mr Haughton – the owner of Fenthorpe Hall – but he might let us cut one down.'

'Good idea,' Brown said. 'You work with Mr Haughton, don't you?' At Pearl's nod, she went on, 'Then I'll leave it with you to ask him and, if he agrees, you and your grandmother can take on the job of identifying a suitable tree and decorating it. I'm sure one of the groundsmen will cut it down for us and carry it inside.'

Great. That was bound to place Deedee in Mr Haughton's path again. But she couldn't object without revealing Deedee's past relationship with him, and she was sure Deedee would hate that. With half a mind she listened to the discussion move to collecting holly, ivy and other greenery, while she resigned herself to leaving Deedee out of anything that might also involve Thomas.

Her focus only fully returned to the meeting when Jenny stuck up her hand. 'We must have mistletoe.'

Most of the other WAAFs gave murmurs of agreement, and a WAAF Pearl remembered from her days in Flying Control said, 'Got your eye on a chap, have you?'

'Any idea where we can get some?' Brown asked. 'I didn't think mistletoe grew around here – not enough trees.'

But Jenny was nodding. 'There's an apple orchard I noticed a mile or two down the road, and I've seen a lot of mistletoe there.'

'Excellent. Then I'll put you and Cooper in charge of asking the owner's permission and, hopefully, collecting it.'

Brown went on to talk about ribbons needed for the wreaths and mistletoe sprigs and said she would buy that from their funds as she could try to arrange a discount for purchasing a large quantity. While Brown was speaking, Pearl's gaze wandered around the ballroom, and she tried to visualise it decorated for Christmas. For the most part, she could see it looking festive, with garlands draped round the huge fireplace and on the high, beamed ceiling, and a large Christmas tree in the corner behind the band. But no matter how hard she tried, she couldn't imagine any garland that would improve the appearance of the boarded windows. The boards clearly covered a vast span of French windows, which must lead to the terrace and lawns. Or what were the lawns before they had been dug up to make vegetable plots. Clearly the RAF, when they had requisitioned Fenthorpe Hall, had decided that the cost of procuring enough blackout material would be prohibitive, so had boarded them up instead. Pearl thought it a great shame. It would have looked spectacular with candles outside on the terrace. Of course, it would have been completely against blackout regulations, which were in place for good reason. Still, she could dream.

And then, just as Brown asked if anyone had any other ideas, inspiration struck. 'We could paint the boards,' Pearl said.

Brown frowned at them. 'What, you mean like in green or red, to go with the decorations?'

Pearl hastened to explain. 'No, I mean we could paint decorations on them.'

Jenny gasped, clearly catching Pearl's meaning. 'We could paint Christmas trees.'

'Exactly.' Pearl shot Jenny a smile. 'I'm no artist, but I think I could manage a Christmas tree and some colourful baubles, given enough paint, of course.'

Thea, meanwhile, was examining the boarded area with narrowed eyes. 'You know, I think there would be space for four trees with a different Christmassy scene in the middle.' He eyes lit up. 'Wouldn't it be wonderful if we had a scenic artist who could paint something for us – a glowing fireplace, maybe.'

This led to a murmur of approval around the group.

'I could ask Geoff Yates,' Pearl said. 'He does the artwork for the *Bombshell*. He was an artist before the war – well, he still is an artist of course, but you know what I mean. I think he'd enjoy it.'

'But that does mean the ballroom will have a Christmas scene all year round. Won't the officers object?' the Flying Control WAAF asked.

'Anything's got to be better than plain boards,' Thea stated. 'Anyway, everyone says the war will be over soon, and then it won't be long before these boards are taken down.'

And so it was agreed that Pearl would speak to Yates and the others would ask around the neighbourhood to see if they could scrounge tins of paint. Annie Brown agreed to buy anything, such as brushes, turpentine and additional paint, to add to any equipment they could borrow in Fenthorpe. Each pair, apart from Brown's, was assigned a space to paint their tree, and the larger middle section would be left for Yates to work his artistic miracles.

However, talk of the war ending inevitably led Pearl's thoughts back to Greg, and she felt her insides twist at the cruel fate that had led Greg to go missing just when it seemed the end was in sight. She sat through the rest of the meeting in a daze.

As they were leaving, Jenny gave Pearl's arm a squeeze. 'Are you all right? You look ever so pale.'

'I'm fine.' Seeing Jenny's doubtful look, Pearl made an effort to smile. 'Really, I'm fine. I had a wobble when Thea mentioned the end of the war, but I feel better now. And you were right, Jenny. It was a really good idea to volunteer for the decorations committee. It's good to have something to think about other than… well, you know.'

Jenny nodded, then said, 'It was an injennyus idea about painting over the window boards.'

Pearl stared at her friend, mentally spelling out *in-jenny-us*, by now used to Jenny's quirk of mispronouncing words she'd read but never heard. However, Thea got there first. She chuckled and said, 'I think you mean ingenious, although your way of saying it is better.'

'No, really?' Jenny wailed. 'I don't believe it! Now I understand why one of the Met Officers gave me an odd look when I told him I thought maximum/minimum thermometers were injenny— in*genious*.'

She soon recovered, though, and chattered on about her ideas for the tree she would be painting with Thea until they were outside. She stopped and fumbled in her pockets for her torch and the other two followed suit. The air was so cold it burned Pearl's nose, and when she turned on her torch she saw a frost was forming on the path.

'Gosh, it looks like we're in for a cold night,' Jenny said. 'I wonder if it will snow soon?'

'You tell us. You're the Met WAAF,' Thea retorted.

'It's not as easy to forecast as rain,' Jenny said. 'Still, we ought to visit the orchard soon and get the mistletoe in case the snow stops us later on. I would hate it if we couldn't get hold of any.'

'Why do you want it so much?' Thea asked. 'I'd have thought— no, forget I said anything.'

Pearl thought she knew what Thea had been about to say. Jenny was clearly sweet on Edwin, yet he had gone missing with Greg. She shut her eyes briefly, battling another wave of misery.

'I know what you were going to say,' she heard Jenny say, 'but I don't mind. I know you're probably thinking that if I'd hoped to get together with Edwin, I've probably left it too late.' Her voice wobbled, but after a brief pause she continued, sounding stronger. 'But until I hear otherwise, I'm going to believe both he and Greg will be there. After all, when I invited him, he promised he'd be there, and I've never known him break a promise.'

Pearl drew a shaky breath. 'You're right, Jenny. That's a good way of looking at it. So' – she did her best to inject a playful tone into her voice – 'you have plans for the mistletoe?'

'I do. When I heard he'd gone missing, all I could think was that I should have told him how I felt. So if… *when* I see him at the dance, I'm going to corner him under the mistletoe and leave him in no doubt.'

Chapter Eight

'Nice room.' Deedee looked around the first-floor bedroom that Pearl occupied in the Rosebery Avenue house. From the outside, Deedee had been fascinated by the turret decorating the corner of the substantial redbrick house, and now she could see it was more than decoration. For Pearl's room was built into it, with a series of sash windows jutting out from the corner of the room, effectively forming a wide bay window. Deedee couldn't resist stepping into the bay and gazing out at the view of the common that opened out on the other side of the road. A cushioned window seat lined the perimeter of the window, and Deedee sat.

Pearl joined her with a smile. 'I knew you'd like the turret,' she said. 'Fancy some cocoa? I've got an electric kettle.' She nodded to a table beside the door that Deedee hadn't noticed at first. Sure enough, it held a kettle, some crockery and a collection of tins and jars, including cocoa, Ovaltine and a tin of household milk.

Deedee shook her head. 'Mrs Stockwell gave me a huge breakfast, and I don't think I could fit anything else in. It's a lovely day. Why don't we go for a walk? I haven't explored Lincoln properly yet.'

Pearl hesitated. 'Are you sure you're not too tired? We kept you up late last night.'

Deedee frowned. It was unlike Pearl to want to stay inside on a sunny day. 'What's up with you? I was expecting you to be raring to pick out the perfect Christmas tree.' For when Pearl, Thea and Jenny had returned to the Gatehouse last night after the decorations meeting, they had told her all about the outcome. Pearl had been apologetic when she'd admitted that they would have to see Tom about the tree, and Deedee had assured her that she and Tom had managed to clear the air. She had to admit, she looked forward to decorating a tree. It felt like an age since she had celebrated Christmas properly.

'It's just' – Pearl twisted the tin in her hands, reminding Deedee painfully of the way Tom had fiddled with his watch – 'I want to be in if there's any news.'

If a telegram arrived, Deedee realised with a sinking sensation. 'But you came out last night. What's changed?'

'It only hit me last night when I came back. I opened the door and suddenly felt sick with dread that there would be a telegram waiting.'

Deedee blinked back tears, wishing she was back in the days when Pearl's hurts could be soothed with a kiss and a jam tart. This was no nightmare that could be explained away but a very real possibility, and Pearl needed practical help, not cuddles and sweets. 'Does your landlady have a telephone?'

Pearl nodded. 'Why?'

'Because you're going to give her the number of the Gatehouse and of Haughton Newspapers. You'll be contactable at one or the other of those numbers.'

'That's not a bad idea.' Pearl wiped her cheek with the back of her hand. 'Why didn't I think of that? I thought I was supposed to be the sensible one.'

Deedee patted her hand. 'You're allowed an off day every now and then. Now get your coat. We're going to pay Tom a visit.'

When she had promised Tom that they could meet in a civilised manner, she hadn't imagined that she would be put to the test quite so early on. But Pearl needed something to occupy her on this sunny Saturday or she would have a miserable day.

It had been the correct decision, for Pearl visibly relaxed as they strode along West Parade, towards the city centre. Deedee also had to admit that Tom had been right to insist they got along for Pearl's sake. As for the fresh layer of powder and lipstick that she'd applied while Pearl had been fetching her coat, well, it was only human to want to look one's best. And if a little voice told her she was trying to make Tom regret what he had rejected all those years ago… again, she was only human.

When would she stop feeling a thud of attraction every time she saw him? When she was eighty? Ninety? One hundred and fifty? The sight of him emerging from the lift when he came down to meet them in the foyer certainly gave her heart muscles some thorough exercise.

'Pearl,' he said, his gaze sliding to Deedee and then back to Pearl. 'I wasn't expecting to see you today.' He frowned. 'You haven't had any news, have you?'

'No news, but we've got a favour to ask, actually. Nothing work-related.'

'Then you'd better come up to my flat.' He gestured for Pearl and Deedee to enter the lift, and a short while later they were walking through a door on the top floor.

'This is amazing. No wonder you didn't mind moving here,' Pearl said, gazing around with wide eyes. The door had opened onto a spacious living room, very much a gentleman's residence in appearance, with deep red leather sofas, floor-to-ceiling bookcases, a writing bureau and a small dining table. Huge windows lined one wall, giving magnificent views of the cathedral.

'Oh yes, it's very comfortable. I suppose I should have moved here when the RAF took over Fenthorpe Hall, but I do enjoy my walks around the grounds, and I couldn't bear to say goodbye to the rose garden. It really wasn't practical to stay there once fuel became unobtainable, though. As you can see, I have everything I need, including a small kitchen.' He indicated one of the doors leading from the living room. 'Speaking of which, can I offer you drinks? I've got tea, or I've even managed to get hold of some real coffee.'

'You've got real coffee? How did you manage that?' In her excitement, Deedee completely forgot she had meant to be as distant as possible.

'I had a meeting the other day with one of the senior staff members at an American base in Norfolk. He sent me the coffee as a thank-you. Would you like some?'

Both women answered with enthusiasm, and minutes later they sat with steaming mugs of coffee in their hands.

'You said you had a favour to ask,' Tom prompted, after a pause while both women did nothing but breathe in the rich aroma of their drinks.

Pearl gave a self-deprecating laugh. 'Sorry, yes. I got a bit distracted. The thing is, I wanted to ask you about the possibility of cutting a Christmas tree from your grounds.' She went on to explain about the Christmas dance and decorating the ballroom.

Deedee, who found it difficult to tear her gaze from Tom, saw his eyes kindle at the mention of Christmas decorations.

'What a marvellous idea,' he said when Pearl concluded her request and took a sip of coffee. 'It's so long since that lovely old ballroom was decked for a party, and I'd love to help. Let me think. Yes, there's a patch of woodland that's got several spruces. Shall we go and choose one now?'

'You mean it?' Pearl looked as though she were having to hold back from throwing herself into his arms. Deedee couldn't blame her.

'Of course. Besides, I've been invited to the dance, and I'd love the room to be filled with that Christmas tree smell. I'm afraid I can't offer you transport, though, so we'll have to go by bus.'

Much to Deedee's relief, Pearl took the seat beside Tom on the journey there, although her relief rapidly faded when the garrulous woman who took the seat next to her insisted on describing her various ailments in vivid detail.

'Thank goodness for that,' she muttered once she'd climbed off the bus at Fenthorpe Hall. 'I was starting to worry I'd catch something.'

'Lead the way, Mr Haughton,' Pearl said.

'How many times have I asked you to call me Thomas?' he said, striding along the drive.

'Hundreds,' Pearl said with a grin, 'but I can't think of you as anyone but Mr Haughton.'

Deedee followed, a wistful sensation tugging her insides. Pearl, whose father had died in the last war, had been forced to grow up without a father figure in her life, and it seemed that Tom had naturally taken that place. Deedee felt excluded from the conversation, yet she couldn't regret Pearl's friendship with her former lover. Sooner or later, Deedee would have to return home, and it was a comfort to know that Pearl would still have Tom's support.

If only she didn't feel a huge sense of guilt whenever she set eyes on him.

'Here we are,' Tom said a few minutes later, when they had walked past the rose garden and the vegetable plots and reached a wooded patch running alongside the Fenthorpe lane. 'I always made sure to plant some spruces among the other trees so we could be sure of a real Christmas tree every year. I'll leave you to choose something suitable.'

Pearl returned to Deedee's side and took her arm. 'We need something a good eight or nine feet high,' she said, brushing her gloved hands over the needles of a small spruce no more than five feet high. 'So this one's safe.'

They weaved around the trees, dismissing some for being too short, others as too tall and one as way too spindly. Finally they stopped by a tree that was about nine feet high with beautifully symmetrical, bushy branches.

'This one's perfect.' Pearl stood beneath it, looking it up and down with a rapt expression. 'How do we go about cutting it down?'

'I'll have a word with the groundsmen,' Tom said. He pulled a length of red string from his pocket and tied it round a prominent branch. 'Always be prepared,' he explained in response to their raised eyebrows. 'This will mark it until we're ready to bring it inside.'

'That's a point,' Pearl said. 'There are still three weeks until the dance. If we cut it too soon, it will lose its needles.'

'How about I ask for it to be cut in two weeks? That will still leave you the best part of a week to decorate it.'

'Perfect,' Pearl declared.

'I suppose now we'll have to spend all our free time making tree decorations,' Deedee said.

'Actually, I might be able to help you there. I've got boxes of decorations in the attic. It's high time they were allowed to celebrate Christmas again. Come with me.'

The officer signing people in and out of the hall waved Tom through, and now Deedee had her first glimpse of the interior of Fenthorpe Hall. As she stepped through the door, she knew a moment's fear that the Haughton family portraits hadn't been removed, and the walls would be lined with ranks of Tom's disapproving ancestors, but thankfully there was not a portrait in sight. They were probably up in the attic, and Deedee hoped they were turned to face the wall.

They ascended three flights of stairs, each narrower than the last. Finally they found themselves in the attic. Or, rather, as Tom pointed out, the attic of the east wing.

'My house has an east wing,' she said as they clomped on creaky floorboards to a pile of boxes at the far end of the room. 'Or, as I call it, the front room.'

Tom snorted. 'Living in the Gatehouse has made me realise how absurd it was for me to live alone in this enormous pile. I shall have to think seriously on the best use for the place when I finally get it back. Ah, here we are. Cover your eyes. This is all very dusty, I'm afraid.'

A waft of dust hit Deedee in the face. It seemed to coat the back of her mouth and made her sneeze. When her vision cleared, she found herself gazing into four enormous open boxes. It was like looking into a treasure chest. She caught glints of gold, silver, emerald, ruby and sapphire, which, when she looked properly, became coiled strands of tinsel and fairy lights. There were also closed tins, each bearing a label written in elegant, sloping letters. The labels said things like 'Bells', 'Snowflakes' and 'Angels'.

'Let's take them to the ballroom,' Pearl said. 'It'll be easier to go through them down there, away from all the dust.'

It took two journeys, but eventually all four boxes were standing on a trestle table in the ballroom, and the three were delving into them, exclaiming with delight at each discovery. Pearl seemed particularly struck with a collection of delicate glass baubles in the shape of pine cones.

Deedee, after pulling out lights, tinsel and strings of glittering gold and red beads, found a pretty silver bell tucked away in one corner. It didn't appear to be part of a set, and she looked at it curiously. It was tied with a ribbon at the top and clearly intended as a tree decoration. Giving it an experimental shake, she was surprised by the light, clear tinkle.

Tom immediately seized it. 'I wondered where that had got to. My wife had it made to mark the year of our silver wedding anniversary. See.' He pointed to an engraving Deedee had missed at first look. There were Thomas's initials, TGH, then a date – 1921 – and then the initials UBH and the words 'Twenty-Five Years' around the base of the bell.

Deedee gave a light smile to show him she was unconcerned at this evidence of his happy marriage. 'You should keep it. Hang it in your flat. It would be safer there.' And out of her sight.

–

Pearl had to blink back tears while Thomas folded the bell in his handkerchief and tucked it carefully away in his pocket. She was remembering last Christmas – her first Christmas as Greg's wife. They had both managed to get forty-eight-hour passes and had stayed at Bakewell in Derbyshire. Pearl had chosen the destination partly because the journey wasn't too far for either of them but mainly, she'd been forced to confess, because of the association with the pudding that she had a great fondness for. Greg teased her incessantly when he discovered this, and the holiday, although too short, had been filled with laughter.

She turned away from Thomas, determined not to descend into self-pity. She and Greg had had one perfect Christmas, and she would take a leaf out of Jenny's book and have faith that there would be many more.

She couldn't help wondering how Deedee was taking this fresh evidence of Thomas's happy marriage and shot her a glance. Deedee, however, was exclaiming with delight over a set of glass icicles and seemed to have already forgotten the silver bell.

There was no chance to ponder if Deedee's unconcern was genuine, for the ballroom door burst open and Thea and Jenny strode in, rosy-cheeked from the cold. They each bore a cardboard box, inside which Pearl could see sprigs of mistletoe.

'Success!' Thea exclaimed, setting the box down on the table next to the tree decorations. 'We've got enough mistletoe to keep everyone's lips chapped for weeks to come.'

'The farmer who owns the orchard was lovely,' Jenny added. 'He insisted on climbing up the trees himself to cut the mistletoe down.'

'Only because he was trying to impress you,' Thea said. 'I think he was hoping to manoeuvre you under it. He looked most put out when I said we had enough and had to go.'

'Urgh, no. He was ancient. He must have been at least forty.'

'Ancient indeed,' Thomas and Deedee said at the same time. They exchanged glances and laughed. It was good to see them getting on, Pearl thought, even if she wasn't convinced by Deedee's reaction to the silver anniversary story.

'Goodness, look at the time,' Deedee exclaimed. 'Izzy – that's Mrs Stockwell – will be expecting me for dinner.'

Pearl shook her head, marvelling at how Deedee was already on first-name terms with a woman Pearl had known for years yet had never dared to address by anything other than her surname. 'Then I'd best get the bus back to Lincoln.'

'Oh, no. She specifically said you were invited. She's making Lord Woolton's pie, using veg the gardeners at the hall kindly supplied, so there's no problem with rations.'

Pearl didn't hesitate. Her landlady had promised to save her dinner if she wasn't back in time, but the prospect of an afternoon on her own didn't appeal. 'In that case, I'd love to come.' She glanced at Thea and Jenny. 'What about you two?'

Thea answered for them both. 'We've got to find somewhere cool to store this' – she indicated the mistletoe – 'then it's sausage and chips at the NAAFI. Our treat for traipsing around the freezing countryside all morning.'

Pearl thought wistfully of eating with friends at the NAAFI, of the camaraderie, the delicious aroma of flap-jacks, of the discussions over the latest articles in the *Bombshell*. She missed her days at RAF Fenthorpe and wondered, not for the first time, if she had made a mistake when she had moved out of the Waafery. It would have been different if Greg was still flying Lancasters there, of course, because she would be with him in married quarters. But lodging in Lincoln could get very lonely. She gave herself a mental shake, telling herself it would have been impractical when her office was in Lincoln.

She tuned in to the conversation in time to hear Thomas offering to store the mistletoe in his shed. 'It will keep longer out there,' he said, 'and you can pop in any time to collect it without needing permission. Come with me. I'll show you where it is. Then, I suppose, I ought to head back to Lincoln.'

'We can't have that,' Deedee said. 'Not after all the help you've given us. Won't you join us for dinner?'

Pearl had to bite back a smile at the look of shock on Deedee's face. It was as if she had surprised herself by the invitation.

She had certainly surprised Thomas, judging from his expression. 'I wouldn't want to intrude,' he said.

'Nonsense.' Deedee recovered her composure. 'It's your house, after all, and I would feel very guilty if I sent you to eat alone in your flat.'

That settled, Thomas followed Thea, Jenny and the mistletoe, promising to join Pearl and Deedee once the mistletoe was safely stored. Pearl set out with Deedee for the Gatehouse.

'Are you sure you'll be okay with Thomas's company at dinner?' Pearl asked once the others were out of earshot.

'I'll have to be. Can't take it back now, can I?'

'So you didn't mean to invite him? I thought you looked shocked.'

'That's one word for it. Flabbergasted is more like it. I didn't know what I was going to say until it burst out. I think I was feeling guilty because he shared his coffee and went to so much trouble for us this morning. It would have felt mean waving him off on the bus when we're eating a hearty meal, cooked in his own kitchen, by his own housekeeper.'

'I suppose you've got a point, although I doubt he helped us expecting any return. He's too much of a gentleman for that.'

'He is.' Deedee gave a fervent sigh that made Pearl slant her a glance. Was there a chance her grandmother still had feelings for him?

She would have said something, but they had arrived at the Gatehouse. Opening the door, Pearl heard Mrs Stockwell's voice drifting out from the study. She must be on the telephone.

'I'm sorry, she's not here at the moment, although I'm expecting her soon. Hang on. I think I can hear her coming in now. One moment, please.'

Pearl went cold, remembering that she had left instructions with her landlady to call should a telegram arrive. She kicked off her muddy shoes and dashed to the study, only to bump into Mrs Stockwell in the doorway.

'Is it for me?' she asked, at the same time as Mrs Stockwell said, 'Telephone for you, Pearl.'

Deedee had come to Pearl's side, and Pearl gripped her arm.

Her agony must have shown in her face, for Mrs Stockwell said quickly, 'It's Flying Officer Fitzgerald.'

Pearl breathed again. Not a telegram. Still, Fitz wouldn't be calling unless he had news, and she dashed into the study and snatched up the receiver. 'Fitz? It's me. Have you heard anything?'

'Nothing about Greg yet, but we've had news of the men who baled out, and I thought you'd want to hear.' Fitz's voice was slightly distorted over the crackly line, but Pearl couldn't detect any hint that he had bad news. She was sure she would hear it in his voice if he had.

'Yes, I would. Thank you. It's good of you to call.' Her legs suddenly unsteady, she sank into the leather desk chair and gripped an arm with her free hand. She was aware of Deedee beside her but focused her gaze on an ink stain on the blotter in front of her.

'It's good news about them, anyway,' Fitz said. 'They all made it down safely and were able to evade capture. They finally ran into Allied troops in the early hours of this morning. They're being treated for cold and dehydration, and they'll be shipped back to England tomorrow.'

'That's good news, at any rate. Do they have any word of Greg?'

'Not at this stage, but I wanted to let you know that the names of the rescued men confirms that it was definitely Greg and Edwin who remained with the aircraft. We'll debrief them once they're back, and I'll be in touch again once that's happened.'

'Do you know when that will be?' If she focused on straightforward, practical questions, she could push out thoughts of the aircrew who needed treatment for cold and dehydration. And that was after a safe landing with parachutes. What state would Greg be in after crash-landing his aircraft?

'Probably the day after tomorrow. I promise to be in touch as soon as I know more. Look, I've got to go, because there's a queue for the phone, but keep your chin up. If I know Greg, he's probably nicked a motorbike from a poor unsuspecting German and is currently tearing through the Dutch countryside, with Edwin riding pillion.'

This raised a chuckle from Pearl, as had obviously been intended. 'Poor Edwin. You'd better have a bottle of strong brandy ready, because he's going to need it, if my experiences of riding pillion with Greg are anything to go by.'

'That's the spirit. Give my love to Thea.' And he was gone.

Chapter Nine

By the time dinner was on the table and Tom had joined them, Pearl had gone through Fitz's news from every possible angle. Seeing how she frequently asked Tom's opinion and was comforted by his answers, Deedee was glad she had invited him.

'Where did Greg crash?' he asked Pearl.

'Somewhere near Blerick.'

Tom nodded. 'I've been studying the maps, and I remember seeing that place. It's not far from Allied territory, and by all accounts the German troops are in chaos. There's plenty of available cover, too. If Greg was mobile, he would stand a good chance of making his way to safety.'

'You really think so?'

Pearl looked so grateful that Deedee impulsively reached across the table and gave Tom's hand a squeeze. 'Thank you. You've been a real comfort.'

Tom looked startled but pleased. 'I'm just glad I can help.'

Deedee sat through the remainder of the meal in silence, listening as Pearl and Tom discussed the positions of the various Allied forces and the likely route Greg and Edwin would attempt. If only she didn't retain such bitter feelings about the way their relationship had ended, she would wholeheartedly welcome his friendship now. As it was, she was grateful for his support but tried to remain distant. How much had he really changed from the man who had used her for fun but had always intended to marry someone more suitable?

–

Before returning to her digs that evening, Pearl announced that she'd like to go to church the next day. She explained that, even though she no longer lived in Fenthorpe, she still occasionally attended the parish church there as that was where she felt most at home. Accordingly, the following morning, Deedee walked into the village with Izzy and met her granddaughter outside the church porch.

Inside, enveloped by the mingled scents of hot wax and the musty smell that always lingered around ancient buildings, Deedee let the peace of the place flow over her. She could immediately see why Pearl felt at home in this place, for more than half of the congregation wore air force uniform, forming a solid block of grey-blue in the rearmost pews. Deedee craned her neck to see if Thea was anywhere in sight, before recalling that she had mentioned being on duty all day.

Then the vicar rose to address the congregation, and the whispered conversations around her died away.

For the most part, Deedee let the service wash over her, murmuring responses automatically, standing or kneeling when she noticed those around her doing so. She was still preoccupied with Tom, remembering his obvious care for Pearl, not to mention his generosity towards herself. It was hard to reconcile this Tom with the one who had used her and then discarded her because she wasn't good enough to be his wife. She also couldn't get the silver bell ornament out of her mind. Something about it prodded her mind, demanding her attention, although every time she was close to making a connection it slipped away before she could grasp it.

An elbow in the ribs jerked her from her reverie and she saw that everyone was standing and the opening chords from the organ announcing the next hymn. Deedee hastily leafed through her hymn book to the right place, just in time to launch into the first verse.

Dear Lord and father of mankind,
Forgive our foolish ways

Deedee snorted, attracting a startled look from the woman in the pew in front. She quickly disguised it as a cough. The Almighty must surely have his work cut out with her and her family.

She gave herself a mental shake and resolved to pay attention to the service to save herself any more potential embarrassment. That was when she became aware of one voice – a female voice – so beautiful it stood out from all the others. This particular hymn had some low notes with which many of the women struggled. Not this singer, who hit the right pitch with ease. The way the voices echoed from the stone walls and vaulted ceilings made it difficult to pinpoint the singer, and it wasn't until the third verse, when a girl sitting slightly closer to the front, in a pew on the other side of the aisle, turned her head that Deedee knew she had found the singer. She was shocked at her youth – surely she could be no more than sixteen, yet her voice had a depth and maturity that belied her tender age. Deedee was reminded of herself at the same age and thought that, if anyone was destined to steal the show in a West End musical, it was this girl.

The hymn ended too soon for Deedee's liking; she could have listened to the girl's singing for hours. It was only when they came to the intercessions and the vicar named Fenthorpe men who had been killed in action that Deedee recalled that she was there to support Pearl. She glanced at her granddaughter kneeling beside her and saw that her eyes were open and her gaze was fixed on her clasped hands. Or, she realised with a pang, her wedding ring. Deedee reached across and squeezed Pearl's clasped hands, shocked at their chill. Pearl gave her a small smile.

'I'm fine, really,' Pearl murmured at the end of the service, as they filed towards the door. 'I mean, it was awful, hearing all the names of the men who have been lost, but it did me good to know I'm not alone. And I've been feeling so terribly alone.'

'But you've got me and Thea.'

'I know, but neither of you are going through the same thing, and Thea... well, she's got Fitz.'

Deedee's heart squeezed. She hadn't missed the way Pearl had snapped at Thea for no good reason on more than one occasion and guessed that Pearl was finding it difficult to see Thea happy with Fitz. 'I know it must be difficult to witness Thea's happiness,' she said, 'but please don't push her away. You'll only isolate yourself more if you can't be around anyone who is happy in love.'

'I know you're right.' Pearl sighed. 'Doesn't make it any easier putting it into practice, though.'

'You'll get there.'

'I hope so. Anyway, as I said, I've realised that others are suffering far worse than me because they know their husbands, sons or fathers aren't coming back. *I* still have hope, and I'm not going to wallow in misery any more. I'm going to follow Jenny's example.'

'Good for you. And when you see Greg at the dance, you can drag him under the mistletoe and snog his face off.'

Pearl choked. 'Deedee, where did you even learn that word?'

'Oh, I heard a group of airmen use it on the train journey here. Did I get it right?'

'Yes.' Pearl's voice was little more than a squeak and there were tears in her eyes, although this time they were tears of laughter.

They joined the queue for the door and shuffled forwards an inch at a time. To Deedee's delight, she saw they were standing just behind the girl who had sung so beautifully. She tapped her on the shoulder. The girl looked round, startled.

'I heard you singing,' Deedee told her. 'You have a wonderful voice.'

The girl glowed. 'Thank you. I love singing. And drama. I want to be an actress.'

'With a voice like that, I'm sure you'll manage it.'

An older woman spun to face Deedee and, from the resemblance to the girl, she guessed this was her mother. 'Now, now, you don't want to go filling my girl's head with nonsense.'

'It's not nonsense. I was on the stage myself in my younger years, and I know star potential when I hear it.'

The girl's eyes sparkled, and she beamed so brightly she outshone all the candles. The mother, on the other hand, scowled and looked Deedee up and down, taking in her appearance from head to toe. 'I see,' she said, managing to convey a world of disapproval in two simple syllables. Deedee was the first to admit she had an unconventional style. She couldn't bear the restrictive girdles and buttoned-up costumes that older women were supposed to adopt and made her own clothes. She was particularly proud of the outfit she had put on that morning; it consisted of a calf-length pinafore that she had made from an old pair of purple velvet curtains, worn over an orange jersey. On her head she wore a cloche hat in a shade that matched her dress, and on her feet her favourite pair of Mary Janes. They had a two-inch heel, because she liked the way her legs looked in heels. While she knew many women found her appearance eccentric, they would have been freezing in church today, in their thin woollen costumes, whereas Deedee had been beautifully warm.

'It's all very well my Georgina wanting to be an actress,' the mother went on, 'but who's going to help me in the shop if she goes gallivanting off to London? That's what I want to know. No, a good steady job is what she needs, not having her head filled with stuff and nonsense.' She turned to her daughter. 'I let you sing in that band, and this is the thanks I get. Be satisfied with what you've got, my girl. There's plenty of young ones that would love the opportunity to work in a nice warm shop.'

The poor girl was looking more downcast by the second, so Deedee turned to the mother. 'Do you have a shop here in Fenthorpe?'

'That's right – March's Bakery. My husband Henry set it up, but he's been gone these five years now, God rest his soul, so I run it now, with Georgina's help when she's not at school.'

'It must be hard work,' Deedee said, feeling more sympathetic towards Mrs March now she knew the circumstances. 'I always admire bakers, having to get up so early each morning.'

Mrs March swelled with pride. 'Oh, it's not so hard when you get used to it. Is it, Georgina?'

The look Georgina shot her mother said otherwise, but Mrs March didn't notice, for the queue had shuffled forward and it was her turn to shake the vicar's hand. 'Such a lovely sermon today,' she cooed. 'I do think it's so important to...' and off she rattled, extolling the virtues of using one's God-given talents wisely.

While Mrs March was occupied, Deedee offered Georgina a compassionate smile. 'You *are* a good singer,' she told her. 'Maybe if you're patient, you'll win your mother round.'

'I doubt it.' Then she glanced at Pearl, who had joined Deedee, having been speaking to the vicar's wife until that point. 'I say, are you stationed at RAF Fenthorpe? Are you coming to the Christmas dance at Fenthorpe Hall? The band I sing with are playing there.'

'We'll be there,' Pearl answered. Her eyes darted to her wedding ring before she added in a stronger voice, 'I've arranged to meet my husband there.'

Deedee couldn't decide if it was helpful or not for Pearl to follow Jenny's example and cling to the conviction that Greg would be there but decided that, if it aided her through the days to come, she would be there for Pearl should it turn out that the worst had happened.

'I look forward to hearing you,' Deedee said to Georgina.

She would have said more, but at that moment Mrs March finished her conversation with the vicar and turned to her daughter. 'Come along, Georgina.'

On her way to her mother's side, the girl shot a glance over her shoulder. 'I love your pinafore. It looks so much more comfortable that this horrible, itchy suit my mother forces me to wear. By the way, my name's Georgie. Only my mother calls me Georgina.'

'Nice to meet you, Georgie,' Deedee called after her, then realised it was her turn to greet the vicar. 'I'm sure it was a very worthwhile sermon,' she told him, 'but I'm afraid I didn't hear a word of it.'

'Deedee!' Pearl exclaimed.

The vicar, however, only laughed. 'Well, there was a section on honesty, and it appears you didn't need to hear that.'

Chapter Ten

A week passed with no more news of Greg. True to his word, Fitz telephoned as soon as the trainee crew from the fateful mission had arrived back at Market Harborough and been debriefed.

'The only extra information I have is that the last the crew saw of them, both Greg and Edwin were uninjured. Otherwise it's as I suspected – Greg refused to bale out and risk the Lancaster crashing onto houses, and Edwin wouldn't leave him. Anyway, it would probably have taken two of them at the controls to keep them airborne for as long as possible.'

Pearl knew she should be proud of Greg, that he had refused to escape to safety while there was a chance the damaged aircraft could kill or injure innocent civilians. Maybe it was something that would comfort her later, but right now she just wanted Greg home and couldn't find it in herself to care overmuch about people she didn't know.

Taking Deedee's advice to heart, she did her best not to resent Thea's happiness and managed to resist the temptation to snap at her sister. However, she had to admit she felt more comfortable with Jenny, who was also facing the prospect of losing the man she loved. Although the pair were no more than friends, Jenny had known Edwin for just as long as Pearl had known Greg and had probably held a torch for him for most of that time. Pearl was mystified as to why Edwin had never asked Jenny out, and knew, that if Edwin didn't return, Jenny would feel his loss bitterly.

On the following Saturday, Pearl returned to Fenthorpe to work on painting her window panel. Although she had managed to get to Fenthorpe Hall for two evenings during the week, this would be the first time since she had enlisted Geoff Yates' help. Geoff had been all too pleased to volunteer for something that required his artistic talents and had promised to paint a 'spectacular' scene on the middle section. He had also suggested that he sketch a Christmas tree outline on each of the other boards so that all the less artistically gifted decorators would need to do would be to slap green paint inside the lines and then paint over with decorations of their own devising. Pearl had immediately seen the advantage of this, as it meant each tree would be the same shape and size, lending a more professional appearance to the window panels.

When she entered the ballroom that afternoon, her gaze flew straight to the windows, and she gasped with delight when she saw the progress Geoff had already made. Three of the four trees were already outlined, and he was putting the finishing touches to the final one.

'These look marvellous,' she told him, standing back to get a good look at the tree she and Deedee would be colouring. 'And you've even added a stack of presents at the base and drawn stars around the outside. I love them.'

'I do admire a person who can draw star shapes,' Deedee said. 'Whenever I try, they always look wonky.'

'I hope you don't mind the additions. I got carried away. It's so long since I've been able to work on a large project. Not that I don't enjoy the cartoons I draw for the *Bombshell*, but they're all line drawings. I can't wait to get started with the paints.'

'Oh, have we got paints yet?' Pearl asked, glancing around.

Geoff pointed out through the door. 'We've got several cans of emulsion out in the entrance hall that some of the others managed to scrounge from the villagers. Brown also bought some more from Lincoln. She's just gone up to the attic to fetch some dust sheets to spread on the floor before we bring everything in. I could never look Mr Haughton in the eye again if I spilled emulsion all over these beautiful floorboards.'

Fifteen minutes later, the floor was protected by the sheets and Geoff had mixed them enough dark-green paint for them to paint their tree. 'When you've done the tree, I'll mix you a midnight blue to colour in the sky,' he said. 'Leave me in charge of mixing the colours, so we can keep them consistent across all the panels.'

Pearl and Deedee donned borrowed overalls, grabbed a brush each and set to work. Pearl found she enjoyed painting around the edge of the tree, as she had to concentrate on not wavering over the line and filling in the sharp points at the tip of each branch. It helped her focus on the moment, and her mind didn't wander to Greg's fate as often as it usually did. Deedee, on the other hand, set to work with enthusiasm, splashing paint in the centre of the tree where there was no danger of any paint escaping outside the outline.

Pearl became so absorbed that she didn't notice Jenny's arrival until her friend gave her a nudge. 'That's looking good,' she said, gazing up at the picture. 'I can't wait until Thea and I can get started on ours.'

'Isn't Thea with you?' Pearl asked, looking around the ballroom.

'She's here somewhere. We've got the afternoon off, so we're going to make a start tying the mistletoe into bunches. It's still too soon to hang them up inside, but they should keep if we keep them out in the shed.' Only now did Pearl notice that she was carrying a box of mistletoe, with green and red ribbon and a pair of scissors balanced on top. Jenny glanced around. 'Where did Thea get to? Oh, there she is.' She pointed to the far side of the ballroom. 'She's chatting to the band members. Apparently they're here to see what space they'll be allocated on the night.'

'Really?' Deedee, who had not appeared to be paying attention to the conversation, put down her brush. 'Was there a young girl of about sixteen in the group? Blond hair, pretty face, snub nose?'

'Yes. I heard she's the singer. I'm sure I recognised her from somewhere.'

'Have you ever been in March's Bakery?'

'Of course – that's where I know her from. She's the assistant.'

Deedee stretched, an all-too-innocent expression on her face. 'Well, I'll leave you to finish your part, Pearl. I need to stretch my legs.'

Pearl wasn't fooled. 'Don't interfere in something when you don't know all the facts, Deedee. Isn't that what you said to Thea when she found out about you and Mr Haughton?'

Deedee gave an airy wave. 'That was different.' And she strolled off in the direction of the group gathered at the far end of the ballroom.

Jenny gave Pearl a quizzical look. 'What was all that about?'

'Deedee met that girl – Georgie, she calls herself – in church. It turns out Georgie wants to be an actress, but her mother doesn't approve. I do hope Deedee isn't going to cause any trouble.'

'I wouldn't pin too much hope on that.' Unnoticed until that moment, Thea had arrived. She placed her box of mistletoe beside Jenny's. 'She is related to me, after all.'

'Yes, and I'm beginning to see where you got your annoying streak from.' Pearl grinned to take the sting from her words.

'So Deedee's determined to stick her oar in.' Thea pulled out a bunch of mistletoe from her box and set about cutting it into smaller pieces, only to pause with a frown. 'Don't you think it odd that Deedee never breathed a word about being on the stage? I mean, she's asked Fitz all about his days at the Vic-Wells. You'd have thought she'd have mentioned that she'd been a celebrated actress back in the Nineties.'

'Maybe she kept it quiet, worried the neighbours wouldn't respect her. Let's face it, even today there's a whiff of scandal attached to the theatre. It must have been a thousand times worse in Victorian times.'

'But when has Deedee ever worried about others' opinions?'

Remembering the many times in her childhood when she had longed for a grandmother who was more conventional and didn't say everything she thought at all times,

Pearl had to admit Thea had a point. 'You could always ask her.'

But her sister shook her head. 'She's hiding something.' Thea started plucking the white berries from her bunch of mistletoe one at a time, apparently without noticing. 'You know what we should do?'

Pearl snatched the mistletoe from her sister's hands before it lost all its berries. 'You can start by paying attention to what you're doing. You're ruining your mistletoe.'

'Oops. Sorry. But I've just had a brilliant idea.'

'Let's hear it.' Pearl wasn't holding her breath. Knowing Thea, it would be completely hare-brained and impractical.

'You work at Haughton Newspapers.'

'It's taken you nearly two years to work that out?'

Thea rolled her eyes. 'What I mean is that you must have access to the archives.'

Pearl suddenly saw where this was leading. 'You want to look for any reference to Deedee?'

'I know it's a long shot, but aren't you a bit curious? I thought you were a journalist!'

'Of course I'm curious.' Not to mention a tiny bit annoyed with herself for not thinking of the newspaper archives herself. 'I'm just worried that anything we find is going to stir up trouble. If Deedee is hiding something, there has to be a good reason.'

'Come on. You know you want to. Don't tell me you bought the story Deedee told us? I mean, it's probably true as far as it went, but she was definitely holding something back.'

'But you haven't seen her as much as I have this visit. Meeting Mr Haughton knocked her for six. She seems to have recovered now, and I don't want to do anything to upset her again.'

'I saw her the first time she set eyes on him at your wedding, so don't tell me I don't know what a shock it was. But I say that she must have really loved him for her to still be hurting decades later, so obviously hiding the truth all these years hasn't done her much good. I want to help her. Aren't you a bit worried about her being all alone? Now I've got Fitz and you're with Greg, I mean.' There was an awkward silence and Pearl felt tears, which were never far away, well in her eyes.

Thea gave her an awkward hug. 'Sorry. That was crass.'

'No, it wasn't. He's coming back, Thea, I'm sure of it.'

Thea regarded her for a moment, head tilted, then appeared to take her at her word. 'Good. And when he does, I'm giving him a piece of my mind for putting you through the mill.' Pearl chuckled, evidently the reaction Thea had wanted, for she relaxed. 'What do you say – are you in?'

'Oh, all right.' Pearl grinned when her sister punched the air. She had to admit she was curious to see if the newspapers would shed any light on Deedee's early life. 'But it will have to be in the evening, because I've got too much work to show you the archives during the day.'

'How about Tuesday evening? It's my day off.'

Jenny, who had until then stayed out of the conversation, occupied with tying her mistletoe into bunches using green and red ribbons, spoke up. 'Can I help? I've never seen a newspaper archive, and it would be fascinating.'

'Don't see why not. Deedee did include you when she told us about Thomas.' Thea grinned. 'Good to see you've learned how to pronounce archive correctly.'

Pearl nodded. 'Many hands make light work. There's one problem, though.'

Thea rolled her eyes. 'Why do you always have to see obstacles everywhere?'

'Because at least one of us needs to try thinking ahead. But listen. What are we going to do about Deedee that evening? She *is* here for moral support, after all. I can hardly say to her, "Sorry, Deedee, I know you've come all the way from Shrewsbury to be a shoulder to cry on, but would you mind awfully spending Tuesday alone because me, Thea and Jenny want to dig through the archives to uncover your hidden past."'

'But you'll be seeing her for lunch, won't you?'

'I suppose so.' Deedee had continued to catch the bus into Lincoln every weekday to meet Pearl for lunch. Although Pearl always protested that there was no need, she was grateful for her grandmother's company each lunchtime, for each morning she would check the news reports to see what progress, if any, had been made in the liberation of the Netherlands. She lived in constant hope that the location where Greg had crashed would fall into Allied hands, and that they would find the plane. After a flare of hope when the Americans had liberated the area around Blerick and Venlo, she had arrived at work every day thinking this would be the day she heard more news. Deedee's support after a morning of continued silence was invaluable in keeping her going through the afternoon.

'Then it shouldn't be a problem,' Thea went on. 'When you see her at lunch, just tell her you're tired and need an early night. I'm sure she'll be glad of a break herself.'

'I suppose so. I don't like lying to her but—'

'But we're doing her a favour really. Wouldn't it be wonderful if we could bring Deedee and Thomas back together?'

'Not this again.'

'No, listen. This is what I was trying to say before. Assuming Greg and Fitz make it through the war, we're going to be starting new lives with them. Goodness knows where Fitz and I will end up, but there's every chance you'll be heading to Australia. Wouldn't you feel happier knowing Deedee had someone to take care of her?'

'I…' But words failed her at the reminder of all the important things she and Greg had never discussed.

Thea frowned. 'Don't tell me you never considered Deedee?'

'It's not that.' Pearl sighed. 'It's the whole business about where I'll live after the war. Greg and I never discussed any of the big issues.'

'That doesn't sound like you.'

'I know. But it was my need for security that nearly tore us apart. When we got back together, the only way I could cope with seeing him fly night after night was to take every day as it came and try not to think about the future. Somehow I never got past that, even after we were married.'

Thea's expression softened, and she patted Pearl's arm. 'You'll be able to talk it all over when he returns.'

Pearl could only pray it was true. And if… when Greg returned, they were due a serious conversation.

–

Deedee couldn't help herself, possibly because Georgie reminded her so much of her younger self. And she had led a happy life as an actress. If life hadn't taken the turn it had, she would have been content to remain an actress for as long as she could find work. If there was anything she could do to help Georgie fulfil her dreams, she would. For if she was halfway as good an actress as a singer, then it would be a crime to hold her back.

She hovered near the back of the room while an officer showed them the area they would occupy and they discussed what they would need on the night. While this was going on, Deedee fiddled with the collection of coloured ribbons that Brown had placed on a nearby table. She pretended to be choosing between a deep green and a red and white candy stripe, all the while waiting for a chance to speak to Georgie alone.

The other band members were young men and women, none of whom appeared to be any older than Georgie. The instrumentalists got into a discussion about setting up music stands, leaving Georgie at a loose end.

Deedee seized her chance. Catching Georgie's eye, she beckoned her over.

'Hello,' Georgie said. 'I remember you from church.'

Deedee, realising she might not have much time, got straight to the point. 'I was interested in you after hearing you wanted to go on the stage. Have you done any acting?'

Georgie's face lit up. 'Yes, well, only school plays.'

'Everyone has to start somewhere. What parts have you played?'

'I was Beatrice in *Much Ado About Nothing* in our end-of-term play. My English teacher said I had real talent.' Georgie wrinkled her nose. 'She's as strict as anything, so she wouldn't have said so if she didn't mean it.'

'Is that what you want to do – Shakespeare?'

Georgie picked up a red ribbon and ran it through her fingers. 'I enjoy it, and I'd jump at the chance to play any part I was offered, but I'm more interested in musicals. I love them.' A faraway look came into her eyes. 'I went to see *Panama Hattie* last year, and it was wonderful. The singing, the dancing, the lights. I felt as though I were up there on stage with the cast, joining in with all the numbers.' Then the light faded from her eyes. 'But you heard my mother. She thinks it's just a phase I'm going through, and I'll change my mind. But acting's all I've ever wanted to do, ever since I got the part of Mary in the school nativity play.' She gave a little laugh. 'I suppose you think I'm silly.'

'Not at all. If that's where your talent lies, then you'd be wasting it if you tried to do anything else.' Deedee thought carefully. The last thing she wanted to do was come between Georgie and her mother. 'If your mother supported your ambition, have you planned what you'd want to do? How you'd go about getting into acting, I mean?'

Georgie bit her lip. 'I hadn't really thought that far. I just thought maybe I'd try to get a job with a company in Lincoln, get some experience before trying for some London shows. You were an actress. What would you advise?'

Deedee spoke gently, knowing there was a fine line between giving realistic advice and crushing a person's hopes. 'I want to help you all I can. But the trouble is, it's over fifty years since I was on the stage, and I'm out of touch with the theatrical world these days.'

'But you must have some idea.'

'True. Well, what I would suggest is the same thing I would say whatever career you want, which is to do some research. Are there any drama classes you could sign up for? You would find it very hard to get a role in a professional production without either any experience or training. A good drama teacher would then surely be able to advise you about what steps to take to get you started in a career.'

'My mother would never let me.' Georgie looked so downcast that Deedee's heart went out to her.

'I'm going to be here for a while. Let me see what I can do. Has your mother said why she's set against it?'

'Two reasons, mainly. First that she needs my help running the bakery.' Georgie bit her lip. 'And to be honest, it is hard work. I don't have any brothers or sisters, so when my father died it was up to my mother alone to keep the business going.'

'It can't have been easy, and it reflects well on you that you care enough not to leave her in the lurch. Maybe given time, though, your mother could find extra help. What was the other reason?'

'Well, that I might not be good enough. That, and that I might fall in with an unsuitable crowd in London. You know what people say about women in the theatre.'

'I do indeed.' Deedee spoke with feeling, remembering all too well what had caused her to flee London. 'There's no easy response to that except to say that, whatever you do with your life, you will always face choices that might lead you down the wrong path. At some point your mother is going to have to start trusting you, and she'll only do that if you have already proved you can be trusted in small ways. It's something to bear in mind. But as I say, I'll be in Fenthorpe for a while, so I'll see if I can say anything that might persuade her at least to let you start drama classes.'

'That would be marvellous. Then at least I wouldn't be wasting my life, forced to do something I hate, and never have the chance to act.'

'Nothing you do is ever wasted,' Deedee told her. 'If you want to act, you are going to have to learn to inhabit another character, see life through their eyes. A good actress will see every experience – good or bad – as a resource for building the characters she plays.'

'I never thought of it like that before.' Georgie opened her mouth to say more, but her band members called to her, evidently having completed their discussion. 'Coming!' she called. She dropped the ribbon back on the table and grinned at Deedee. 'I'm glad I've met you. I hope I see you again soon.'

'I'm sure you will.' For Deedee was resolved to visit the bakery at her earliest opportunity.

Chapter Eleven

Although Deedee had promised Georgie she'd speak with her mother, she couldn't find the right opportunity at first. At church the following day, she took a seat near the Marches, hoping to catch Mrs March at the end of the service. But when they were filing out, she happened to catch Georgie's eye, and smiled and nodded, only for Mrs March to intercept the look and scowl.

'Come on, Georgina,' Mrs March said, grasping her daughter's arm. 'Don't dawdle. We've got veg to prepare if you want to have your lunch at a reasonable hour.' And she hauled her away before Deedee could corner her.

On Monday, Deedee decided to visit the bakery in the morning before catching the Lincoln bus to meet Pearl for lunch. However, the queue was so long, stretching out onto the pavement, that Deedee knew Mrs March would never have time for a serious talk, even if she wanted to speak to Deedee, which seemed unlikely.

It was the same story the next morning, and Deedee was starting to worry that she was going to let Georgie down. Therefore, when Pearl professed herself to be tired when they met for lunch and said she would rather not meet Deedee that evening but have an early night, Deedee didn't protest. As soon as they parted after their sausage casserole at the church hall, Deedee made for the bus. Hopefully the queues would have dispersed after the morning rush for bread and Deedee could catch Mrs March alone in the shop. Georgie would also still be at school, and Deedee preferred to have this discussion without her as a witness.

The bus pulled up on the opposite side of the street to the bakery, giving Deedee a clear view into the shop as she crossed the road. As there was a customer being served, she made a show of admiring the wreath on the door of the newsagents next door and only entered March's bakery when she saw the customer leave.

She bestowed her most cheerful smile upon Mrs March. 'Good afternoon. Lovely day, isn't it?'

Mrs March merely shot a pointed glance out into the freezing fog, making Deedee feel rather foolish. 'How can I help you?'

'Oh… ah, a loaf of bread, please.'

Mrs March wordlessly handed her a loaf. Too late did it occur to Deedee that she hadn't brought a basket with her, so she had to tuck the bread awkwardly under her arm.

'Anything else?'

This wasn't going to script at all. In her head, Mrs March had replied to the 'lovely day' comment with her own observations about the weather, and the conversation had naturally progressed to Georgie. Thankfully Mrs March chose that moment to throw her a bone. 'Are you sure you need bread? Mrs Stockwell bought some earlier.'

'It's my granddaughters,' Deedee said, seizing the opportunity, thinking she might be able to guide the conversation from her granddaughters to Mrs March's daughter. 'They're always hungry. Like gannets. It must be all their hard work. And I'm terribly worried about Pearl at the moment, of course. She's so anxious about her husband she'll hardly eat a thing. Ah… apart from bread, of course,' she added hastily, before Mrs March could question how Pearl could be devouring everything in sight one moment and refusing all food the next.

Fortunately Mrs March didn't seem to notice her blunder; her face softened. 'I heard about your grand-daughter's husband. I was sorry to hear it. I hope he'll soon be back, safe and sound.'

'So do we all.' At that moment Deedee happened to glance at the few pastries left on display, and she temporarily forgot all about her promise to Georgie. 'Those custard tarts look delicious. I haven't had one of those for ages.' Possibly it was all the talk about gannets, but Deedee found her mouth watering at the sight of the individual pastry case filled to overflowing with a generous portion of set custard. Best of all was the fine dusting of grated nutmeg on the top. 'I have to have one of those.' Then she recalled Izzy. 'Actually, make that two. I'm sure Mrs Stockwell would like one too.'

The delectable treats were wrapped up – another item for Deedee to juggle on the bus ride back to the Gate-house, but she was prepared to suffer if she had the reward of a tasty treat at the end of it. Now Mrs March's attitude seemed to have thawed, Deedee decided it was now or never. 'I am sorry if I spoke out of turn to your daughter the other day. As her mother, you must know her best.'

Mrs March's mouth turned down. 'I always used to think that, but now I'm not so sure. I thought she'd be bound to grow out of this acting phase, but she's been obsessed for years, so what do I know? I mean, this band she and her friends have put together – I let her do it, thinking she'd soon tire of fitting rehearsals around schoolwork and her shifts here, but she's stuck with it, and they've made a success. They're even playing at the RAF Christmas dance, would you believe.'

'How old is she?'

'Just turned sixteen.'

'Then I'd say she's proved she's a hard worker, if nothing else. And you need to work hard if you want to make it as an actress.'

'But she hasn't even taken her school cert yet,' Mrs March wailed. 'She's got an intelligent head on her shoulders, and I want her to stay on for her higher cert.'

'Why can't she do both?' Deedee eagerly seized the opening. 'She's already shown she can handle lots of responsibilities. Why not encourage her to take a drama class? There must be one in Lincoln. That way she'll soon find out if she's got the talent or not.' Mrs March looked dubious, so Deedee decided to go for the jugular. 'I think I mentioned I was an actress in my younger days. I met several girls who had run away to London because their parents refused to let them be actresses. If you outright ban Georgie from doing what she yearns to do, you risk losing her.'

Mrs March blanched. 'Run away to London – with those awful V2s? I couldn't bear it.'

'Then you'll think about letting her take a class right here?'

'If you think that's the best option?'

'I do. And I agree that it makes sense for her to stay on at school to take her higher certificate. That way she would have plenty of other options should she not make it in acting.' She suddenly thought of Jenny, who had longed for an education but been forced to leave school at fourteen and go to work. She had been hard on Mrs March when they'd first met, but hearing that she wanted her daughter to get a good education raised her in Deedee's estimation. She reached across the counter and patted Mrs March's hand. 'You clearly want the best for your daughter. I'm sure you'll work it out.'

It was a tearful but smiling Mrs March who bid Deedee farewell, and Deedee felt she had done her best for Georgie. She could only hope the girl would see the sense in staying on at school and not do anything she might regret.

–

'I've just realised there are only eleven days till the dance,' Jenny said as she, Pearl and Thea walked down the stairs to the basement, where the newspaper archive was kept.

'That's eleven days for Greg to get home,' Pearl said. There had still been no news, and she was starting to grow despondent again.

'He'll get here,' Thea said. 'And when he does, not only will you have plenty of mistletoe to celebrate beneath, but with luck we'll also be able to tell him all about Deedee's scandalous past and the happy news that she's back together with Mr Haughton.'

Pearl had given up cautioning her sister not to try forcing Deedee and Thomas together. Instead she simply rolled her eyes, pushed open the doors to the archive and made for the catalogue. 'Mr Haughton has plans to transfer the archive to microfilm, but at the moment all the papers are stored the old-fashioned way,' she told the others. 'I think the best newspapers to look at would be the *Eastern Express* and the *Lincolnshire Bugle* because they deal with national as well as local news.' She found the drawer for the *Lincolnshire Bugle* and slid it open. 'They're weekly papers, so there will be an awful lot covering the 1890s. Can we narrow it down at all?'

Jenny leaned over the drawer and ran a finger across the index cards. 'Do you know when she left London?'

Pearl thought back over what Deedee had told them. 'I can't remember her mentioning any specific dates, just that she got a leading role some time in the Nineties. At the Gaiety Theatre, I think.'

'I suppose knowing she was at the Gaiety is something,' Thea put in. 'Wait. Our mother was born in Shrewsbury, wasn't she?'

'Of course! That was April 1894. Good thinking. So we can narrow down our search to before 1894 and after she started in that musical. What was it called?'

'*The Milliner's Girl,*' Jenny supplied.

'I wish I could remember what year that started.' Pearl shook her head as though doing so would bring the date to the front of her mind. 'I suppose we ought to start at 1890, then.' She flicked through the index cards and jotted down the locations of the newspapers covering the relevant dates. 'Follow me.'

She led them past towering shelves, stacked high with boxes, until she reached the ones where the *Lincolnshire Bugle* was stored. 'Right.' She found the box containing the January 1890 editions and placed it on a nearby table. 'You two take the *Lincolnshire Bugle*. Start with this box and, for goodness sake, keep them in order. And be sure to put each box back in the right place. Actually, to save you both fighting over the same paper, Jenny, why don't you start at December 1893 and work back?'

Leaving them to it, she went to find the *Eastern Express*. Soon she had a copy of that spread on the table, and there was silence for a while as all three pored over their papers.

'Good grief,' Thea said after she had turned two pages, 'this print is minute. How did they read this without damaging their eyes?'

'Magnifying glasses,' Pearl replied. 'Hang on.' She went and rummaged in a cupboard and returned armed with three magnifying glasses.

'Good idea. Now I can examine my text, feeling like Sherlock Holmes.' Jenny took one of the glasses and peered through it. 'I don't know what the great detective would have made of this advert for Beecham's Pills. They claim to cure consumption.'

Thea chuckled. 'I've found an advert for laxatives. Listen to this—'

'If you're going to read every advert out loud, we'll be here until the new year. Focus!'

'Sorry.' Thea ran her glass down a column and quickly turned the page.

The trouble was, it was all too easy to get absorbed in articles that weren't remotely connected with the theatre, let alone Deedee. Even Pearl forgot herself and read something out that she found particularly amusing. An hour and a half later they were stretching aching spines, having found not one single mention of Hope Burnell or the musical comedy she had starred in.

'I'm beginning to think Deedee made the whole story up,' Thea muttered, rotating her shoulders with a wince.

Pearl replaced the newspaper she'd just finished and pulled out the next one. 'I told you it was a long shot. Remember this is a provincial newspaper, so not all the London news would have made it in. It would depend on how much local news needed to go into each edition.'

'You mean they might have missed out an item about a talented young actress in London in favour of a report on a champion marigold grower winning an award at the village fete?' Thea said, scowling into her magnifying glass.

'Something like that.'

They all returned to their copies.

'Hang on,' Jenny said a few minutes later. 'Listen to this.'

Thea groaned. 'If it's another advert about Tidwell's Tantalising Tisanes, I'd rather not.'

'No. Listen. This is from a column called "London Life".' Jenny cleared her throat. '"All the gossips of London are speculating this week about the burgeoning relationship between a celebrated actress and a young gentleman about town. Hope Burnell—"'

Thea snapped her fingers. 'That's Deedee!'

'We know,' Pearl said, her nerves tingling. 'Go on, Jenny.'

Jenny peered back into her magnifying glass. '"Hope Burnell, the actress who shot to fame playing the title role in *The Milliner's Girl*, has recently been seen walking out with—"'

'Thomas Haughton,' Thea finished for her.

'No!'

'What? Who, then?'

'If you'd listen instead of interrupting me every couple of seconds, you might find out.'

'Sorry. Go on.'

Pearl felt as confused as her sister obviously did. She, too, had been convinced that the gentleman associated with Deedee would have been Thomas. She leaned closer to Jenny, waiting in growing impatience while her friend struggled to find her place in the tiny print.

At last Jenny started reading again. '"…has recently been seen walking out with Lord Gerald Dorsey. London society waits agog to hear what Hope Burnell will get up to next."'

Jenny stopped and Thea glared at her. 'Well? Don't stop there. What else does it say?'

'That's it. The column carries on with a mention of a new play at the Garrick Theatre. Nothing more about Deedee.'

Thea asked the question that was foremost in Pearl's mind. 'Who on earth is Lord Gerald Dorsey?' Then her face cleared. 'No, wait. I think I might have seen his name before, but it didn't register because I was looking for Deedee – or, rather, Hope.' She turned to her own newspaper and flicked back a couple of pages. 'Yes, here he is. No mention of Hope, though. Just that he was seen dining with a load of other people I've never heard of. I suppose he must have been a notable playboy of his day.'

An idea occurred to Pearl. 'What's the date of your newspaper?'

Jenny peered at the front page. 'July the twenty-first 1893.'

Pearl checked the date of the one she was reading. 'I've only got to January 1891 with mine. Perhaps we ought to focus on 1893. The piece about Deedee and this Lord Gerald Dorsey seems to expect readers to have already heard of them both, so maybe there's more about them closer to July 1893.'

'Good idea.' Thea put back her copy and brought an issue from the end of June 1893 to the table. Pearl swapped hers for one dated 15 July of the same year. They returned to their reading with renewed enthusiasm.

Over the next half an hour, they discovered several mentions of Hope Burnell, all praising her performance in *The Milliner's Girl* and predicting a rosy future for the young actress. There were no other mentions connecting her with Lord Gerald, although he occupied many of the column inches in his own right. The girls had soon built up a picture of him as a noted playboy who seemed to be seen with several different women every month. He was the younger son of the Duke of Redmarch and seemed to have more money than he knew what to do with. Curiously, although they found several other accounts of Lord Gerald dated after the first item Jenny had read, there were no more mentions of Hope Burnell. It was as though she had disappeared from the scene.

Finally Thea, who had been poring over a newspaper from October 1893, said, 'Listen to this. "Crowds flocked to the opening night of *The Shop Girl* at the Gaiety Theatre last night. Ada Reeve, stepping into the shoes of the popular Hope Burnell, charmed in the role of Bessie Brent."' Thea looked up. 'There's a lot more about the new play, but nothing more about Hope. What does it mean about Ada Reeve stepping into her shoes?'

Pearl, however, was counting on her fingers. 'I think I know. Mother was born in April the following year, so

Deedee would have been three months gone by this time. I suppose she had already left for Shrewsbury. That means' – a sudden sick feeling hit her in the pit of the stomach, and she gazed at Thea with wide eyes – 'she must have fallen pregnant around the time she was seen with Lord Gerald Dorsey.'

Thea looked aghast. 'You're not saying—'

Pearl held up a hand. She was surprised to see it shake slightly. 'I'm not saying anything yet. I need to think.' There was a pause while she scribbled some notes. Eventually she put down her pencil and flexed her fingers. 'It's getting cold in here. Why don't we go back to my digs and talk it through there? I told Mrs Dale I'd be out this evening, so she won't have cooked for me. Shall we get some fish and chips on the way?'

The others agreed this was a good plan, so they gathered their notes, put away the newspapers and returned the magnifying glasses. Then they walked out into the freezing night.

Half an hour later they were sitting in the window seat in Pearl's room, eating fish and chips from their laps, the unfolded newspaper placed on plates to keep the grease off their clothes. Pearl scowled at the newspaper on her lap, thinking she wouldn't mind if she never saw another gossip column in her life. It was almost a relief to see that the paper shortage had evidently caused this newspaper to cut all unnecessary items, even if the remaining news made grim reading, consisting as it did of the latest news of the war and more on the story about the young woman from Cambridge who had gone missing. In her worry over Greg, she had neglected to keep up to date with any news that didn't impact upon the *Bombshell*, and so she read the article partly to satisfy her curiosity but mostly to attempt to stop her imagination running away with her regarding Deedee's past. The report said that the police were linking the disappearance with that of other young women in the south and east of England, although it failed to state how they had drawn that conclusion. As she read, she found herself idly editing the article in her head and working out the questions she would have asked the police to produce a more thorough account of the investigation.

Finally Thea peeled her last chip from its wrappings and popped it in her mouth. Then she folded her newspaper and put it into the salvage basket. 'Right. I've been bursting to say this for ages, and I can't hold it in any longer. Do you think this Lord Gerald bloke is our mother's father? Our grandfather?'

'It certainly looks that way.' Pearl picked at a piece of batter, then regretfully threw her own paper into the basket, doing her best to dismiss the fate of the missing women from her mind. She had enough on her plate without worrying about something that was none of her business and beyond her control.

Jenny was looking from one sister to the other, her brow furrowed. 'I feel like I shouldn't be here,' she said. 'When we started, it felt like a bit of fun, but I can see you're both hurt and confused. Maybe I should leave you to talk.'

But Pearl shook her head. 'Please stay. I can't speak for Thea, but I feel all at sixes and sevens, and it would help to have someone around who's able to see things with a clearer head.'

But Thea was grinning. 'Yes, stay, Jenny. Have you read any books on etiquette? How do you address the granddaughters of the younger son of a duke?'

'No differently from anyone else,' Jenny said. 'Anyway, you don't know that Lord Gerald Dorsey was your grand-father.'

'I know, but wouldn't it be fun if he was.'

Pearl could bear this nonsense no longer. 'Aren't you at all bothered that Deedee's lied to us all these years? She's always led us to understand that our grandfather died before we were born.'

'Perhaps he did. We should look him up. He'd be in *Who's Who* or *Debrett's*, wouldn't he?'

'Thea, listen to yourself. It doesn't matter if he is or isn't our grandfather. What matters is that Deedee's led us to believe she was happily married to our grandfather after she moved to Shrewsbury. Yet now we've found evidence she was most definitely in London and unmarried when our mother was conceived. She's been living a lie all these years.'

Jenny spoke up. 'I can understand why you're upset, Pearl, but can you think of any reason why Deedee would lie?'

Pearl tried to think back to all the things Deedee had said whenever the subject of their grandfather had come up but couldn't remember her ever saying he had died. 'The funny thing is, I think I might have just assumed that he was dead. I don't recall Deedee ever saying she'd been married either, do you, Thea?'

Thea shook her head. 'Looking back, I think we put words in her mouth, and she never actually confirmed they were right. I suppose we just assumed they were.'

'She didn't deny them, either. I hate that she's deceived us all these years. I mean, it doesn't bother me one bit that she wasn't married, but I do wish she'd told us the truth. Did she think we would think less of her?'

Jenny rose. 'Why don't I make us a drink?'

Pearl gave her a wan smile, feeling bad that Jenny had been dragged into this murky family matter. 'Good idea. There's some cocoa in the cupboard. You'll have to use powdered milk. You'll find that in the cupboard too.'

While Jenny went to make the drinks, Pearl tidied away the remaining chip papers and plates. Thea helped. 'I'm sorry if I didn't seem to be taking you seriously,' Thea said as she rinsed the plates under the tap in the little washbasin. 'You're right, though. It is strange that she never told us the truth.'

'I suppose she was trying to protect our mother. You know how people talk behind their hands about illegitimate children.'

Thea nodded. 'Do you think that's why she went to Shrewsbury – to be well away from anyone who might have known about her past?'

'It makes sense.'

'Are you seeing her tomorrow?'

'Yes. We're meeting for lunch as usual. I don't know what to say to her, but I can't ignore it.'

'I suppose not.' Thea suddenly seemed to notice that she'd been rubbing the same spot on the plate for a while now. She picked up a tea towel and dried it briskly. 'I wish I could be there, but I can't get away at all tomorrow.'

'It's fine. I understand.'

'I'll be at Fenthorpe Hall the next evening though. We could meet in Fenthorpe half an hour early so you can fill me in on what Deedee says. Then we can both go and collect her.'

Pearl agreed and, as they drank their cocoa, she tried to work out how on earth she was going to approach the next day's difficult conversation.

Chapter Twelve

Deedee spent the evening by the living room fire in the Gatehouse. She had intended to carry on with her knitting, which had been rather neglected what with all the trips to Lincoln and Fenthorpe Hall over the past week. She wasn't surprised Pearl had said she'd needed an early night – Deedee felt the same and was feeling glad of the break.

She was also grateful for the space to think. Ever since she had seen Tom's tree decorations, she'd had the niggling feeling that she was missing something important, but she couldn't think what it was. She wasn't finding knitting as relaxing as usual, either. Probably because she couldn't stop remembering Tom's happy domestic tale of how he had learned to knit. Everywhere she turned there were bitter reminders of the woman Tom had chosen over her. There were the photographs on the mantelpiece, the books in the bookcase, all with her name written in an elegant female hand. Even the cushions and curtains were surely chosen by a woman. The interior of the Gatehouse was far different from the masculine decor of Tom's flat. Her only comfort was that he couldn't have lived here with his wife; he had only moved here when Fenthorpe Hall had been requisitioned at the start of the war.

Eventually, Deedee flung aside the knitting and went to choose a book instead. She ran her finger over the spines as she perused the titles. *Testament of Youth* – definitely not. Deedee didn't need to be reminded about how harrowing war could be. She was after escapism. *Wuthering Heights*? Way too much melodrama. *Middlemarch*? She could feel her will to live seeping away. Where were the frothy romances? Eventually she selected *Northanger Abbey*, remembering she had read it and enjoyed its humour when Thea had studied it at school.

Even when she was back beside the warm fire with the book open on her lap, her concentration started to slip. Was it Jane Austen who had published under a male pseudonym at first? No, it was the Brontë sisters. That was it – they had used the names Currer, Ellis and Acton Bell.

Bell... what did that remind her of? The next moment she had sprung to her feet, the book sliding to the floor. The silver tree decoration for Tom's twenty-fifth wedding anniversary. There had been a date on it: 1921. It had been nagging away at her subconscious for days. But why?

She counted on her fingers. If they had celebrated their silver wedding anniversary in 1921, they must have married in 1896.

A chill trickled down her spine. That couldn't be right. Tom had been about to marry in 1893. She'd had it on good authority, from his father, no less.

But she hadn't heard it from Tom. Hadn't waited long enough. Had she thrown away her entire life based upon a lie?

Deedee woke the next morning, heavy-eyed after only an hour or two's sleep. She had tossed and turned all night, running the events of her last days in London through her mind. Despite hours of fretting, she had ended up no closer to an answer than when she had gone to bed, and, even when she drifted into sleep, her dreams were disturbed by images of silver bells and the portrait in the foyer of the Haughton Newspaper Group. If Tom had been on the point of returning to his family home to marry the woman he'd always intended to marry, why had the wedding not taken place until three years later? It didn't make sense.

There was only one thing for it. She had to see Tom as soon as possible and ask him to explain. That was going to require some explanation on her part as well, and, as she ate a hurried breakfast, she thought carefully about what she would reveal and what she must never let him know.

Thanks to a light doze on the bus, she felt more refreshed by the time she climbed out. The freezing air finished the job, and she was fully alert and ready for battle by the time she reached the office. She asked for Tom at the desk, darting glances at the lift, terrified that Pearl was going to see her. Although she would probably have to enlighten her granddaughters in due course, she needed to get the truth from Tom before she decided what to tell Pearl and Thea.

Luckily Tom was available right away and within minutes he emerged from the lift. 'This is unexpected,' he said.

'Not unwelcome, I hope.'

'Never that. What brings you here? It's not Pearl, is it? Have you had any news of Greg?'

'No, nothing like that. This is' – she hesitated, seeing the receptionist regarding them with undisguised curiosity – 'something best discussed in private.'

'We'll go up to my flat, then.'

The first thing Deedee saw when Tom ushered her into his living room was the silver bell, in a prominent position at the centre of a shelf. While he went to make some coffee, Deedee wandered across to it and picked it up to study the inscription. She hadn't made a mistake – the date of Tom's silver wedding had indeed been 1921.

When Tom returned to the room carrying a tray, she held up the bell. 'I see you've put this in pride of place.'

Tom set the tray on a low table before replying. 'I was so pleased to find it again. I'd never meant it to be packed away with the rest of the decorations.'

Deedee set down the bell, joined him by the table and took the cup he handed her. She took a sip, savouring the rich flavour, trying to organise her thoughts.

'Now why don't you tell me what brings you here,' Tom said, setting down his cup and looking her straight in the eye.

Deedee drew a deep breath. 'I need to know if the date on that bell is right. Did you really not get married until 1896?'

Tom's eyebrows twitched together. 'You came all this way just to ask me that?'

Deedee nodded. 'Please. It's important.'

His frown didn't disappear, but he answered readily enough. 'Ursula and I were married in December 1896. Why's that important?'

Here was the moment Deedee had dreaded. 'When we met in the rose garden, you wanted to know why I left without a word, and I didn't really answer.'

She could swear he turned a shade paler. 'Are you going to explain now?'

She nodded. Her mouth had gone dry, so she took another sip of coffee before speaking. 'The day before I decided to leave, I sent you a letter. It said... well, it doesn't matter what. Thinking about it now, it must have gone astray, or you wouldn't have wondered why I left.'

'I never got a letter. Trust me, the first days after you disappeared, I looked everywhere, thinking you would never have gone away without an explanation.'

Deedee closed her eyes briefly, fighting tears. He hadn't had her letter. At least she had that to be thankful for.

'What did it say?' Tom asked.

'I'll explain in a minute. The main thing you need to know now is that the next day I went to your rooms. I... I couldn't believe you hadn't come to me right away, after reading what I had to say. And that was when I met your father.'

Tom's hand twitched, spilling coffee onto his knees. Pulling out his handkerchief, he glared at her. 'My father? But I never saw him.'

She gave a bitter smile. 'No, I imagine not.'

'He did come to see me the following week, though. That's when he persuaded me to return to Lincoln, take up my position as his second. You know I'd resisted it for ages, but I was so bitter at losing you I couldn't bear to stay in London another day.' He finished mopping the coffee stain on his knee and stuffed the hanky back in his pocket. 'He said something to make you leave, didn't he? What did he say?'

'He told me that you never intended to marry me. That you'd been sowing your wild oats before returning to Lincolnshire and marrying the heiress you'd been engaged to from the age of eighteen.'

Tom's lip curled. 'Oh, yes, that's what he told everyone. Penelope Fairchild. I had no interest in her, nor she in me, I might add, but our families kept throwing us together. It was one of the reasons I went to London, because my father simply wouldn't accept that I refused to marry the woman he'd lined up for me. I knew that if I didn't get away, sooner or later he was going to corner me into having to propose to the poor girl.'

'You never told me that.'

'Because I was determined to forget the whole business. London was new and exciting, and I was enjoying my work as a Fleet Street reporter, no less. Lincolnshire felt like a bad dream.'

'Then you *were* serious about me?'

'So serious I wrote to my father to tell him all about you.'

The horrible truth was dawning on her. 'And so he dashed up to town to separate us.'

Tom's face was grim. 'It's starting to look that way. It wouldn't surprise me if he intercepted your letter. It's the obvious explanation.'

It certainly was. Deedee supposed she should have worked that out, but she'd been so despairing about what Mr Haughton senior had told her that she hadn't been able to think straight. 'All this time I thought you were married straight after I left London, and you didn't get married to the heiress at all. It was someone completely different.'

Tom nodded, his eyes sad. 'I was broken-hearted, but I told my father in no uncertain terms that I wasn't going to marry Penelope. He died not long after that, and so I was forced to take over as head of Haughton Newspapers. If it hadn't been for that, I might have returned to London to look for you, but there was never the time. Anyway, I was convinced you had forgotten me.'

Deedee swallowed, blinking back tears. 'Never.' But she didn't want to think about what she had done next, so she asked, 'When did you meet your wife?'

'A year after I left London. It started as friendship. We were both nursing broken hearts, and we turned to each other for companionship, to help each other through our hurts. It was over a year before we fell in love. It was a very gradual thing.'

Nothing like how it had been for them, Deedee thought, remembering how she had bumped into him on a walk through Kensington Gardens and had fallen hard in more ways than one. She dabbed her eyes, then said, 'Do you think we can be friends again? Proper friends, I mean, not just two people who tolerate each other's company for Pearl's sake. I've missed you.'

Tom didn't reply straight away. He pulled his watch from his pocket and gazed at it as he spun it between his fingers. Deedee, unable to drag her gaze from him, became convinced that he was trying to find the words to turn her down gently. Finally he looked up and said, 'If you can answer me two things.'

'What?' Her dread of the next questions was so great it was a strain to look him in the eye.

'First, is it true that you left me for Lord Gerald Dorsey?'

Deedee choked, struggling not to spit out her mouthful of coffee. 'No, it's not. I only met him once, and when he propositioned me I told him in no uncertain terms where he could go.'

Tom's shoulders sagged; he pocketed his watch. 'My father showed me a piece in the paper that implied you were his mistress. It was what persuaded me to leave London.'

'Well, it was a lie. I wouldn't have touched him with a bargepole.'

'I should have realised that but, in case you haven't realised, my father was very manipulative.'

'Oh, I worked that out all by myself. What's the second question?' *Please let it be as easy as the first.*

'What was in the letter?'

Not so easy. What should she do – tell the whole truth or just a part? But if she wanted to be friends, she couldn't hide this any longer. She placed her cup carefully on the table before saying, 'I had tried to tell you something to your face, but I couldn't get the words out. So I put it in a letter. You see, I'd realised I was expecting a baby. Your baby.'

Thomas went white. 'And my father read the letter and never breathed a word to me.'

Deedee thought about what had happened later. 'I'm almost positive.'

His face contorted as though he were in severe pain. 'I knew he was manipulative, knew he wouldn't approve of you, but I never dreamed he could have done something like that.' He gazed at her imploringly. 'You have to believe I would have stood by you. Married you.' He passed a hand over his eyes. Deedee waited in silence for him to speak again, her throat uncomfortably tight. 'I would have married you even without the child. I loved you. But to think my father sent you away, knowing you were going to have his grandchild, beggars belief.' There was another pause, then: 'The child – did you lose it?'

Deedee slowly shook her head. 'I went to live in Shrewsbury, put on a wedding band and passed myself off as a widow. The child was my daughter, Clara.'

'But then…' Sudden understanding flared in his eyes, and he sprang to his feet. 'Pearl and Thea are my grand-daughters?'

She could only nod, heart pounding, unable to read his reaction in his suddenly frozen expression.

When he spoke, it was as if to himself. 'All these years, I had a daughter and never knew her. My son had a sister.' His mouth convulsed. 'She died and I never knew her.'

She could have withstood his anger, had been braced for it. But this sorrow for a daughter he had never known was far worse than anything he could have said in anger. 'I know there's nothing I can say to make it right,' she said. 'I'm not using this as an excuse, but you have to understand how very alone… how *betrayed* I felt. I thought we would have the child together, only to discover – or so I thought – that you had no interest in me beyond a brief bit of fun.'

She saw anger in his eyes then and she shrank from him, tears welling. 'I'm sorry you never got to know Clara. Blame me if you want, but please don't take it out on Pearl and Thea.'

She was starting to babble, and he held out his hands in a soothing gesture. 'I am angry, but not at you. It's my father I'm angry with. You didn't choose to bring up Clara alone; he forced you into it. He kept me from my own daughter.' He sighed, burying his head in his hands. When he spoke again, it was to the floor. 'Do Pearl and Thea know?'

'No. They know I was involved with you, but they don't know any more than that. They assumed I got married and moved to Shrewsbury afterwards. I admit I haven't had the courage to tell them otherwise.'

'When are you going to tell them?'

Not *if* she was going to tell them but *when*. And there was no getting away from it. He was their grandfather and he had every right to be a grandfather to them. And Pearl and Thea deserved to know the truth and have a relationship with their only other living relative. After all, they were already good friends, so there was no reason to keep them apart.

'I will tell them soon. But you have to let me do it my way. I'll do it the next time I see them both together. It wouldn't be fair on Thea if I told Pearl first.'

'Very well. As long as you do it on this visit. I've lost my son, and the daughter I never knew. I want to have as much time as I can with my granddaughters.'

This was fair enough, and there was no good reason to deny him. 'I'll do it the next time I have them both together. I promise.'

Tom straightened up and picked up his coffee cup with hands that shook. He went to take a sip, apparently not noticing that the cup was empty. 'When my son died, it took me a long time to reconcile myself to the fact that I was the last of my family line. And now I have not one but two grandchildren. It's a gift I never thought I'd have. And to cap it all, I already know them and know what wonderful young women they've grown up to be. I'm sorry I couldn't be there for Clara, but I want to be part of Pearl and Thea's lives.'

And it would be unreasonable of Deedee to demand otherwise, not that she would. The trouble was, there was still a huge untold part of the story hanging over her, one she could never confess. It was the reason she felt shame every time she remembered those dark days and the reason she had never told Thea and Pearl the truth about their grandfather. Even if she could cope with losing Tom's regard – and she wasn't sure if she could – she knew the truth would change the way Pearl and Thea regarded her, and she couldn't live with that.

Chapter Thirteen

Pearl left her office at dinnertime, content that she had put in a good morning's work and that the bulk of the next edition of the *Bombshell* was ready. Although she still jumped every time the phone rang, her concentration was less scattered than it had been in the first week following Greg's disappearance. Funnily enough, with each passing day where there was no further news she grew more confident that Greg had survived. Surely by now the occupying force would have discovered the crash site and, if any bodies had been found, news would have filtered back to the authorities via the Red Cross. Something told her Greg and Edwin had survived. She would continue to believe that until she heard otherwise.

Another reason for her absorption was the question of the mysterious Lord Gerald. From the reference books available in the office, Pearl had discovered that he had died without issue in 1913.

When she emerged from the lift on the ground floor, she was astonished to see Deedee and Thomas standing together near the door. What was Deedee doing here? Knowing how uncomfortable she was around Thomas, Pearl had always gone to meet her at the bus stop to save her grandmother the potential embarrassment of bumping into him at the office. Yet there they both were, chatting as though there had never been a fifty-year-wide rift between them. She hoped that Deedee hadn't invited Thomas to eat with them, because it would prevent her from quizzing her about Lord Gerald. Thea had told Pearl she was going to ring when she got a break that afternoon and had threatened dire consequences if Pearl had no answers for her.

So absorbed were they that they didn't even notice Pearl's arrival until she greeted them.

'I wasn't expecting you to meet me here,' she said to Deedee.

Deedee gave a start, and Pearl had the fleeting impression that she was as surprised as her granddaughter. But she immediately dismissed the notion. What else would have brought her here apart from a desire to see Pearl?

The look was gone in no time, and Pearl might almost have thought she imagined it. 'I arrived a bit early and thought I'd save you the wait out in the cold,' Deedee said and gave an exaggerated shiver. 'It's cold enough to freeze the—'

Pearl leapt in before Deedee could finish the expression. 'I see. Well, that was kind of you.' Even though she was sure Deedee had had no such thought.

It wasn't only her grandmother who was behaving oddly. Thomas kept staring at her but looked away each time Pearl glanced in his direction. He shot her a swift sideways glance now, as if it was his first time seeing her. What was that all about?

Whatever was going through his mind, he seemed to make an effort to shake it off. 'Well, I'll leave you two ladies to it.' He sounded falsely jovial, not at all the usual

Thomas. He looked from one to the other and seemed on the point of speaking, but Deedee cut in.

'It was lovely to bump into you. We must dash.' Now it was Deedee's turn to sound completely unlike herself. She sounded more like the matronly grandmothers who liked to chat in the street, not at all the outspoken Deedee who always said the first thing that came into her head.

Pearl didn't get a chance to question her grandmother until they were seated at a rickety table in the church hall with plates of steaming corned beef hash and slices of bread and margarine. Although she hadn't forgotten her determination to ask about Lord Gerald Dorsey, the question of her and Thomas's odd behaviour took priority.

'What was all that about with you and Thomas?' she asked before even taking her first mouthful, despite her gurgling stomach.

'I don't know what you mean. He just happened to be walking through the foyer when I arrived.' Deedee still didn't sound quite herself, and Pearl eyed her suspiciously.

'That's not what it looked like to me. You've always been uncomfortable with him before, but when I saw you today you looked more relaxed. And so occupied you didn't notice me until I spoke.' And, it suddenly struck Pearl, they had both looked as though the years had fallen away. She could almost imagine them as the young couple barely out of their teens that they must have been.

Deedee brushed off the statement with a negligent wave. 'I suppose I've always been aware of you or Thea watching the two of us together. Maybe I did feel more relaxed with him when I didn't have to consider what you might be thinking.'

It might have been the truth, yet Pearl didn't believe a word of it. She could see she was going to get nowhere, though, and as her dinner hour was ticking away, she changed the subject. 'Anyway there was something else I wanted to ask you. Thea and I wanted to ask you, in fact.'

Deedee relaxed fractionally. 'What was that?'

'Is there any truth in the rumour that you had a liaison with Lord Gerald Dorsey?'

Deedee hunched over her food, her shoulders shaking. For a horrible moment Pearl thought she had burst into tears, but then she emitted a snort of laughter. Pearl scowled at her grandmother, who was now wiping her eyes. 'What have I said?'

'Oh, my goodness. Where did you dig up that morsel of gossip?'

It was only then that it dawned on Pearl that she was going to have to come clean about the reason why she had not wanted to see Deedee the evening before. Oh well, if she expected the truth from Deedee, it would be hypocritical not to be open in return. 'We – Thea and I – were curious about your life in London, and we thought we might find out something about you in the newspaper archives.' She might as well leave Jenny out of it.

'I see.' Deedee had recovered from her laughing fit, and now her expression was unreadable. 'And what did you find?'

'Well, nothing much apart from a few reviews praising you in *The Milliner's Girl* and then this piece linking you with Lord Gerald Dorsey.' Pearl glanced at her plate, only belatedly realising she was tearing her bread into tiny pieces.

'And why are you so curious to know more? I told you I was involved with Tom at the time. You know that an actress only had to glance in a notorious man's direction in those days and tongues would start wagging.'

There was nothing for it. Pearl was going to have to be more direct. 'The thing is, the date on the article was the year before our mother was born. I'm sure you can understand why we're curious.'

Deedee's lips twitched. 'Yes, I can see why your attention was caught. I'm going to have to disappoint you, though. You and Thea are not descended from the nobility. That article was pure speculation and gossip, with no foundation behind it.'

'Oh, thank goodness. I didn't want to think badly of you.'

This elicited the first scowl of the conversation from Deedee. 'Think badly of me? Why would you have thought badly of me?'

'I—' Pearl had no idea how to answer, so was relieved when Deedee carried on without pausing to allow her to speak.

'I would very much hope that anything you might discover about a woman's past involvement with a man wouldn't make you think any less of her. I hope I brought you up better than that, whatever opinion society might hold.'

Pearl felt her face burn, ashamed. 'No, you're right. Anyway, it was more your judgement I was questioning, considering the trail of broken hearts and marriages Lord Gerald left behind.'

'I should hope so.'

Then it dawned on Pearl that Deedee's scolding hadn't been genuine. She had been trying to divert the conversation. Again. This always seemed to happen when the subject turned to her and Thea's grandfather. 'You're doing it again.'

'Doing what, dear?' Deedee's innocent look clinched it for Pearl. She was definitely hiding something. She opened her mouth to ask Deedee outright, but her grandmother held up her hand. 'Please don't ask me anything you know I can't answer just yet. Let's talk about something else.'

'Like what – the weather?' Pearl was feeling mutinous, but it was no good trying to force Deedee to say something she clearly wasn't prepared to talk about.

'No, dear, because that would be as dull as all the books on Tom's bookshelves.'

This elicited a grudging smile. 'Ah, well, I think I can help you there.' Pearl rummaged in the pocket of her greatcoat and pulled out a dog-eared paperback. She knew all about Deedee's reading tastes. 'Mr Haughton's secretary has similar reading tastes to you, and I've discovered she runs an informal book exchange with other like-minded women at the office.' Pearl paused. 'And, actually, I suspect quite a few men. Anyway, I managed to get hold of this, and Mrs Norris promises she can lend you more when you finish that one.'

Deedee took the book, and her eyes lit up when she read the title. '*Passion in Paris*, ooh, that sounds right up my street.' Suddenly she reached across the table and patted Pearl's hand. 'Be patient. Just because I won't answer your questions here, it doesn't mean they'll never get answered.'

And so, as the conversation turned to the other books Mrs Norris might be able to lend Deedee, Pearl did her best to rein in her curiosity.

–

Having found the events of the morning emotionally draining, not to mention the difficulty of evading Pearl's questions, Deedee decided a bracing walk was required once she'd parted company with her granddaughter. So rather than taking the bus back to Fenthorpe, she opted to explore Lincoln. The sharp climb up Steep Hill was a most effective way of taking her mind off her various worries and troubles, for it was impossible for her mind to wander when the necessity of drawing breath into her starving lungs took all her concentration. Finally, puffing and panting, she staggered to the top and looked out over the town and across into the countryside to the south.

The wind really was bitter up here, so she made her way to the cathedral and sank gratefully onto a chair, glad to be out of the wind. She let her gaze wander around the interior, allowing the peace and grandeur of the place to sink in. A pool of candlelight cast quivering golden lights on a nearby pillar, and Deedee went to investigate. She found a little side chapel alight with a mass of tiny candles. A handwritten card on the altar explained that the chapel had been set aside for quiet prayer. Beyond the altar rail was a raised platform that must usually hold a table. In its place, however, was a crib scene, lit by the tiny candles. Looking at the baby in the crib and the adoration on the faces of Mary and Joseph, Deedee thought of all the people who had lost or feared for their children because of the war. She supposed many of the candles had been lit by parents praying for their offspring. These thoughts inevitably led to Greg. Pearl had still had no further news, and Deedee dreaded to think how she would cope should she hear the worst.

Moved by a sudden impulse, she dropped a few pennies into the box and lit a candle, adding her prayers to the multitude. She remembered Clara's inconsolable grief when her husband had been killed, tragically close to the end of the Great War. Deedee had always believed that Clara's grief had contributed to her own death from the influenza epidemic, soon after Thea's birth.

She placed the candle in the holder, then gazed at the little figures in the crib scene, thinking of all the parents and grandparents for whom the unthinkable had happened – the loss of a child or grandchild. She thought of Greg's parents, so far away in Australia, who must be feeling as lost and helpless as Pearl. A flash of anger took her by surprise. It was like all the candle flames had united deep in her chest and were bursting to escape. How much longer was this war going to go on? How many more deaths? How many more grieving families? It felt as though the latter half of her life had been dominated by conflict, and she longed for it all to be over.

She lingered in the chapel for some time, and gradually her inner turmoil ebbed away. Stiffly, she rose and began the trek down the hill to the bus. Bundling her coat tightly around her, she saw that the wind had cleared the mist from the surrounding countryside. Occasionally, the sun peeped through gaps in the high cloud and glinted on the water in streams and ditches like tiny sparks of starlight.

The view lifted her spirits and, despite being cold and tired, she was in a better mood by the time she reached the bus stop. She got even more of a boost when the bus rolled up scarcely a minute after she arrived. Just as she was taking her seat, a hand grabbed her elbow.

'Deedee! Fancy seeing you here.' It was Georgie, looking much younger in her school uniform, her hair in a neat plait down her back. She took a seat beside Deedee and unwound her scarf. 'It's perishing cold, isn't it? I wouldn't be surprised if we had snow.'

'I hope not. Steep Hill would become impossible if it got icy.' Deedee studied her young friend. 'You look happier than the last time I saw you,' she remarked. 'Dare I hope your mother's allowed you to join a drama class?'

Georgie practically bounced on her seat. 'She has! We had a lovely talk the other day, and she admitted she had been hard on me. She said if I agreed to stay on at school, she would pay for drama lessons. And we've found an awfully good teacher. She reminds me a bit of you. She's old, too, but a lot of fun,' she said, squashing Deedee's notions of being considered a wise, mysterious benefactress. 'The group puts on a play every term and there will be auditions and everything.' She rattled on for some time, and it did Deedee good to know that her talk with Mrs March had helped. 'Of course, I've joined too late to be in the Christmas play, but I'm going to be helping backstage. Next term, though, I have a good chance of getting one of the main parts,' Georgie said happily. 'Mrs Stokeley has already said I have the makings of a fine actress. Will you still be here at Easter? I'd love you to come and watch, if I do get a part.'

'I expect I'll have gone home before then,' Deedee told her. And she sincerely hoped it would be because Greg had returned safe and sound. 'I'd love to see you in your first play, though. I tell you what. If you get a speaking part, I promise to come.'

Georgie chattered happily about her hopes and dreams for the remainder of the journey.

Chapter Fourteen

Pearl was still mulling over Deedee's reluctance to speak of her grandfather when she caught the bus to Fenthorpe Hall later that evening. What she had said at the end of lunch seemed to imply she *was* going to tell her about him at some point, just not yet. What was she waiting for?

She called in at the Gatehouse, expecting to meet Thea, Jenny and Deedee before heading straight across to the hall to carry on painting their panels. However, it was Thea who answered the door when she rang the bell, and there seemed to be a strange air of expectancy about her.

'Deedee's got something to tell us,' her sister said. 'She won't tell me what, but she asked Jenny to go on up to the hall and meet us there later. She's being very mysterious. I'm half expecting her to confess to a murder or something.'

Pearl, her curiosity aroused, was on the point of going into the living room when Thea clutched her arm. 'Any news of Greg?' Before Pearl could reply, Thea rushed on. 'I mean, I'm sure there isn't or you would have said so straight away, but it seems unfeeling not to ask.'

Pearl gave her a wan smile. 'No news, no.' She blew out a breath. 'I try to comfort myself by telling myself there's still hope, but it's hard to stay positive, especially with the news that's getting through of the starvation in the Netherlands. It's been two weeks now. If he is alive and free, he must be suffering. How's Jenny holding up?'

'Much the same.' Thea grimaced. 'I wish there was more I could do to help. I… I feel guilty whenever I get a letter from Fitz or speak to him on the phone.'

'You mustn't. I'm just glad that at least Fitz is safe.' Pearl felt a twinge of guilt herself and hoped that her jealousy and resentment of Thea hadn't shown. What kind of person was she if she wished this pain on her sister, wished that Fitz was dead or starving, outside in the freezing cold winter all alone instead of Greg? Because, deep down, wasn't that the logical conclusion of her jealousy? 'Come on. Let's see what Deedee has to say.'

Deedee, however, seemed to be unable to say anything. She greeted Pearl with a strained smile, then launched into a long and completely irrelevant explanation of how Mrs Stockwell was visiting her sister that day, obliging Deedee to make the tea herself, which she now offered to Pearl. Then she spent a long time fiddling with the sugar tongs and asking how many lumps Pearl and Thea wanted, despite the fact that neither had changed their preferences since they were in their teens.

Finally Pearl could bear the suspense no more. 'Please tell us whatever you have to say. You're putting me on edge.'

Deedee sat back with a sigh, not quite meeting either of her granddaughters' gazes. 'You wanted to ask me a question earlier, Pearl, but I stopped you because I had a good idea what you were going to ask, and I didn't want to say anything without Thea hearing it too.'

Pearl swallowed. 'I was going to ask you to tell us the name of your husband.'

Deedee winced. 'Ah. Well, that's where it could be difficult.'

'Why?' Thea asked. She glanced at Pearl. 'We have a right to know!'

'Of course you do. All I meant was that it would be difficult to tell you my husband's name because I never had one.'

Pearl found she wasn't surprised. After all, Deedee had still been in London less than nine months before their mother had been born. She opened her mouth, but Thea got there first.

'I don't know why it never occurred to me. You can tell us, Deedee. Was our mother the secret illegitimate offspring of Lord Gerald Dorsey?' Too late, Pearl realised she hadn't updated her sister on her earlier conversation with Deedee.

Deedee's lips twitched. 'Pearl told me all about your theory. As I said to her, I'm afraid you're barking up the wrong tree.'

Thankfully Thea didn't look disappointed. 'So no chance of finding I'm really Thea, Duchess of Redmarch, then.'

'Athena,' Pearl put in.

'Shut up, Aphrodite.'

Pearl winced.

Deedee snorted. 'Not even Lady Thea of Frankwell,' she said, naming the area of Shrewsbury where they had grown up.

Thea gave a mock sigh. 'Shame. I fancied myself in a tiara.'

'If you're quite done with the fantasies, I'll tell you your grandfather's real name.'

Pearl exchanged a disbelieving glance with her sister. After all this time it seemed impossible that Deedee would freely offer up that information. 'Go on, then. Who is it?'

Beside her, Thea was leaning forward in her chair, gripping the arms. 'It's Thomas, isn't it.' It was a statement, not a question.

Deedee simply nodded. Pearl stared at her, unable to grasp how she had failed to work that out for herself.

It seemed so obvious now Thea had said it. She could only suppose it was because, until now, she had been convinced that Deedee had been married to the man who was her grandfather, so she had just assumed it couldn't possibly be Thomas. 'Does Thomas know?'

'Yes, I went to see him this morning. He had no idea, and I was expecting him to be angry. I never told him before, but he' – here Deedee paused, a soft smile lighting her features – 'he seemed more delighted than angry. He thought he'd lost everyone, and now he has two grand-daughters.'

Pearl swallowed, trying to get her head around the news. She had known Thomas for over two years and had grown very fond of him, to the point where she had asked him to give her away at her wedding. 'I can't believe it. What are the odds that the man who's been a good friend for most of the time I've been in Lincolnshire is actually my grandfather?'

Thea was grinning – a delighted smile that stretched from ear to ear. 'I always felt that he was reminded of someone every time he looked at me, and now I know who.' She looked at Pearl. 'At least now we know where you got your love of journalism from.'

Deedee was looking from one to the other of her granddaughters, a furrow between her brows. 'You really don't mind?'

'Mind?' Thea sounded incredulous. 'This is the best news we could have. We already know and love Thomas. If I could have chosen my own grandfather, he's the one I would have picked.'

'What about you, Pearl?'

Pearl couldn't help being more cautious. For most of her life Thea and Deedee had been her only family and, whatever Pearl perceived to be Deedee's shortcomings as a traditional grandmother, she was and would always be the heart of the trio. But now it felt as though the sudden reappearance of her grandfather threatened to change everything, and Pearl didn't want to lose the closeness of the little group that was all the family she had known for so long.

This, coming at the same time as the dreadful uncertainty surrounding Greg's fate, was too much for her to contemplate. All she could do was deflect the question. 'More importantly, how do you feel, Deedee?'

Thankfully, Thea seized on the question. 'Yes, what's going to happen now? Are you and Thomas going to get back together?'

Deedee laughed. 'What's this obsession with getting me and Thomas back together? There's too much water under the bridge for that. Isn't it enough that we're friends again?'

Thea's eyes twinkled as she shook her head. 'You gave up everything to look after our mother and then you had to do it all over again for us when she died. Now Pearl and I are grown up, it's your time at last. I'd like to see you happy and cared for.'

Thea's attitude put Pearl to shame. At this rate, she wouldn't even be able to stick to her claim of being the sensible one. Her reaction had been purely selfish, worrying how Thomas's reappearance in Deedee's life would affect her. She forced a smile. 'Thea's right.'

'Ring the bells. A miracle has happened. Pearl's finally admitted I'm right.'

Pearl shot her a glare. 'As I was saying before I was so rudely interrupted, I agree with Thea. You've done so much for us, Deedee, but it's time you did what's right for you without worrying about us. If you think there's a chance you and Thomas might have a future together, you should consider it.'

–

Was there a chance she and Tom might get back together? Pearl's statement refused to leave Deedee and it was almost a relief, when she met her for lunch the next day, to hear that Tom was in Grimsby, involved in meetings, and would probably need to stay there overnight. She had gone to Lincoln that morning, her stomach in knots, wondering if Pearl had already spoken with her new-found grandfather, and if Tom would expect Deedee to meet him. Now she had a day's grace, one in which she could try to sort out her feelings.

She still hadn't been able to answer the question to her satisfaction by the time she was on the bus back to Fenthorpe. Did she even want more than friendship? But as she had said to Thea, too much had happened in her life since those heady days in London. Now she knew Tom had not knowingly abandoned her and their unborn child, it was as though her happier times in London had been restored to her. She could look back on her time there with fondness, and she could even welcome the prospect of Tom being in Pearl and Thea's lives. Hopefully she and Tom could build a genuine friendship on the ashes of their former love, but she couldn't allow herself to consider anything more. Because surely then she wouldn't be able to conceal how low she had stooped in those desperate days when she had thought Tom had abandoned her.

She reached that conclusion just as the bus pulled up in Fenthorpe. Feeling happier now she had made her decision, and seeing the inviting displays in the bakery window, she decided to get out here, buy a treat for herself and Izzy, and then walk the rest of the way to the Gatehouse.

The warm scents of yeasty bread enveloped her as she stepped inside March's Bakery. She was surprised to see not Mrs March but Georgie at the counter. 'Hello. Shouldn't you be at school?'

The girl wrinkled her nose. 'We've got exams. I don't have one today, so my mum said I could stay here and take care of the shop.'

Deedee spied a dog-eared exercise book on Georgie's side of the counter. 'So you're fitting in study between customers?'

Georgie grinned. 'Don't tell my mother, but I'm reading the script for the Christmas pantomime we're putting on at the stage school. Part of my work involves prompting, and I think it'll be better if I'm familiar with the script.'

'What's the pantomime you're doing?'

'*Robin Hood*.' Georgie's eyes shone. 'It's wonderful. The costumes are so colourful, and the dialogue is hilarious.' She paused as though struck by a sudden idea. 'Would you like to come? It's on Saturday. Tickets are two shillings.'

'I'd love to. Perhaps I should buy two tickets, and I'll try to persuade Pearl to come with me. I'm sure it would do her good.'

Georgie promised to reserve two tickets and gave Deedee the details of how to find the church hall where the performance was to be held, then Deedee bought two gingerbread men and returned to the Gatehouse for a brief rest before it would be time to meet Pearl at Fenthorpe Hall to finish painting their Christmas tree.

The following day, when Deedee opened the curtains to let in the morning light, she caught her breath at the magical transformation that had occurred overnight. A heavy frost had etched glistening ferny fronds on the window panes and decorated the landscape with sparkling diamonds. Everything was starting to look Christmassy, and it was a sharp reminder that there were only ten days until the day itself, yet she had bought nothing for Pearl or Thea.

She therefore took an earlier bus into Lincoln with the idea of using the extra time to choose suitable presents. When she arrived in the bustling city centre, she was too busy at first admiring the effects of the frosty weather to want to step indoors, so she wandered up the hill, marvelling at the low sun casting its golden light on the timber-framed shops and the stone cathedral towering above them all. As she walked, something about the beauty of the day helped her settle her thoughts regarding Tom and, by the time she had paused to catch her breath at the top of the hill, she felt prepared to meet him. Knowing he would want to spend time with Pearl and Thea as their acknowledged grandfather at the earliest opportunity, she decided to seek him out at the office after her usual lunch with Pearl and suggest they meet up at the Gatehouse that evening.

Her mind made up, she set about gift buying with enthusiasm. She finally chose a new fountain pen for Pearl, who had been complaining that the one she had was too narrow and made her fingers cramp on days she did a lot of writing. For Thea she found a pretty enamel-backed hairbrush and matching hand mirror. She was about to seek out a tearoom to while away the time until lunch when she remembered Jenny and Tom. It would be mean to leave Jenny without a gift, when she suspected the poor girl would be getting very little from her family. And as for Tom, she wanted to get him something as a sign of their renewed friendship.

It wasn't difficult to think of a suitable present for Jenny, as she made no secret of her love of books. Remembering a conversation from the other day where Thea had mentioned enjoying Dorothy L. Sayers' books, and Jenny confessing she had never read any, Deedee bought her *Strong Poison* and *Have His Carcase*, thinking Jenny would appreciate the character of Harriet Vane. For Tom, she bought a pair of silver and mother-of-pearl cufflinks. By the time she had completed her last purchase, she was nearly due to meet Pearl, so she strode out down Steep Hill.

After a morning spent thinking of gifts, it struck her with a sudden twist of guilt that she hadn't thought of Greg at all. Perhaps Pearl had received news. Deedee quickened her pace. The whole reason she had come to Lincoln was to support Pearl, and instead she had become so wrapped up in the past that she had neglected her responsibilities.

Her head was so full of her own shortcomings that she failed to notice where she was walking. One moment she was hoping and praying that Greg was still safe, the next her feet slipped on the icy cobbles and shot out from under her. She landed on her back, knocking the air from her lungs. She lay still for a moment, trying to force her dazed brain to understand what had just happened. But the chill of the icy ground soon seeped through her clothes, and she struggled to sit up. The moment she put her right hand to the ground, a pain shot from the tips of her fingers all the way up her arm, and she couldn't suppress a yelp of pain.

Then she felt hands under her shoulders, supporting her and easing her upright. She looked up to find herself looking into the concerned face of a young woman. 'How badly are you hurt? I saw you from my shop window. Do you think you can stand?'

'Give me a moment.' Deedee was embarrassed at how weak her voice sounded. By this time more passers-by had gathered and added their voices to the chorus of concern. Deedee tried to block them out as she shifted her legs experimentally, testing to see if she had any pain other than the discomfort of her arm, which she now felt mainly in her wrist. Much to her relief, apart from feeling bruised and sore, her wrist seemed to be the only real pain. 'I think I can stand,' she said to the young woman. 'Do you think you can help me? I've hurt my wrist.'

In reply she felt a firm hand support her under the elbow and she staggered to her feet. 'Thank you,' she said to the woman. 'You're very kind. I think I can manage now.'

But the woman shook her head. 'I don't like to leave you after a fall like that. Come into my shop for a moment and sit in the warm. I'll make you some tea.'

Deedee tried to take a couple of steps and soon discovered that she felt far more shaky than she had at first realised. 'I think that might be best,' she said.

Another lady said, 'Is there anyone you'd like us to fetch?'

Deedee seized on the suggestion gratefully. 'I was going to meet my granddaughter at the Haughton Newspapers office. Do you know it?'

'Oh yes, I live not far from there. What's your grand-daughter's name?'

Once Deedee had given Pearl's details, she allowed her first benefactress to help her into the shop. There, she was settled into a chair behind the counter.

'I'm Mrs Little,' the woman told her. 'You're welcome to sit here as long as you need. I'll make that tea.'

'Are you sure you can spare it?' Deedee felt bad enough taking up Mrs Little's time at a busy time of year, let alone using her precious rations.

'I was about to make a pot for myself,' Mrs Little assured her, 'and it will easily stretch to two cups.'

'Thank you. That would be lovely.' Then she added, 'I'm Deedee, by the way.'

While Mrs Little slipped into the back room to make the tea, Deedee took her first look around the shop and took in the shelves stacked with folded shirts and pullovers, the rails hung with men's jackets, and deduced that she was in a gentlemen's outfitters. Still feeling shaky, she examined her injured wrist and saw it looked a little puffy. Her palm was also grazed, and she realised she must have injured it when she had flung out her hand to break her fall.

Mrs Little returned, bearing a tray with the tea things. Seeing Deedee's hand, she said, 'I've got a first aid kit in the back. We should clean up that graze, although you should really see a doctor about your wrist. Can you move your fingers?'

Deedee managed to waggle them and, although it was painful, she didn't think she had broken anything. Once Mrs Little had poured the tea, she disappeared again into the back room and re-emerged carrying a basin of water that smelled strongly of TCP. As Mrs Little gently rinsed the grazes with a soft cloth, the antiseptic smell brought back vivid memories of treating Pearl and Thea's childhood injuries.

By the time her hand was clean and she had finished her tea, Deedee was feeling much improved. She was on the verge of saying she felt well enough to leave when the door opened with a merry jingle of the bell and Tom walked in, his face set in lines of concern.

'How are you? I came as soon as I heard.'

Deedee could only gaze at him in confusion. 'What are you doing here? I was expecting Pearl.' The moment the words were out of her mouth, she realised how ungrateful she sounded, and she hurried to undo it. 'I mean, it's nice of you to come.' It was more than nice. She couldn't deny she felt slightly flustered at the sight of his obvious concern, not to mention the hair, ruffled from his brisk walk – in his hurry, it seemed he had forgotten his hat.

Tom ran his hands through his hair, smoothing it down, much to Deedee's disappointment. 'I happened to be in the foyer when the lady arrived at reception, and I overheard her saying you'd had an accident. I dare say Pearl will be here soon, but I couldn't wait. How badly are you hurt? Do you need a doctor?'

Deedee was both moved and pleased that Tom evidently cared enough to dash to her rescue. Not that she needed rescuing, but it was heartwarming to know that the man she had once loved still harboured friendly feelings for her after all that had passed. 'It's mostly just bruises.' She inclined her head with a smile at the shopkeeper who was tidying a display of neckties. 'Mrs Little has been very kind and taken good care of me. I've sprained my wrist, but I don't think it's too bad.'

'Let me look.'

He cradled her wrist in one hand and, when he explored the bruised area with gentle fingers, she shivered suddenly. He immediately stopped. 'Did that hurt?'

'No.' Feeling the need to explain away her reaction to his touch, she said, 'It's a bit tender but not too bad.' For she wasn't about to confess that she had felt a sudden wave of the desire she had thought long dead. She could feel heat rushing into her cheeks and had to hope that he either didn't notice or thought she was flushed from the hot tea. Now they were on friendly terms, she didn't want anything more complicated. As things stood, she could comfortably stand to be in his company when he wanted to spend time with Pearl and Thea; yet if he got an inkling that her feelings were taking a deeper turn, things would get awkward again, and she didn't want that. Anyway, he had clearly transferred the feelings he had once had for her to his wife, and she didn't want his pity if he thought she wanted more than friendship. Which she absolutely didn't. She was happy with the way things were, thank you very much.

It was probably a good thing that Pearl burst in at that moment.

'Deedee, are you—? Oh, hello, Mr Haughton. I mean, Thomas.'

Tom's whole attention turned to Pearl, although he kept hold of Deedee's arm. His face lit with a smile. He opened his mouth to speak, then hesitated and glanced at Deedee, a question in his eyes. Words were unnecessary – she knew he was asking if she had told Pearl and Thea that he was their grandfather. She gave him a small smile and a nod.

'Now you've finally got used to calling me Thomas, I wonder if you would consider using a different name. Grandpa, perhaps?'

Pearl stepped closer, her hands clasped. Her whole stance spoke of her uncertainty, and she darted glances between Tom and Deedee. 'You don't mind?' she asked, and Deedee couldn't tell who she was addressing.

'Nothing would bring me greater joy.' Tom's voice was husky, and Deedee found herself blinking away tears.

'Hello, then, *Grandpa*.'

Deedee could tell that Pearl wasn't altogether comfort-able with the new name, but she was clearly determined to give it a try. Tom was beaming with pride. However, if Deedee had expected to be forgotten, she was proved wrong when Tom immediately turned back to her. 'Well,

I don't think your wrist is broken, but we should get a doctor to take a look to be sure.'

Pearl hurried to Deedee's side. 'Are you hurt anywhere else? The lady who gave me the message just said you'd had a fall. She wasn't able to tell me anything more.'

Deedee struggled to her feet, wincing as stiff muscles protested. 'It's just my wrist and a few bruises.'

Pearl took her uninjured arm. 'Why don't I see you back to the Gatehouse?' She glanced at her watch. 'I should be able to get there and back in my dinner hour.'

'I don't want to take you away from your work.'

Tom interjected. 'I've got a suggestion. You're very welcome to rest in my flat. I do think you should see a doctor and, if you don't object, I'll telephone mine and ask him to visit you there.'

Pearl's face cleared. 'That's a good idea.'

Deedee tried to object, but Pearl wouldn't hear of it. 'Please, Deedee, I don't like to think of you all alone at the Gatehouse if you start to feel unwell. This way I can come back with you this evening and make sure you're all right.'

There was no arguing with this, so after Deedee had thanked Mrs Little one last time and said her goodbyes, she allowed herself to be escorted to the flat. Although it wasn't far, she found she was more wobbly than she'd expected, and was grateful when she reached the offices and even more grateful for the lift to the top floor. As soon as she was settled on the couch, Tom insisted on making them both sandwiches to make up for the meal they would be missing. Then he went to telephone the doctor.

An hour later, the doctor had strapped up her wrist and agreed with her that it was just a sprain. 'Take it easy for a few days,' he said as he packed his bag. 'You'll be stiff and sore for a while, but there's no lasting damage.'

'Thank goodness for that,' Pearl said, once she'd seen the doctor out. 'I got quite a scare when I heard you'd had a fall on Steep Hill. It's a wonder there aren't more accidents there when it gets icy.'

Deedee gave a rueful glance to her bandaged arm. 'I'm afraid I won't be much use with the decorations. You'll have to finish painting our panel without me, I'm afraid.'

'Will you be all right on your own?'

'You heard the doctor. I'm fine. I'll sit by the fire and read.' A thought struck and she glanced at Tom, who had returned now the doctor had left, having hovered outside the door while he had been examining her. 'Actually, would you be free to pop round this evening, Tom? I think Thea is also free.' She glanced at Pearl for confirmation before saying, 'I know you wanted to spend some time with the girls now they know you're their grandfather.' Then she added to Pearl, 'We'll invite Jenny too. I'm sure the poor girl won't want to walk back to the Waafery alone, and she's as good as family.'

And so it was arranged, and Pearl returned to her work, making Deedee promise not to return to Fenthorpe alone but to wait for Pearl, who would accompany her on the bus.

Tom looked as though he was about to follow Pearl, but Deedee called him back. 'What do I owe you for the doctor's bill?'

Tom waved it off. 'I'm happy to pay.'

'I can't let you do that.'

'You can and you will.' Tom looked unexpectedly serious. 'I can't get out of my head that you provided for and cared for Clara and then Pearl and Thea all alone, and it pains me to think of the struggle you must have had, when I would have willingly provided for you had I but known. I can't go back and change the past, but please let me do this for you, little as it is.'

There was no arguing with him, so Deedee had to accept. When he took his leave, she followed him to the door, and when she had closed it behind him she rested her forehead against the cool wood. His kindness was almost too much to bear. Would he still feel the same if he knew how she had provided for her family?

Chapter Fifteen

Pearl stood back to admire her finished panel. That evening she'd lost herself in painting the decorations on the tree, using the brightest colours available. Now her tree was daubed with brilliant red, gold and blue baubles, with splashes of pale yellow for the candle flames. She had also painted the presents at the foot of the tree, using the same colours as the baubles, and she had to admit that, although it looked a bit messy close to, now she was standing back the effect, when seen with the other painted window panels, was pleasing and festive, especially now that the real Christmas tree had been cut and placed in its corner, waiting to be decorated. The only panel she couldn't see was the central one that Geoff Yates was working on, for he refused to let the others look until he had finished, and it was currently draped in a long sheet.

'Go on, have a look. You know you want to.' Thea was standing at her shoulder, paintbrush in hand, mischief sparkling in her eyes.

'No, if Geoff wants to keep it as a surprise, I'm not going to spoil it for him.' She arched a brow at her sister. 'Why, have you looked?'

'Not on your life. Knowing my luck, I'd end up smearing the paint and ruining the whole thing.'

'Glad to hear you're finally learning sense.' Pearl turned back to her panel. 'Right. Just the stars to fill in. Shouldn't take long. Then we can all head to the Gatehouse to see Mr Haugh... Thom... Grandpa.' She gave a rueful shake of the head. 'I'm never going to get used to calling him that.'

On the point of returning to her task, she paused when she noticed Assistant Section Officer Brown heading in her direction.

'Message for you, Pearl.' She held out an envelope.

Pearl's vision tunnelled, until all she could see was the envelope. An icy chill filled the pit of her stomach. She was aware of Thea moving to stand beside her, weaving a supportive arm through hers, and Jenny coming to stand on her other side. 'Who... who from?' she managed.

Brown clapped a hand over her mouth, her face a mask of horror. 'Oh, it's nothing official. Sorry – I didn't think. No, it's just someone who'd left a report for the *Bombshell*.' She named an officer who regularly contributed articles.

Pearl released a shaky breath and pressed a hand to her chest in a vain attempt to calm her pounding heart. 'Thank goodness.' She tried to smile but, judging from Brown's expression of pity, she failed dismally. She took the envelope and stuffed it in her pocket. 'It's fine, really.'

'No, it's not. That was thoughtless of me. Take a seat and I'll fetch you some tea.'

But Pearl shook her head. 'Honestly, I'm fine. I'd much rather finish my panel. I need to keep busy.'

After giving Pearl one last doubtful look, Brown walked off.

Jenny squeezed Pearl's arm. 'Are you sure you don't want to take a break? You look terrible.'

'By terrible, she means your face actually turned green. I thought that was just an expression until now,' Thea added helpfully.

Pearl set her jaw. 'I want to finish the stars.' She picked up a paintbrush, dipped it in yellow paint and filled in the closest star outline. But she felt sick and shaky and could no longer close her mind to frightening thoughts. What was Greg doing now? Was he even alive? And, worst of all, was he suffering?

Finally she flung her brush into a jar of turps and dropped onto a nearby chair. 'It's no good. I can't concentrate any more.'

Jenny picked up the brush and wiped it on a rag. 'I'm not surprised, after the scare you had. Thea and I will clear up, then we'll go to the Gatehouse.'

Jenny's voice shook a little, and Pearl only belatedly realised that she hadn't been alone in getting a fright from the unexpected message. And at least Pearl had the comfort of knowing she would be the first to hear as soon as there was any news of Greg. Jenny wouldn't get any news of Edwin unless Fitz remembered to tell her. Pearl made a mental note to tell Fitz that next time she spoke to him.

By the time the brushes and paints were cleared away, Pearl was feeling less shaky, and she strolled out into the dark grounds with Thea and Pearl, looking forward to spending time in Thomas's company.

'Are you sure you don't mind me coming?' Jenny asked.

'Deedee made a point of inviting you,' Pearl told her. 'Just because you're not related by blood doesn't mean you're not family.'

'That's a really nice thing to say.' Jenny's voice was husky.

'I'm not just saying it. I mean it.'

'Now that's sorted, will you two use your eyes for a moment and look up?' Thea had stepped between them, and now grabbed the arms of both women.

Pearl looked up and gasped. Earlier that evening, the sky had been cloudy; now the clouds had all dispersed, revealing a sky glittering with stars. There was no moon, making each minute point of light so brilliant Pearl fancied they almost cast a shadow.

'I don't think I've ever seen so many stars before.' Jenny's voice was awed.

They stood in silence for a while, and Pearl felt some of her anxiety ebb. She traced out the constellation of Orion and in a low voice she muttered, 'Per ardua ad astra.' Through adversity to the stars – the RAF's motto.

'And don't you forget it,' Thea said. 'Think about it, both of you. Somewhere Greg and Edwin are gazing at the same stars. And Edwin's a wizard at using them to navigate. So they're not lost. We don't know where they are, but Edwin will know exactly where they need to go to reach safety.'

The thought was comforting, and Pearl felt the serenity of the stars seep into her. 'You know, until now I never really understood the significance of candles at Christmas,' she said, not shifting her gaze from the sky. 'But looking at the stars has really brought it home to me how tiny each one is when compared to the huge expanse of nothingness each one is in. Yet it's the stars that draw our attention. They inspire hope. And that's what Christmas is about – shining the light of hope into the darkness.'

Beside her she heard Jenny sniff, and, on her other side, Thea spoke. 'There's your editorial for the Christmas issue.'

Pearl gave a shaky laugh. 'I must remember to write it down.'

'Don't worry,' Jenny said. 'I won't forget.'

Pearl walked the rest of the way to the Gatehouse in silence but felt fully at peace for the first time since hearing about Greg's doomed flight.

They had just reached the porch when they heard the sound of footsteps from the lane. A dark figure emerged. 'Good evening, ladies,' came Thomas's voice. 'I feared I was late, but I seem to be right on time.'

His arrival broke the spell the stars had cast upon the group, and they trooped into the drawing room, chattering and laughing.

Deedee rose to meet them. 'Well, there's a sight for sore eyes,' she said. Then, with a rueful glance at her bandaged arm, added, 'And sore everything else, too.'

Pearl waved her back into her chair. 'How are you feeling?'

'I've got to admit I'm feeling a little stiff, but I think that's more from having been sat down all evening. I couldn't even do any knitting with my wrist all strapped up.'

'Well, now we're here, it's our job to keep you entertained,' Thea said. She looked at Thomas. 'What do you say, Grandpa – do you think you can beat us at rummy?'

The look of startled delight on Thomas's face made Pearl smile. 'I thought I was going to have a struggle on my hands to get you to call me that.' He shot a glance in Pearl's direction. 'I can tell it makes Pearl feel awkward.'

Thea shrugged. 'Maybe it's different for me. I never knew my father, or my grandparents on his side, so you're the first father – or grandfather – figure I've ever known.'

Thomas pulled his handkerchief from his pocket and dabbed his eyes. 'The cold always makes my eyes water,' he explained, fooling nobody. 'I never thought I'd ever have grandchildren, and now I've got two.' Then, looking at Jenny, he inclined his head. 'Plus an honorary grand-daughter.'

Struck by a sudden impulse, Pearl gave him a hug. She didn't know who was the more startled, Thomas or herself. 'Welcome to the family,' she said. 'I may find it awkward at first, but you're the only person I could ever imagine calling Grandpa. I'm more pleased than ever that you gave me away at the wedding.'

Thomas's cheeks turned pink, and he pulled a bottle of sherry from the bag that Pearl only now noticed he was carrying. 'I think this calls for a toast, don't you? Then, by all means, let's play rummy, although I should warn you, I don't like to lose.'

The rest of the evening passed in toasts, laughter and several rounds of rummy. Finally Pearl glanced at the clock. 'I suppose we ought to make a move,' she said to Thomas. 'We wouldn't want to miss the last bus. What about Thea and Jenny – did you get late passes?'

Thea rolled her eyes. 'Yes, Mummy.'

Deedee choked, eliciting a glare from Pearl. 'Anyway, it's high time you went to bed, Deedee. Don't try and tell me you're not aching all over. I'll come and check on you first thing tomorrow. Good thing it's the weekend. We can stay right here for a day or two. No need for you to come into Lincoln.'

'Actually there is. I nearly forgot.'

'What? If you left something in the shop or office, I'll fetch it for you.'

'I didn't leave anything. But it's Georgie's Christmas show tomorrow, and I promised to go. I got two tickets. I thought you'd come with me.'

The bubble of security that seemed to have been cast around Pearl after the starlit walk burst. Surely soon she would hear news of Greg, and she needed to be contactable at all times. She couldn't bear it if she missed a vital message because she was out of contact. 'Are you sure you're up to it? Wouldn't you rather stay here?'

Deedee shook her head. 'I'm right as rain, and I won't need my wrist to watch a show. I'm sure it'd do you good to get out and about.'

Pearl opened her mouth to reply, but Thea, who had given her sister a knowing look, broke in. 'I think what Pearl's too proud to admit is that she doesn't want to be out of contact for that long. I think you should go, though, Deedee. What time does it start?'

Deedee rummaged in her handbag and pulled out a ticket. 'Seven.'

Thea's face fell. 'I'm on duty until eight, or I would have been happy to go. What about you, Jenny?'

Jenny pulled a face. 'Sorry. I don't come off until eight either.'

'I'll go,' Thomas said.

Deedee stared at him. 'Seriously? I wouldn't have thought it was your thing.'

'Why not? I seem to remember rather enjoying musical theatre back in the Nineties. There was a certain actress I was rather taken with.'

Pearl was amused to see Deedee look uncharacteristic-ally flustered. 'Well, if you're sure. But I don't like to think of Pearl all alone.'

'She won't be,' Thea said. 'She'll be with you all day, and she'll have Mrs Stockwell here until Jenny and I come off duty.' She looked at Pearl. 'That's okay, isn't it?'

Pearl bit back a grin, knowing Thea was determined to get Deedee back with Thomas. 'I'll be fine.'

The next morning Pearl left Rosebery Avenue and strode out, determined to reach her destination in the shortest possible time. It was getting harder to leave a place where she could be easily contacted. Although it wouldn't take long for her to reach the Gatehouse, she couldn't bear to think of missing a message. She comforted herself with the knowledge that there was a telephone there, and she had left the number with her landlady, together with instructions to call straight away if she received a telegram. Thea had already spoken to Fitz before leaving the night before, so he knew to call the Gatehouse if he had any news on Saturday.

When she reached the bus stop, a glance at her watch showed her that she had made record time and might even be able to catch an earlier bus than anticipated. She hurried to join the queue, not looking where she was going, and bumped into a girl.

'I'm terribly sorry,' she said, and stooped to pick up the girl's hat, which had fallen off in the collision. 'Oh, it's Georgie, isn't it?'

The girl nodded and took her hat. 'Thanks. Don't worry. It was my fault. I wasn't looking where I was going.'

'My grandmother's looking forward to your show tonight.'

Georgie's face lit up. 'I'm so glad she's coming. And I had amazing news last night. The girl who plays Maid Marian has the mumps.'

'How wonderful.' Pearl was unable to hide her grin.

Georgie's dimples deepened. 'I know. That sounded heartless. But it means the girl who plays her maid is now Marian, and I get to play the maid.'

'That *is* good news. I'm really pleased for you. I look forward to hearing how it goes.'

'Oh, aren't you coming? I thought Deedee bought you a ticket.'

'She did, but I can't make it.' Pearl didn't feel like explaining why she didn't want to go, so simply added, 'She's bringing… a friend instead.'

At that moment her bus arrived. 'There's my bus. I must dash. Break a leg!' And she hurried to climb on board.

She found Deedee stiff and sore but still determined to go to the show, especially after Pearl related Georgie's news. Pearl didn't attempt to dissuade her, knowing it would be pointless, but insisted she spend a quiet day by the fire to avoid tiring herself out before the evening. Deedee read her book while Pearl struggled with a letter to Greg's parents. However helpless she was feeling, it must be worse for them, being so far away in Australia. They had written her some lovely letters since the wedding, welcoming her to the family with whole hearts, and Pearl had maintained a correspondence with them, patchy though it was, owing to the unreliable post across such a vast distance. However, since Greg had been reported missing she had held off writing, hoping for more certain news before she put pen to paper.

'What do you think I should do, Deedee – write now or wait until I get fresh news?'

Deedee put down her book. 'What did you say when you wrote to them after he went missing?'

'I didn't. I mean, I didn't write.'

'Why not? They must be worried sick.'

'I know. I feel awful. But I kept thinking I would hear one way or the other soon, and it would be better to wait until I knew. Anyway, letters take ages. Chances are I'll know more long before any letter reaches them.'

'That's not the point. If anything had happened to Fitz, you would have expected Thea to write to his mother by now.'

Pearl looked down at her hands. 'I know. I just... I've no idea what to say.'

'Write from the heart. Tell them you hope you'll have better news for them soon and let them know you're thinking of them.'

It sounded so easy put like that, but even so Pearl struggled to find the right words. As she wrote, it dawned on her that the true reason she hadn't written earlier was that putting the words down on paper made them seem more concrete and forced her to face the reality of the situation.

She had only just finished when Thomas arrived, at tea time. She studied her grandfather across the table and thought he looked younger and happier than she had ever known him. Was he falling in love with Deedee all over again? Whatever his intentions, she hoped neither of them would end up getting hurt.

Thomas glanced up and caught her eye. 'You're looking very thoughtful, Pearl. Are you feeling all right?'

'Just the usual. You know how it is.' Not wanting to put a dampener on the evening by speaking of Greg, she said, 'I was wondering earlier if you are planning to make it generally known that Thea and I are your granddaughters. I was speaking to Georgie earlier and caught myself about to tell her that my grandfather was going with Deedee to the show. I didn't know what to say, so I said you were her friend.' Would he want everyone to know he'd had an illegitimate daughter?

Thomas looked at her gravely. 'That was very considerate of you, but frankly I'm delighted to have you and Thea as granddaughters, and I want the world to know. Finding you has made me so proud and happy.'

Was it her imagination, or did Thomas's gaze stray to Deedee as he spoke? Thea would be delighted, but Pearl wasn't so sure. Not because she didn't want to see her grandparents together but because she was unsure how Deedee felt. She desperately hoped no one would end up hurt.

Once Deedee and Thomas had left, Pearl picked up her pen again, this time to work on an article on New Year's resolutions. She had asked personnel in the various stations in 5 Group to write in with their resolutions and now she was compiling them and adding her own thoughts to turn it into an amusing item. She was just chuckling over one WAAF who had said she had resolved to decide which of her boyfriends to keep when she heard the phone ring.

She flew out of the living room, but Mrs Stockwell had got to the study before her. Pearl froze, straining her ears to hear Mrs Stockwell's side of the conversation. 'Hello? Yes… she's here, yes… please hold on while I fetch her.'

Pearl dashed to the study, heart pounding, only to barge into Mrs Stockwell coming the other way. 'Who is it?' she gasped.

'It's Flying Officer Fitzgerald.'

Pearl scarcely knew how she reached the desk in the study; she couldn't remember walking into the dim room, but all of a sudden she was standing by the desk with the receiver pressed to her ear. 'Fitz? What have you heard?'

'Nothing definite yet, but I thought you should know.'

Something about his tone of voice made her insides freeze. 'What is it?' She groped for the office chair and managed to reach it before her trembling legs gave way and she sank into it.

'American troops moved into Blerick some days ago, and they've found Greg's Lanc. At least, they've found a Lancaster we presume must be the one Greg was in.'

'What do you mean? Why don't you know for sure?'

She heard Fitz release a heavy sigh. 'Because it's nothing more than a burned-out shell.'

Pearl couldn't speak. All she could do was grip the receiver and draw one steadying breath after another, only half listening to Fitz's next words.

'They've been able to identify it as a Lancaster, but all other identifying marks have been obliterated.'

Pearl clutched this one slender hope and finally found her voice. 'Then it might not be his.'

'Maybe not, but it's right where we expected to find it, given the information we got from the crew members who returned.'

'But you can't be certain.'

'Not certain, no. But Pearl, there's something else.'

'What?' Although she already knew what he was going to say.

'They found a body. Too badly burned to identify.'

'Oh God.' Then her brain caught up with what Fitz had just said. 'Only one?'

'Only one,' Fitz confirmed in a bleak voice, reminding her that he was close to both Greg and Edwin, and he must be suffering too.

A few seconds of silence passed, interrupted only by the steady tick-tock of the grandfather clock in the hall and the faint crackle down the line. Finally Pearl bestirred herself. 'What happens now?'

'Difficult to say. Remember how chaotic things are in the Netherlands at the moment. Obviously attempts will be made to identify the body, but I've no idea how long it will take or even if it's possible.' Another pause, then: 'Don't give up hope, Pearl. I wanted you to be prepared in case it turns out to be Greg, but we've no idea who it is yet. He could still be out there.'

Chapter Sixteen

Deedee laughed, wiping away tears of laughter as she watched Maid Marian, helped by her feisty maid, fool the Sheriff of Nottingham into giving his Christmas presents to the poor children of the town. While Georgie's role was small, she shone, and Deedee heard more than one whispered enquiry in the audience regarding the identity of the clever maid with the amazing singing voice.

When the company burst into a fast-paced number, Deedee listened in satisfaction as Georgie's voice rose clear and strong above the others. Not that any of the performers had weak voices, but Georgie's grabbed the attention in a way that none of the others did. Deedee had no doubt that she would be given a starring role in the next production. It wasn't just luck that had secured her this role, but the dedication she had displayed in getting to know the script even when she had thought she wouldn't be getting a part in this production. The fact that she had then been ready to make the most of her opportunity when it arrived was a testament to Georgie's hard work.

A voice hissed behind her. 'See the maid? That's my daughter. Isn't she wonderful?'

Deedee turned to see Mrs March sitting two rows behind her. She shot the woman a grin, and Mrs March waved back. Deedee was amused to hear the next comment Mrs March addressed to her neighbour. 'That lady who I just waved at? She used to be a famous actress herself. Discovered my Georgina, she did.'

She belatedly became aware of Tom's gaze on her. He leaned across to murmur in her ear, 'You did a wonderful thing in encouraging that girl. I'll be sure to give her a glowing mention when I review the performance.'

Deedee opened her eyes wide. 'I didn't think you actually wrote any articles.'

'I don't often have the time, but I like to keep my hand in. And this deserves a special mention, don't you think?'

'Of course.' Deedee smiled at him, then caught her breath at the smile he gave in return. It was as though the years since they had last been together had dissolved, and he was the same young man he had been then, giving the smile that was reserved for her alone.

It would be so easy to lean against his shoulder, weave her arm through his and pretend they had never been separated. But so much had happened since then. She turned back to the stage and tried to focus on the performance, ignoring the longing she felt to place her hand in his.

When the show ended, Deedee applauded as best she could given the state of her wrist, ignoring the pain and clapping as hard as she could when Georgie took her bow. She wished the moment could go on for longer, so that she could extract every last bit of enjoyment from Georgie taking her applause with starry eyes, but all too soon the curtain fell for the last time, the lights went up and the audience rose and filed out, pulling torches from their pockets so they could find their way in the blackout.

Acting on impulse, Deedee said to Tom, 'Wait here. I want to congratulate Georgie.'

Fighting against the crowd, she made her way to the front of the hall to a doorway at the side of the stage. This was clearly the way to the backstage area, for a few of the performers emerged, still in costume, and waved to their friends or family. Knowing that everyone backstage would be frantically busy getting changed or clearing away costumes and props, Deedee doubted she would be welcome, so she approached one of the cast members – the boy who had played Little John. He had just finished his conversation with a friend, and Deedee stopped him before he could return backstage. After congratulating him on his performance, she said, 'Could you tell Georgie March that Deedee would like to speak to her, please?'

The boy nodded and disappeared. While she was waiting, Deedee found herself humming the closing number while watching the crowd as they queued for the exit. A favourite pastime of hers was making up stories about the various people she observed, and she found herself doing it now. A prim middle-aged woman ushering two boisterous children became an heiress who had lost her fortune to a scheming cousin; a pale young WAAF had, Deedee decided, joined up to keep alive the memory of a man she had loved. No, that made her think of Pearl and Greg. As she tried to think of a more cheerful scenario, a young man emerged from the stage door and knocked her wrist as he pushed past, causing sparks of pain to shoot up her arm. He didn't even have the manners to apologise, just forced his way through the milling crowd and was soon out of the hall.

While Deedee usually refused to entertain the kind of gossip that wondered why certain young men were not in uniform at this time of national crisis, she made an exception for this obnoxious specimen. Everything from the cut of his suit to his hat screamed 'spiv', and Deedee decided that he had falsified his medical records to avoid conscription and was now making money on the black market. Her happy imaginings of his arrest and humiliating trial were interrupted by Georgie.

'Deedee! I'm so glad you came. What did you think?'

'I thought you were wonderful. If you don't get a lead role next time, your drama teacher is a fool.'

Georgie glowed. 'I've had loads of people say lovely things, but it means so much more coming from you. Thank you for everything you've done.'

'It was a pleasure, dear. I enjoyed every minute of the show, but your performance made me look forward to visiting London in the not-too-distant future and seeing your name in lights.'

Georgie clasped her hands. 'Do you really think so?'

'I do. Assuming you continue to work hard and don't let your head get turned.' ·

Georgie pulled a face. 'That could never happen with my mum making me work extra shifts to pay for my drama lessons.'

'Well, it's all good experience for you. Most actors need to turn their hands to another job to see them through lean times. It's good that you're no stranger to hard work.'

'Anyway, guess what?' Georgie was bouncing on her toes, and Deedee doubted she had listened to many of her cautionary words. 'A man came to see me just now and said he was a theatrical agent. He even gave me his card.

Look.' She pulled the card from her pocket and waved it before Deedee's face. Deedee was just able to make out the words: 'David Mountjoy, Theatrical Agent.' There was also an address and telephone number, but they were no more than a blur as the card sped past her eyes.

'Well, that's very encouraging, but you must take care. There are a lot of men out there who would take advantage of a young girl's dreams.' This was something Deedee's parents, who had been in the theatre themselves, had impressed upon her and, from everything she read in the papers, nothing had changed in the intervening years. She didn't want to squash Georgie's excitement on today of all days, however, so she simply added, 'Your drama teacher will be able to give you the best advice on things like agents and auditions, so always check with her before agreeing to anything.' She would save her serious lecture for a time when Georgie would be likely to be more receptive.

Although Georgie nodded, Deedee wasn't convinced the girl had taken in her caution, for she cradled the card in the palm of her hand, treating it as a precious object, and gave it a loving stroke. She frowned. 'I think he's given me two stuck together. Yes, look.' She peeled them apart, then brightened. 'At least I have a spare if I lose one.'

'Actually, could I have it?' Deedee scarcely knew what impulse caused her to blurt out her request, unless it was a vague sense of unease.

Georgie shrugged and handed it over. 'Why, are you thinking of going back on the stage?'

But there was no need for Deedee to reply, for someone called Georgie from backstage. The girl glanced over her shoulder. 'I'd better go. I've still got loads to do.'

But as Deedee returned to Tom, her qualms about the agent wouldn't leave her. Surely a reputable agent would have no need to look for talent at a provincial drama class production. And the memory of the ill=mannered spiv flashed into her mind. She would be sure to have a serious word with Georgie at the earliest opportunity, and in the meantime she would hold on to his card in case she wanted to investigate him.

With her hand tucked in the crook of Tom's arm, humming a song from the show, Deedee picked her way over the dark pavements with care. 'I can't remember when I last enjoyed an evening so much,' she said. Her vague disquiet was fading and in Tom's company, her head still buzzing with the light and laughter of the show, she let it go completely.

'Same here,' Tom said. Then, with a slight catch in his voice, he added, 'I think it must be the company.'

Deedee did her best to ignore the thrill his words gave her. *Be sensible for just once in your life*, she told herself. But being sensible didn't come naturally, especially not when she was enjoying a starlit walk with Tom that reminded her of their late-night strolls in London, the rapturous applause still ringing in her ears some hours after the end of another successful performance and every inch of her flesh thrilling at Tom's nearness. On one memorable night, they had dared each other to squeeze through a gap in the fence into St James's Park and walked around the lake by the silvery light of the full moon. Tonight, the moon was the merest pale crescent, but the stars were dazzling, much brighter than she had ever known them in London. It was so magical she could almost imagine time had gone backwards and they were once more young and in love.

The throb of aero engines cut across her musings, pulling her back to the present. She looked up, automatically seeking out the aircraft, but it was impossible to find in the dark. Presently the growl faded away.

Tom cleared his throat. 'I hope you've enjoyed the evening as much as I have.'

'It was wonderful,' she said. 'Thanks for coming. I didn't think you'd be interested.'

'I'd be interested in going anywhere as long as you were there too.'

Something about his tone of voice made Deedee give him a sharp look, even though he was only visible in silhouette. 'Tom, I don't think—'

'Wait. Hear me out, please.'

Her warning had been half-hearted to say the least, so she gave in. 'Go on.'

'I know there's a lot of time and hurt between us but, now we know it was my father who separated us, why can't we start again? I won't deny I loved my wife, but I never really stopped loving you.'

Deedee couldn't be anything other than truthful. 'I never stopped loving you, either.' It didn't mean she had to tell the whole truth, though. There were some things she would never be able to tell him. And that was why she added, 'I think it's too late for us, though. We're both too settled in our lives as they are.'

'You were never afraid of change, and I don't think you're so very different now. Deedee Pritchard is very much the same woman Hope Burnell ever was.'

Deedee couldn't deny that those words gave her a thrill. She still felt like the same girl she always had been. While Pearl and Thea might see a woman in her early seventies, she didn't feel any different than she had at twenty, and it was nice to be with a man who still saw her that way. Regardless, she summoned up her most sensible voice, one that sounded very much like Pearl, and said, 'I hope we'll always be friends now you know about Pearl and Thea, but I don't see how anything else could work, given I'll be returning to Shrewsbury before long.' That gave her a bit of a jolt, remembering that she was only in Lincoln for Pearl. She could only pray that she would be returning because Greg had been found safe and well.

She'd thought that would put an end to this line of conversation, but Tom said, 'I don't want my father to win. He kept me from the woman I love and my daughter. If we don't even try to make it work, now that everything that separated us no longer exists, it will feel like he's won all over again. There's nothing to keep us apart now.'

Nothing that Deedee was prepared to admit to, anyway. She tried to make light of the situation. 'Is that the only reason you want us to have a relationship – because it would annoy your father?'

'No, of course not. I still love you. If you didn't feel the same, I would be content to accept your friendship and nothing more, but you've just said you also love me. There's no reason to go through the pain of separation again.'

In many ways, Deedee couldn't argue with him. While she couldn't tell yet if her affection was strong enough to contemplate a life together, wasn't that the whole point of courtship? It was oh so tempting to agree. After all, there was nothing to keep her in Shrewsbury any more. She loved her snug cottage, but there had been a time when she would have given it up like a shot if Tom had asked her forgiveness and asked her to marry him. But in the back of her mind an insistent voice continued to prod at her and ask if he would still love her if he knew what she had done. She didn't want to find out, so the safest thing was to keep him at arm's length. At the same time, she couldn't bring herself to give him a firm no right now and spoil what had been a wonderful evening. She wanted to keep one more fond memory close to her heart. So she said, 'Maybe you're right. I can't say anything for sure yet. Will you give me time?'

He squeezed her hand. 'Take as long as you need.'

This was so much the gallant Tom of fifty years past that she longed to be done with caution and kiss him there and then in the street, in the starlight. Maybe she would have done if Tom hadn't added, 'And if you want me to remove my father's portrait from Haughton Newspapers' foyer, just say the word.'

Memory of Mr Haughton senior sent a cold trickle down her spine. Tom could take away the portrait, even destroy it, but the ghost of his father would always come between them.

If Deedee had been in any doubt about her decision, what she found when she returned to the Gatehouse would have decided her. Pearl was sitting by the fire, staring at the flames with dull eyes, Thea and Jenny hovering over her. Deedee immediately flung off her coat and went to sit beside her eldest granddaughter, all thoughts of romance and starlit walks evaporating. Fearing the worst, she scarcely dared ask what had happened. Some of the ice-cold lump of dread lifted from her chest when Thea explained.

'So you don't know for sure if it's Greg.' Then she caught sight of Jenny's haunted expression and hastily added, 'Or if it's the right plane at all. For all we know, Greg and Edwin could be taking shelter somewhere, or meeting Allied troops at this very moment.'

Pearl bestirred herself and spoke for the first time since Deedee had arrived. 'But the burned-out Lancaster was right where the crew estimated it was going to crash. I don't think there's any doubt it's Greg's plane.' She grimaced, shooting a glance in Jenny's direction before lowering her voice to a whisper. 'And if I hope the body's not Greg, that's the same thing as hoping it's Edwin. What kind of person does that make me? Edwin's my friend.'

'It makes you human.' Deedee was firm. She perched on the arm of Pearl's chair and pulled her into a hug. At first Pearl remained stiff and unmoving, but eventually she relaxed and returned the embrace, resting her head on Deedee's shoulder with a sob.

'I'm glad you're here,' she said, her voice muffled against Deedee's shoulder.

Deedee patted her back. 'I'm not going anywhere.'

She shouldn't have left Pearl alone all evening. Deedee went cold at the thought that Pearl had only had Izzy for company when Fitz called. Izzy would have done her best, of course, but it wouldn't have been the same as having family or close friends around her. This was all her fault, allowing herself to get over-involved in Georgie's life when Pearl needed her more. And more than that, enjoying her evening with Tom and allowing herself to be overtaken by fond memories. What had happened with Tom was in the past and should stay there, and she shouldn't have gone out with him when Pearl needed her more. The next time she saw him, she would tell him it was impossible for them to have anything more than friendship.

Chapter Seventeen

The next morning, Pearl dragged herself out of bed when she heard her landlady clattering in the kitchen downstairs. She had lain awake all night and couldn't face food, but also couldn't face her landlady's gushing sympathy if she said she didn't feel up to breakfast. On the whole, despite her shortcomings as a cook, Mrs Dale was a good landlady who kept a clean, comfortable home, but she also loved to gossip, and Pearl deeply regretted telling her that Greg was missing in action. Now she could hardly walk down the street without some concerned housewife stopping her and asking if she had any news. And heaven forbid she should ever show signs of being off her food without Mrs Dale dropping hints that she might be 'in the family way'.

It was the one thing she and Greg had actually talked through before getting married. Both had wanted to delay starting a family until after the war. Pearl because it would mean leaving the WAAF – while WAAFs were allowed to marry, if they became pregnant, they were required to leave – and she wasn't ready yet to give up doing the job that she loved. Greg had said he didn't want to become a father until he was able to be there for any children and be a part of their lives. Although he didn't say it, Pearl knew he couldn't bear the thought of leaving her to bring up children alone should he be killed. The trouble was, as she faced the very real prospect of a life without Greg, she couldn't help thinking that if they'd had a child, it would have brought her comfort knowing a part of him still lived on.

Typical. The only decision they had actually made about their future, and already Pearl was regretting it.

With a heavy heart and heavy eyes, she got herself washed and dressed and went down to breakfast. She was just spreading butter onto her toast, taking care to use the butter set aside for her own use, when the doorbell chimed.

'I'll get it.' She flung her knife onto her plate with a clatter and hurried to the door, feeling sick. She sagged with relief when she saw not a messenger boy bearing a dreaded brown envelope but Deedee. 'I thought we'd arranged that I'd come to you this morning.'

'We did, but I decided to come and meet you instead. I didn't like the idea of you being alone any longer than necessary.'

'I was just finishing breakfast. Why don't you wait in my room? I won't be long.' Then, as Deedee was on the point of going upstairs, Pearl caught her arm. 'Thank you. I do feel better now you're here.'

Indeed, when she returned to the breakfast table she found that she now had the appetite not only for the toast but also for a small bowl of porridge, accompanied by chopped apple and walnuts.

'It's good to see you with a bit more colour in your cheeks,' said Mrs Dale with a smile. 'Here – I saved you the top of the milk.'

Pearl took it, feeling bad about her uncharitable thoughts towards her landlady, although not so bad that she was going to turn down the extra-creamy milk on her porridge. She ate with relish, the hollow, empty feeling inside lessened just knowing that Deedee was nearby.

'I'm really glad you're here,' she said again to Deedee when she returned to her room. 'I didn't know how scared and alone I felt until I saw you at the door.'

Deedee gave her a hug with her good arm. 'I thought you must be feeling that way. I didn't like to see you leave last night, but there isn't a spare bed at the Gatehouse. I shouldn't have left you to go to the show. I feel terrible that you were all alone when Fitz called.'

'You mustn't,' Pearl said. 'I'm just grateful that you're here at all. Anyway, I wasn't alone. Mrs Stockwell was there, and Thea and Jenny arrived not long after. I would have felt awful if you'd stayed in when you'd promised to see Georgie in her show.'

'That's all very well, but I should have been there for you. You're the reason I'm in Lincolnshire, after all.'

Seeing how serious Deedee was, Pearl didn't argue the point. Instead she asked, 'Do you have any plans for the day?'

'That's what I was going to ask you. Did you want to go to church?' Deedee glanced at her watch. 'We should be able to make it to Fenthorpe in time if we get a move on.'

Pearl hesitated. 'I would like to go to a service, but I don't think I can face everyone asking after Greg.'

'What about the cathedral? We'll be nice and anonymous there, and if we sit at the back, we can slip out if it gets too much.'

This sounded like a good idea to Pearl, and so, instead of a rush to catch the bus, they took a leisurely walk up the hill to the cathedral. Mindful that Deedee must still be suffering from her fall, Pearl took a route that avoided Steep Hill and had a gentler incline.

Attending the cathedral service turned out to be the perfect way to spend the morning. They sat near the back, and Pearl let the peace of the ancient building wash over her, taking comfort in the familiar words of the service. She found the sermon particularly appropriate, for the dean was preaching on the theme of Advent.

'It's a reminder to us to hold on to hope and not to give in to despair, even when the world around us is plunged into darkness. Dawn always follows night and spring follows winter.'

Pearl blinked back tears and thought of the other times in her life when all had seemed dark. Although she had been very young at the time, she still had vivid memories of her father's death near the end of the Great War, closely followed by her mother's not long after Thea's birth. That had been a very dark time indeed, yet, although she still missed her parents, she had gradually found joy in life again. It was a reminder that, whatever happened, she would get through it. And she still had plenty to be thankful for.

So when they emerged from the cathedral and Deedee told her Mrs Stockwell had performed some wizardry with rations and had invited her, Thea and Jenny to lunch, Pearl didn't shy away from spending time with her sister, who still had Fitz, but agreed, looking forward to spending time with her loved ones.

'What about Thomas – is he coming?'

There was a slight pause before Deedee answered, and when she spoke, although her tone was breezy, Pearl could have sworn she sounded awkward. 'Oh, I'm not sure. We can invite him if you like, but we'd need to ask Izzy first, to be sure there was enough food to go round.' Pearl got the impression that Deedee wasn't so keen.

'We'll invite him if we see him, assuming Mrs Stockwell doesn't mind.' For Pearl found that Thomas, like Deedee, was a comfort to have around. 'Also, I think we should decorate the tree for the dance this afternoon, seeing as Thea and Jenny will be around to help.' The last thing Pearl wanted to do was sit around helping Deedee with her knitting. She needed to do something to keep her busy, preferably something to lift her spirits. And nothing could lift the spirits like a pretty Christmas tree.

When they reached the Gatehouse, Mrs Stockwell told them that she had already spoken to Thomas on the phone earlier and, although she had invited him to lunch, he had said he would be busy but would visit later. Pearl shot her grandmother a sideways glance when she heard that, and tried to see if it was welcome news or not. Deedee, however, simply said, 'It will be lovely to see him, whenever he can make it.' And her expression gave nothing away.

Her curiosity piqued, as soon as they were alone in the living room Pearl said, 'I never asked you how your evening went yesterday.'

'No, well, your mind was understandably elsewhere by the time I returned.'

'I know. But now I'm asking. How did it go?'

'It was wonderful. Georgie was a complete star. I heard ever so many people compliment her, even though she only had a small part. Even her mother was pleased.'

'Good for her. Although I really meant how was your evening with Thomas. You could almost say it was a date.'

'It was not a date.' Deedee drew a deep breath. 'But if you must know, Tom did say something about wanting us to start courting again. Although courting's probably the wrong word for what we did back in the Nineties, considering your mother was the result.'

Honestly, it was a good thing Mrs Stockwell was out of earshot. How did Deedee always manage to say such embarrassing things? 'What did you say?'

'He took me by surprise, to be honest. I said I'd think about it, but now I think too much has changed. We aren't the same people we were then.'

Was Deedee trying to talk herself out of it or into it? Despite studying her carefully, Pearl couldn't tell. 'Of course you're not the same people. But it doesn't mean you can't be happy together. What do you want, deep down?'

Pearl wasn't asking out of mild curiosity. This seemed like a question Deedee needed to work out the answer to, if she didn't already know. When Deedee didn't answer straight away, she added, 'You obviously need to think about this. Your happiness is important. Don't throw it away out of some misguided idea that Thea or I need you. We're both grown up now, and it's time you put yourself first.' Then she gave a wry smile. 'Well, I say Thea and I are grown up, but I still have my doubts about Thea.'

'I feel my ears burning.' Thea breezed through the door, Jenny close behind. This put an end to Pearl's tête-à-tête with Deedee.

'So they should be,' Deedee said. 'Pearl was expressing her doubts over your ability to look after yourself.' This was said with a brief but meaningful look at Pearl, warning her not to mention anything about Thomas's romantic leanings towards Deedee. Pearl could appreciate that, considering how enthusiastically Thea had promoted Thomas and Deedee's relationship, and so she held her tongue.

'She's probably right,' Thea agreed. 'That's why I'm so lucky I've got Fitz to look out for me. While I look out for him, of course.'

This gave Pearl a jolt. It sounded a lot like an engagement. Thea must have read her mind, for she looked horrified. 'Don't take that the wrong way. We're not engaged or anything. Even I wouldn't be so crass as to announce my engagement at a time like this.'

Pearl forced a smile, hating herself for the stab of jealousy. 'I don't expect you to put your life on hold just because of my situation.' After all, hadn't she just said something similar to Deedee? Then why could she mean it with all her heart when she said it to her grandmother yet be eaten up with jealousy when considering her sister's happiness? All in all, she was grateful when Mrs Stockwell announced that lunch was ready, putting an end to the conversation.

They trooped into the kitchen, to discover a huge fisherman's pie waiting to be served.

'The fishmonger managed to get some fresh cod yesterday,' Mrs Stockwell explained. 'So I was able to make a substantial meal without making much of a dent in our rations.'

There was enough for a hearty portion each, plus carrots and swede. When Pearl carried her plate to the table, she made sure to sit next to Jenny so she didn't have to pick up the conversation about Fitz. Jenny, after all, had her own worries about Edwin, and being with her made Pearl feel less alone.

'I don't suppose you've had any more news?' Jenny asked once they were all tucking into their meal.

Pearl shook her head. 'I promise I'll let you know as soon as I hear anything,' she said.

'Could you pass the salt, please, Pearl?' Deedee asked. She gave Pearl a searching glance that made Pearl feel quite uncomfortable. She wondered if her grandmother had picked up on her reluctance to sit with Thea.

Deedee thanked Pearl, then addressed the table. 'Pearl and I thought we would decorate the tree in the ballroom today. Will you join us, you two?'

Thea nodded. 'Sounds like a good idea. What about you, Jenny?'

'Anything that keeps us indoors. I enjoy my work, but at this time of year I can understand the appeal of a desk job.'

Accordingly, when the last morsel had been eaten and the dishes washed and put away, the four women set out across the grounds.

'Lend me your arm, will you, Pearl? I'm still not feeling completely myself.'

Pearl gave Deedee a curious look as she dropped back from Jenny's side and offered her arm to her grandmother. Deedee had appeared to be back to her usual sprightly self, apart from her wrist, and hadn't needed any assistance walking through Lincoln earlier. Still, she didn't comment and slowed her pace to match Deedee's until a considerable gap had opened up between them and the others.

'I wanted to speak to you alone,' Deedee said. 'I couldn't help but notice you seem to be avoiding Thea.'

Pearl sighed. She had been naive to think Deedee wouldn't notice. 'I'm just finding it hard,' she said. 'I don't want to resent Thea, but every time she mentions Fitz it hurts. It's a reminder of what I've lost.'

'You haven't lost him yet. Don't give up hope.'

'It's getting harder to hold on.'

'Anyway, would you prefer it if the situation was reversed – if Fitz was missing and Greg were still safe?'

'What? No, of course not.' Pearl was horrified. 'I'd hate to see Thea miserable. And Fitz is my friend too.'

'Well then, don't you think Thea feels the same? She's hurting because you're hurting. Is it really so difficult to believe?'

'I didn't say I liked being jealous. I can't help feeling that way.'

Deedee nodded. 'And so you're avoiding Thea because you feel guilty as well as jealous. But you're doing yourself no favours by placing a distance between you and your sister. She wants to support you. And consider this – the war isn't over yet. How would you feel if Fitz was killed and your resentment had created such a chasm between you and Thea that you couldn't offer her the support she needed?'

Pearl swallowed. She had become so closed in on herself that she hadn't thought of that. 'I'd feel awful.' She fixed her gaze on her sister and Jenny. While she couldn't hear their conversation, she could guess the subject, for Thea had her arm round Jenny's shoulders, and Jenny, who had seemed particularly down earlier, stood a little straighter. 'You're right,' she said finally. 'I'll try not to push her away.'

Deedee gave her hand a squeeze. 'And don't be too hard on yourself. What you're feeling is only natural. I'd just hate to see you let it drive a wedge between the pair of you.'

After that, Deedee miraculously recovered her energy, and they caught up with the others at the door. They trooped into the ballroom and regarded the Christmas tree, which was just as tall and bushy as Pearl remembered it and would look wonderful once decorated.

Thea tilted her head to the side, pulling a face at the bucket the tree had been wedged into with earth and stones to keep it stable. 'It looks like something carried in from a building site. It doesn't exactly scream Christmas.'

'I've got an idea.' Jenny purloined one of the sheets that they had used to protect the floor where they had been painting their window panels and draped it artfully round the bucket to give the impression of snow.

Thea stepped back to study the effect. 'It looks good,' was her verdict. 'I don't think the paint splotches matter, because we can cover them over with something. Holly or ivy, or something similar.'

This set them off singing 'The Holly and the Ivy', and the merry tune gave Pearl's spirits a lift. Determined to keep her word, she went to sort out suitable decorations from Thomas's collection with Thea, while Jenny and Deedee set to work unwinding the sets of fairy lights and testing them.

'Some of these baubles are far too fragile,' Thea said, cradling a glass ornament painted in bright reds and blues like a stained-glass window. 'We can't use anything that would smash if it got knocked off. With people dancing, they're bound to brush against the branches.'

'You certainly are, if you and Fitz insist on dancing a lindy hop.'

'We usually prefer the jitterbug.'

'Oh, like that's going to end well in a crowded ball-room.' Pearl had images of Thea being swung round directly into the tree. Although it probably wouldn't happen given Fitz was a trained dancer.

Suddenly Thea engulfed her in an awkward hug. 'Anyway, I won't dance a step if Greg isn't back by then. It wouldn't feel right.'

Pearl allowed herself to relax into the embrace and accept Thea's support. 'And it wouldn't feel right if you didn't enjoy yourself.' She pulled away slightly and gave her sister what she hoped was a convincing smile. 'If I've learned one thing, it's that you must make the most of the time you have together.' True, she still felt a twinge of jealousy, but she also meant what she said. She accepted that she wouldn't be truly free from envy unless Greg returned safe and sound, but Deedee's words had shaken her. There was still no guarantee that Fitz or any of their RAF friends were going to make it through the war in one piece. Although they were clearly in the endgame, fighting was still fierce, and who knew how many of those attending the dance would still be around next Christmas?

Feeling closer to Thea than she had for a while, Pearl worked at her side to sort through the boxes, packing away the fragile or clearly expensive ornaments and leaving out the more robust ones. Then, with Deedee directing the proceedings, they set to work on the tree, first winding strings of fairy lights criss-crossing up and down the full height of the tree, then adding tinsel and baubles. Finally, when there was hardly a bare branch left, they admired their work.

'You do the honours, Jenny,' Pearl said, pointing to the switch.

Jenny turned on the lights, and the tree was lit in sparkling blue, red and gold. The baubles swung gently in the draught, and with each turn the lights glinted on them, creating a magical sight.

When Jenny pointed at them with a delighted smile and announced, 'They look like skintillating stars,' Pearl decided to correct her later. She didn't want anything to spoil this moment.

Thea breathed deeply and closed her eyes, a blissful smile stretching from ear to ear. 'Now it smells like Christmas. This is perfect.'

And it was perfect. A cosy moment of pure joy amid the worry and strain of recent days. This was how she would have to cope from day to day, moment to moment, appreciating each glint of light when it appeared and not looking too far ahead.

Chapter Eighteen

It did Deedee's heart good to see Pearl make a serious effort to enjoy Thea's company and even speak of Fitz. She knew it must still be paining Pearl to compare Thea's happiness with her own inner turmoil, but the main thing was that she was trying, and Deedee could see her gradually lose herself in the task at hand.

Now the tree was finished, the ballroom was looking wonderfully festive. Some of the other WAAFs had collected greenery and had started the work of winding garlands round the doorways and the huge mantelpiece. There were also colourful paper chains – another find from Tom's decorations – hanging from the ceiling. The room was starting to look like a scene from a Christmas card or jigsaw. She experienced a sudden flash of how it must have looked before the war and when Tom's wife had still been alive, with her, Tom and friends gathered around the tree, singing carols.

Well done, Deedee. There you go, jealous of a dead woman, and after all you said to Pearl, too. But it was a reminder that she had promised Tom to think about their relationship. The trouble was, every time she decided to do the sensible thing and tell him they couldn't be more than friends she felt a twist of disappointment. But anything more was impossible, and it would be cruel to keep him dangling.

She would have stern words with Pearl and Thea if they treated a man like that, and she couldn't hold her granddaughters to a higher standard than herself. Therefore, as she made the return walk to the Gatehouse, she promised herself that the next time she managed a moment alone with Tom she would break it to him.

They returned to the Gatehouse with the boxes of decorations that had been too fragile or precious, reluctant to leave them anywhere they might be broken. The women hadn't long settled beside the fire in the living room, cradling mugs of steaming cocoa, when there was a ring on the doorbell. Deedee felt a flutter, thinking it might be Tom. She couldn't decide if she longed or dreaded to see him. However, a lurch of pleasure won out when the man himself staggered into the room, carrying a small spruce in a pot.

'I thought the room could do with some festive cheer,' he said as he placed the tree in front of the French windows. 'I don't know what we can use for decorations, though, what with all mine being up at the house.' Then he caught sight of the boxes that the women had left on the dining table, unsure where to store them. 'Wonderful! We can use these.'

'Oh, but these are the ones we were too scared to use in case they broke,' Pearl protested.

'Nonsense. What's the point of having unused decorations?'

This tree was easier to decorate than the one in the ballroom. That one had reached almost to the ceiling, whereas this stood only about four feet high in its pot. They festooned it with a string of colourful lights that they had judged too small to show up on the larger tree, and then hung it with the delicate glass baubles and strings of beads. As they worked, Pearl told Tom about the latest news she'd had from Fitz.

Tom listened with a grave face. 'That must have been a terrible shock,' he said. 'I wish there was something I could do. The thing about my job is that I've built up a huge network of contacts around the country, so I'm used to having someone I can contact for help in practically anything. But I don't know anyone who could help with this. I'm sure you need a quick answer so you can know for sure.'

'It's fine,' Pearl assured him. 'That's not why I told you. I just wanted you to know.' She paused to dab her eyes, and Deedee moved to put an arm round her. Tom, however, got there first, and Pearl rested her head against his shoulder for a moment before stepping away and hanging another bauble on the tree. Deedee was pleased to see how easily Pearl seemed to have accepted Tom as her grandfather and even more how readily Tom had taken to the role. The way he offered emotional support reminded Deedee of how she had always been able to rely on his strength.

She felt a wave of loss as it hit her all over again just what she, Clara, Pearl and Thea had missed all these years. And now Tom was asking if she would let him into her life again, it was hugely tempting to agree. Not just because he made her feel like a giddy twenty-year-old again but also because she longed to be in his company all the time. The trouble was, for her being in a full relationship meant holding nothing back, and if she did that, she stood to lose him altogether. What should she do – risk everything by telling him the truth, or keep him as a friend? It was an impossible decision.

When the tree was finished, they turned off the main electric light, keeping the room illuminated by nothing more than the firelight and the twinkling lights on the tree. Tom opened the gramophone and put on some Christmas carols.

'This feels magical,' Pearl said from her seat on a cushion at Thea's feet.

Thea nodded. 'I could almost believe that any wish we make now will come true.'

'That would be perfect,' Pearl said with a sad smile.

While Deedee had never been one for wishes, she found herself picturing Greg walking into the room, making the little family huddle complete. She was sure Pearl's thoughts were running along similar lines.

And if she could make a wish for herself? She would wish that Tom would understand and forgive her if she confessed all. In a way, it was a relief that Deedee didn't get a moment alone with Tom that evening. It being a Sunday, the last bus to Lincoln left earlier than the other nights, and so he and Pearl couldn't stay late. Being still undecided over her answer, she made no attempt to catch him alone, and waved them off after extracting a promise from Pearl to call her should she hear any more news, no matter the time.

The next day she was feeling much recovered from her fall. Her wrist was less swollen and much less painful, and her other aches and pains had almost disappeared. She didn't want to stray far from the Gatehouse in case Pearl tried to contact her, so she spent the morning wrapping her gifts for everyone. The paper shortage meant the only wrapping available was newspaper, but she chose her pages carefully – nothing with news of the war and certainly not the tragic report concerning the young Cambridge woman who had gone missing three weeks earlier. She glanced at the offending page long enough to read the headline: *Cambridge Girl Found Murdered in London* and the accompanying subheading: *Police losing hope in search for three other missing girls*. With a sad shake of the head, she set it in the salvage basket with the rest of the grim reading, then selected pages filled with lighter news and adverts and set to work. A search in the writing bureau turned up a tin of coloured pencils, giving her the idea of drawing sprigs of holly and mistletoe on each parcel to make them look more festive. Once the gifts were arranged under the tree, she stepped back to admire them, pleased that they made the room feel Christmassy.

That done, she saw it was almost time to catch the bus to Lincoln for her usual lunchtime meeting with Pearl. She hurried upstairs to apply some lipstick and powder, but when she picked up her powder compact she made the mistake of using her injured hand. She fumbled and dropped it, breaking the compact powder into thousands of fragments.

'Damn and blast,' she muttered. There was no saving any of it; all she could do was fetch a dustpan and sweep the scattered powder from the floorboards. She would have to buy some more, because she hated going out without all her make-up on. For now, she had to content herself with just a slick of lipstick before dashing to catch the bus.

When she arrived in Lincoln there was still twenty minutes before she was due to meet Pearl, so she decided to see if she could buy more face powder. She set out for the high street and soon found a little chemist with a small selection of cosmetics. To her joy, she found the same Yardley powder that she always used. With cosmetics in short supply, this was a major triumph, and she was smiling when she left the shop with her latest purchase. As she was turning to head for Haughton Newspapers, she caught a glimpse of a man leaving a nearby tobacconist. She walked on a few steps, feeling she had seen him before somewhere; that flashy suit looked familiar. As the term *spiv* floated into her mind, she remembered. It was the man she had seen at the show. She suspected he was the agent who had introduced himself to Georgie.

Without making any conscious decision, she changed direction to tail him from an unobtrusive distance. She only had to follow him for fifty yards or so before he pushed open the door to a cafe and disappeared inside. Quickening her pace, Deedee drew level with the cafe's leaded windows and peered in, making a show of adjusting her hat in her reflection. It didn't take her long to find the spiv. He was at a table with his back to Deedee, but there was no mistaking the cheap suit. And he wasn't alone. Facing him was a young woman smiling at him with a rapt expression. Deedee thought she looked familiar, although it took her a moment to place her. Then she had it – she had played Maid Marian at the pantomime. She was holding something, turning it over and over between her fingers. Squinting, Deedee saw it was a tiny rectangle of card, and she would bet good money it was the same business card Georgie had shown her. So this *was* David Mountjoy, and he was evidently scouting for talent in

Lincoln, although Deedee didn't think the girl who had played Maid Marian had the same star quality as Georgie.

Deedee turned away and resumed her walk to Haughton Newspapers, unable to shake off her suspicion. It just didn't make sense that a successful agent would need to come all the way to Lincoln to find talent; he must have any number of hopeful actors clamouring for his attention.

She stopped abruptly, earning herself an irate glare from a woman who had to dodge to prevent a collision. Deedee ignored her and felt in her pocket. Until now, she had forgotten all about the card Georgie had given her, but she was sure she'd put it in her coat pocket. Then her fingers closed around the little card rectangle and she gave a grunt of satisfaction before setting off again, this time at twice the speed. The evening before, Tom had lamented that his plentiful contacts didn't stretch far enough to help Pearl locate Greg. However, there was a good chance they included someone who could help her find out more about David Mountjoy. Having encouraged Georgie in her ambitions, she felt responsible for the girl, and something about this Mr Mountjoy made her uneasy.

Of course, that did mean seeing Tom again. Before going into the building, she got out her new compact and found a sheltered spot out of the wind to apply a little powder. This wasn't for Tom's benefit; she always liked to look her best. Satisfied that her lipstick hadn't smudged and her hair was tidy, she went inside and asked to see Mr Haughton.

Tom was delighted to see her. He met her in the foyer and insisted on escorting her to his apartment, despite her protests that she really needed to meet Pearl. He settled the matter by asking the receptionist to telephone Pearl and ask her to meet them in the apartment.

Once in his living room, he offered her a drink, which she refused, then he said, 'Dare I hope you've come to a decision?'

Despite her earlier resolution to turn him down, she knew she couldn't do it now. Not when she was about to ask a favour. 'I'm sorry. I don't want to mess you around, but I still need more time. I—'

He raised his hands, palms out, to stop her. 'It's fine. I'm sorry. I obviously misread the situation.'

Deedee stared at him, torn between guilt and relief. Guilt because she hated to give him false hope and relief because she could pretend for a while longer that they could make this work. If she was being totally honest with herself, she had to admit that she could see herself falling in love with him all over again, and didn't she deserve just a few days of imagining them together before facing reality? Yet because she didn't want to deceive him, she forced herself to say, 'I don't want to mess you around, but so much has happened since we were together that I need to be sure I'm doing the right thing. Whatever happens, I do want us to be friends, and I'm scared that if we try and rekindle the old romance, it won't work out and I'll lose your friendship all over again. I couldn't bear that.'

'You'll always have my friendship,' he said. 'I couldn't bear to lose that either.'

He was fiddling with his watch again, and it was such a sharp reminder of old times that she had to resist the temptation to throw caution to the wind and kiss him.

'I just need more time to work things out,' she told him, putting a little more space between them to ensure her resolve didn't weaken.

'Of course.' After a pause, he added, 'Anyway, as you didn't come all this way to throw yourself into my arms, why did you want to see me?' This was said with a deprecating grin. He was obviously trying to make light of his disappointment.

Feeling a complete heel, she pulled out David Mountjoy's card. 'I can't remember if I mentioned it to you on Saturday night,' she said, 'but Georgie said she'd been approached by a man calling himself a theatrical agent. I was instantly suspicious, but there's nothing I can put my finger on. Anyway, I saw him again just now.' She related what she had seen before ending with, 'I wondered if any of your contacts could find any information about him. If he's genuine, I don't want to do anything to jeopardise Georgie's chances, but I just don't see a reputable London agent coming all the way to Lincoln for an amateur show.'

'More fool them.' Tom took the card. 'They were excellent. I know what you mean, though.' He glanced at the name on the card. 'It doesn't ring any bells, but I'm a bit out of touch with London society these days. Leave it with me and I'll see what I can do.'

'Thank you. And I'm sorry about… well, you know.'

His eyes twinkled. 'You mean sorry for stringing me along but still expecting me to be at your beck and call?'

She chuckled. 'Something like that. I thought I was supposed to be the outspoken one.'

'Maybe it's infectious.'

It was probably a good thing Pearl chose that moment to arrive, because Deedee needed reminding that she was there for her, not to lose herself in Tom's company.

–

'Shall we go to the canteen again?' Deedee asked as they stepped outside into the icy breeze.

'I suppose— no.' Pearl felt strangely out of sorts, and found her voice approaching a wail as she added, 'I'm fed up of the same thing day in, day out. I need a change. I need— oh, I don't know.' She was aware of the startled looks from passers-by but couldn't seem to stop herself.

Deedee spoke as one would attempt to soothe a nervy horse. 'It's not a problem. We can go somewhere else. How about the Bishop's Pal?'

Pearl shook her head, as much to dispel the nervous tension as to show her disagreement. She had been there with Greg too many times, and the same could be said for the cafe at the Regal cinema. 'I'm fed up with that too.'

'Then where would you suggest?'

'I don't know. I can't think.'

'Thea often mentions the cafe above Boots. We could try there.'

'I suppose so. It's not far.'

It turned out to be a good choice. Pearl didn't often go there and so it didn't carry the same associations with Greg as her usual haunts. The cafe had a string quartet playing, so it was possible to talk without being overheard, and potted plants dotted around that made the tables feel secluded. Pearl and Deedee found a corner table and they both ordered soup and tea and then sat in silence until their drinks arrived. Pearl listened to the music, and it gradually soothed her restless spirits. Finally she poured tea for herself and Deedee. 'I'm sorry for getting upset earlier. I don't know what came over me.'

'I do, and there's no need to apologise. This endless waiting is wearing for me, so I can only imagine how it's affecting you.'

Pearl treated herself to two lumps of sugar and stirred her tea before replying. 'Even so, it's no excuse. I've snapped at you, snapped at Thea. I'll be lucky if anyone still wants to speak to me when this is all over.' She let out a heartfelt sigh, releasing all the minor irritations of the morning. 'So thank you for your understanding and please accept my apologies for being so crabby.'

Deedee reached across the table and patted her hand. 'There's really no need, but thank you.'

The waitress arrived with their food and there followed a lull in the conversation, broken only by comments of appreciation as they ate the delicious lentil and vegetable soup. Pearl, whose stomach had felt too knotted to manage much breakfast, felt considerably better after a few mouthfuls, and tucked in with relish. Eventually she said, 'I don't know how I would have managed if you hadn't come to stay. I appreciate it's caused some awkwardness for you, what with meeting Thomas again, but I'm so glad you came.'

'You and Thea are the most important things in the world to me. I'll always be there for you both. And don't fret about me and Tom. I've missed him a lot over the years, and now, thanks to you and Thea, we're friends again. It means a lot to have him back in my life.'

'But only as a friend?' Pearl was curious to learn whether Deedee had come to a decision.

'I think that's best. Whatever else we once meant to each other is in the past. I don't want any more complication.'

It seemed to Pearl that Deedee was trying to convince herself more than Pearl. 'As long as you've made that decision for yourself and not from some misguided belief about what you think is best for me or Thea. Or Thomas, come to that.'

'I have.'

Pearl wasn't wholly convinced, yet short of accusing Deedee of lying there wasn't anything more to say. Only then did it occur to her to wonder why Deedee had been in Thomas's flat earlier. 'Is that what you were doing with Thomas this morning – telling him you wanted to remain just friends?'

Deedee grimaced and waved the salt shaker over her soup, apparently not noticing that nothing was coming out. 'I couldn't bring myself to do it. Anyway, I actually wanted to ask him for help. Something to do with Georgie.'

'Is it something I could help with?'

'I don't know. You've got enough on your plate at the moment. I don't want to bother you with more.' She ate another spoonful of soup and pulled another face. She picked up the salt pot again and shook it vigorously over the palm of her hand. 'Blasted thing is all bunged up.'

Pearl reached back to the empty table behind her and grabbed the salt from there. She gave it an experimental shake over her own hand. 'Here, this one's working.' Once she was satisfied that Deedee had seasoned the soup to her taste, she carried on, 'Honestly, it's no bother. Trust me.

The more I have to occupy my mind, the less time I spend worrying.'

'If you're sure.'

And Pearl listened, intrigued, as Deedee described Georgie's excitement at being approached by a theatrical agent. 'And after I saw the same man earlier, talking to another girl from the panto,' her grandmother concluded, 'I suddenly remembered what Tom said to you yesterday about having many contacts. So I thought I'd ask him to see what he could uncover.'

'Good thinking,' Pearl said. 'Well, I'm sure if anyone can find out anything, it's Thomas, but I'll keep my eyes and ears open too. I agree it's strange to hear of a successful agent coming to an amateur production in Lincoln. Unless he was visiting family for Christmas or something like that.'

'Yes, I suppose that would explain it.'

They went on to discuss what little information they had from all angles. Finally Pearl caught sight of the time. 'Goodness. I must fly or I'll be late.'

As Pearl's office was on the way to the bus stop, Deedee walked back with her, and they said their goodbyes in the foyer. Pearl told Deedee she would need to work late for the next few evenings to put the finishing touches to a Christmas double edition of the *Bombshell*, which was due to go to the printers on Thursday. 'Once that's all done, we're closing down until the new year, so I'll be able to come to Fenthorpe to see you.' Her voice wobbled and she swallowed to control it. It was impossible to forget that Greg had planned to take leave to coincide with her own break. But she was sure she and Deedee would find plenty to do in Fenthorpe, even if it meant removing all the ballroom decorations and starting them all over again.

She was about to go up to the office when Thomas emerged from the lift. His face lit up when he saw Deedee, making Pearl wonder all the more about her grandmother's feelings. She hoped for Thomas's sake that his obvious affection was not one-sided. 'I'm glad I caught you,' he said, addressing Deedee. 'I've managed to find something about that matter you mentioned earlier.' His gaze strayed to Pearl, then back to Deedee.

'Don't worry,' Deedee said to him. 'I've already told Pearl everything I told you.'

Thomas's face cleared. 'Oh good. Well, I telephoned a friend of mine in London, because he knows anyone who's anyone in the theatre. Apparently David Mountjoy is a well-known agent. Totally above board.'

Deedee's eyebrows shot up to her hairline. 'That's good to know. Just goes to show you can't judge people on appearance.'

Chapter Nineteen

In the two days that followed, Pearl claimed to be so busy that she couldn't even spare an hour for lunch. Both days, Deedee would have none of it and forced her to accompany her to the crowded church hall and ensured that her granddaughter ate all the food on her plate. She could tell Pearl was losing hope, and her heart bled, knowing that it was all too likely that Greg was indeed dead. It was hard to know how to comfort her.

Help came from Tom when Deedee accompanied Pearl back to the office after lunch. He happened to be entering the building at the same time and glanced at Pearl's downcast face. 'I take it there's still no news?'

Pearl shook her head. 'It's hard to summon up the enthusiasm for the Christmas and new year edition under the circumstances.'

'Come up to my office. We got a letter today that I was going to forward to you, but I think I'd like to give it to you personally.' Tom's gaze switched to Deedee. 'Do you have to get back? I think you'd like to see it too.'

Deedee firmly squashed the flutter of pleasure she always felt when Tom was around and told herself it was purely curiosity that prompted her to agree.

Once in his spacious office, Tom invited them to sit and then picked up his telephone and spoke to his secretary.

'Do you still have the letter I was going to forward to Corporal Tallis? Good. Could you bring it here, please, Mrs Norris?'

A moment later, the secretary appeared and handed Tom a handwritten letter.

'Thank you, Mrs Norris.' Once the secretary had returned to her own office, Tom addressed Pearl. 'This arrived just this morning. It's... well, it would be quicker just to read it to you.' He put on his spectacles, cleared his throat and read: '"Dear sir"' – Tom gave Pearl a crooked smile – 'Believe it or not, this is written for you, but apparently the writer couldn't believe a newspaper editor could be a woman. "Dear sir,"' he continued, '"I have two sons in the RAF, both in Lincolnshire, and between them they always send me a copy of the *Bombshell* as soon as it comes out. I should have said I *had* two sons, for my younger son, Neil, was killed in action in October."'

Pearl gave a little gasp and covered her mouth. Deedee put an arm round her shoulder and shot Tom a glare. 'How is this helping?'

Tom grimaced. 'Sorry. Maybe I should have explained before reading, but hear me out. I think you will find this helpful.'

'It's okay,' Pearl said. 'I want to hear it.'

Tom nodded and resumed. '"My other son stopped sending copies after that, thinking they would upset me, but I found I missed them and asked him to send me more. I wanted to let you know how much reading your newspaper has helped me come to terms with Neil's loss. It's been a great comfort to read about the daily life on a Bomber Command station and vicariously experience the same camaraderie that Neil enjoyed. These glimpses of daily life have been a godsend and have helped to bring me closer to Neil's life in the RAF. Reading about the dedication of the men and women of 5 Group has brought home what Neil always used to tell me – that he was doing important work that was worth risking his life for. I will grieve for him for the rest of my life, but the *Bombshell* has helped keep him alive in my heart.

"'I know that your readership is aimed at RAF personnel, but I wanted you to know how much your newspaper means to me as a mother. Keep up the good work!

"'Yours faithfully, Mrs Lester.'"

Deedee looked at Pearl, who was dabbing tears from her cheeks. 'Thank you,' she said. 'I was starting to wonder if I'd made a mistake working here instead of in my old post at Fenthorpe, but this has helped me see that what we do here is important too.'

Tom took off his glasses, then handed Pearl the letter. 'Hold on to it so you can read it if you ever start to doubt your worth. I thought you could use something to cheer you up today.'

Pearl tucked the letter into a pocket. 'It really helped. Not just knowing how important the *Bombshell* is to families but because it makes me feel a little less alone.' Then she glanced from Deedee to Tom, looking distressed. 'Oh, that didn't come out right. I know I'm not alone. But the letter's a reminder that I'm just one of many people missing a loved one.' She drew a shaky breath. 'And I'm luckier than most, because I still have hope.'

Tom patted her hand. 'Hold on to that. And remember we're all here for you.'

'I will.' Pearl rose and squared her shoulders. 'Well, I've got a paper to get to the printer, so I'd better get back to work.' Tom hastened to open the door for her, and she took his hand and squeezed it, her lips quivering, although now she seemed to be overcome with gratitude rather than despair. She marched out, and Deedee felt happier about her state of mind than she had for some days.

Deedee made to follow suit, then hesitated. On impulse, she seized both Tom's hands and kissed him on the cheek. 'Thank you,' she said. 'I've been getting so worried about her, and you've given her a real boost.'

He pressed her hands in return, holding them a moment or two before releasing her. 'I'm just trying to be a good grandfather.'

But all the way back to Fenthorpe, Deedee couldn't forget his expression as he said those words, for, in addition to the love and concern he clearly felt for Pearl, there had been love for her as well. Was she being cruel to string him along without giving him a definite answer to the question he had asked after the show? The trouble was that, despite the awful conviction that she would need to tell Tom the complete truth if she agreed to a courtship, the more time she spent with him the more she found herself picturing life with him. He had so much love to give and already poured it out onto his new-found grand-daughters. Now she knew that Tom had not married for some time after she had left London, she bitterly regretted not having more faith in him and trusting that he would do right by her and her unborn child. He would have made a wonderful father, and it pained her that he had never known Clara, had never had the joy of cradling his baby daughter in his arms, had not seen her grow into the lively, caring young woman she had become and had not been there to walk her down the aisle on her wedding day. And that was all her fault. He would never have abandoned her; she knew that now. But she had believed otherwise at the time and had been forced to take an action that would taint her in his eyes if he ever found out. And now she knew his heart was true, she couldn't bear for him to think less of her.

The following day, Deedee prepared for her trip to Lincoln, humming a cheerful tune as she dabbed powder on her face. The *Bombshell* had been due to go to the printers that morning, so Pearl would officially be on holiday once it had left her office. Tom had suggested that Pearl might like to stay at the Gatehouse over Christmas, saying that there was a folding bed that could be made up in Deedee's room, and Deedee had been relieved when Pearl agreed. She was sure it could only be a matter of days before they had more information about Greg, and she wanted to be there when the news arrived. Therefore she was going to meet Pearl as usual for lunch and then return to Fenthorpe with Pearl when she finished work. It was a weight off her mind to know that she would be close to Pearl for the next week. Now all that was left to do to make Christmas a time of true joy was pray that Greg was found safe and well. Better still, that he would be home in time for the party on Saturday.

Wanting to buy some treats as a welcome for Pearl, Deedee decided to visit the bakery before catching the bus and walked into Fenthorpe. Dark clouds hung overhead, and it was cold enough for snow. She could only hope it didn't fall before she and Pearl were safely back at the Gatehouse.

The warm, yeasty scented interior of the bakery provided a welcome refuge from the chill. 'Georgie not here today?' she asked while Mrs March wrapped up two large Chelsea buns for her. She'd expected to see her young friend, as the schools had already broken up for the Christmas holidays.

'She had to go to Lincoln. Said she'd forgotten about a drama class.'

Deedee was surprised by this. She imagined that the drama teacher would have needed a break after the show as much as her students. Nevertheless, she said nothing, just paid for the buns and put the package into her basket.

She was about to leave the shop when Mrs March said, 'Actually, are you going into Lincoln today?' When Deedee replied that she was, Mrs March continued, 'I wonder if you could do me a favour?'

'Of course.' Pearl had already said she wanted to spend a bit of time after lunch sorting her office, meaning Deedee needed to find a way to occupy herself. It might as well be helping the harassed-looking baker.

'Well, I don't want to put you out, but I wondered if you could pop into the church hall and leave a message for Georgie? I had a note from my dressmaker saying a dress of mine is ready, and if Georgie could collect it for me, it would save me a trip.'

Deedee readily agreed, and so Mrs March jotted down the details on a scrap of paper.

It was so cold in Lincoln that, once she had said goodbye to Pearl after lunch, Deedee was glad to have a task. As she set off at a brisk pace, the first flakes of snow dropped from heavy clouds. By the time she had made it up the hill to the church hall where Georgie attended her class, the snow was falling steadily. When she approached, she was surprised to see no sign of life by the main doors but, remembering Georgie had told her the class usually used the side door, which she called the stage door, Deedee walked down the poky side alley. However, her surprise turned to uneasiness when she opened the door and heard no chatter or any sound at all coming from the hall. She stepped inside and found herself in a dim corridor.

'Hello?' she called.

There was no reply. All she could hear was the distant sound of footsteps and bicycle bells from the street. This was very strange. Perhaps Mrs March had made a mistake and the classes were held elsewhere.

She was about to leave when she heard a clatter coming from behind one of the closed doors. She opened it to see a middle-aged woman, dressed in apron and headscarf, picking up a mop and bucket from the floor. The women shrieked, clasping a hand to her chest, before relaxing.

'You gave me the fright of my life.'

'I am sorry. I did call.'

'Ah. Well, I didn't hear you. I had a cold last week, and my ears are still bunged up something chronic. Can I help?'

'I'm looking for a girl who's attending the drama class, but I must have got the wrong place.'

'No, Mrs Stokeley holds all the classes here, but they're closed down for the Christmas break now. It's made my job much easier this week, let me tell you, because they don't half leave a mess. Won't be back before the middle of January.'

'That's strange. Her mother said I'd find her here. Are you sure Mrs Stokeley isn't holding individual classes?'

'She can't be. She's away in Market Rasen, visiting her sister. Left the day after the panto.'

Deedee thanked the woman and walked back out onto the street, unsure what to do next. Her experience of bringing up Thea had taught her that a girl misleading a parent about her whereabouts didn't necessarily mean she was in trouble; with Thea it had simply been a desire for independence and a need to get away from Pearl's interference. Deedee had always known that Thea would turn up when she was hungry or tired without any harm done. Georgie was probably in a cafe with friends, enjoying her freedom from school and wanting to spend the day with friends instead of working behind the counter at the bakery. If that was the case, she didn't want to get the girl in trouble with her mother. She had, after all, worked hard all term, and deserved a day off. On the other hand, if she really was in trouble and Deedee had known she was missing and said nothing, Deedee would never forgive herself.

She glanced at her watch. There was still half an hour before she had agreed to meet Pearl, giving her plenty of time to search for Georgie in Lincoln. If she didn't find her by then, she would drop in on Mrs March on her way home. In all probability she would find Georgie already there, and Deedee needn't give away her secret.

However, as the minutes ticked by and Georgie was not to be found in any of the shops or cafes, Deedee was aware of a growing cloud of dread. She even went into the dressmaker Mrs March had mentioned to ask if Georgie had been there. It was a forlorn hope, and she was not at all surprised when the dressmaker denied all knowledge of her. For some reason David Mountjoy's face appeared in her mind, but Deedee knew Georgie's whereabouts could be nothing to do with him; a reputable agent wouldn't entice a young girl away from her family. The worry wouldn't go away, though, so she collected Mrs March's dress herself and went to meet Pearl.

She found Pearl ready to leave, so, once she had fetched the small case packed for the holiday, they left to catch the bus. On the way, Deedee confided her worry.

Pearl heard her out with a furrowed brow, brushing the snow from the brim of her cap. 'Did you try the Bishop's Pal?' she asked when Deedee had finished. 'Or how about the cafe above the Regal?'

'Yes, those were the first places I looked. I—' Deedee stopped as a thought struck. 'Hang on. I looked in the cafe, but I never thought to check the cinema. I bet that's where she is.'

Pearl's face cleared. 'I think you're right. Where else would a girl go who dreams of being an actress?'

Deedee checked the time. 'Do you know when the matinee finishes? We could wait for her to come out.'

'No, sorry. Anyway, the Regal's not the only cinema in town. I still think you're going to have to tell Mrs March you couldn't find her.'

Deedee bit her lip. 'I suppose you're right. I hate to get her into trouble, though.' She pointed to the parcel containing the dress. 'Good thing I collected this. It might soften Mrs March up to have it back.'

They found Mrs March dealing with a queue of customers, which gave Deedee an excuse not to betray Georgie just yet. When Mrs March glanced up from serving some tasty-looking sausage rolls, she beckoned Deedee and Pearl behind the counter.

'I picked up your dress for you,' Deedee said, somewhat unnecessarily considering it was draped over her arm.

'That's very kind of you. I take it Georgie was too busy with her friends to help me out. I'll be having words with her when she gets back. I'm run off my feet.'

'Er…' Deedee began, unwilling to explain the truth in front of a crowd of customers.

In the event, she needn't have worried. Mrs March gabbled on without waiting for her to finish. 'Would you be a dear and take it upstairs for me? It'll get ruined down here, and I can't leave my customers.'

'Of course,' Deedee said and, following Mrs March's instructions, she left via the storeroom and went up the stairs to the flat. Pearl said she would wait outside.

Deedee hung the dress on the back of Mrs March's bedroom door as instructed and was about to go back downstairs when she noticed that the door next to Mrs March's room was ajar. Guessing it must be Georgie's room, she glanced inside in case the girl had crept up unseen by her mother. The room, however, was empty, the bed neatly made and a pile of scripts vying for space with brushes, combs and hair ribbons on her dressing table. As she was on the point of backing away from the room, Deedee's gaze fell on a handwritten note on the bedside cabinet.

Her curiosity got the better of her, and she picked it up and read.

> *Dear Mum,*
> *I'm sorry for leaving without telling you, but I know you would try and stop me, and I've been*

given an opportunity that's too good to miss. A London agent has told me that there's a part in a West End theatre that I'd be perfect for. He's sure I'll get the role, but I have to get to London by Friday morning for the audition. Please don't worry about me. I'll send a telegram when I arrive. Just think – the next time you see me, I could be a leading lady!

    xxx

Deedee leaned against the wall, fighting a wave of nausea. In her distress the letter slipped from her hands and disappeared down the gap between the cabinet and the wall. It hardly mattered, though. Every single word was etched on her brain. Could she have stopped this? She should have come straight to Mrs March the moment she knew Georgie had deceived her mother about being at a class, instead of trying to protect her from a scolding. And now, with the cabinet being much too heavy for her to shift unaided, she'd even managed to lose the note Georgie had left for her mother. The note she hadn't even bothered to sign. In a way, Deedee was glad she wouldn't be able to show it to Mrs March, because she would never have believed the girl capable of such thoughtlessness.

There was no putting off the awful moment, though. She trudged downstairs and, catching Pearl's eye through the shop window, beckoned her inside. Thankfully, the queue had now subsided, so Deedee hovered in the background until the last customer had left.

Mrs March straightened, rotating her shoulders. 'Thank goodness that rush is over. I think the snow's made everyone want to stock up.' She looked at Deedee. 'There was no need to wait, but thanks again for collecting my dress.'

'Actually, I've got some disturbing news.'

As Deedee related her tale, from finding the church hall empty to discovering Georgie's letter, Mrs March's expression gradually changed from puzzlement to anger and then to downright distress. Finally she sank onto a stool, her hand pressed to her chest. 'Why would she do that?'

Deedee could only shrug. 'Heaven knows. It seems so out of character.'

'What can we do?' Mrs March grasped Deedee's hand.

Pearl stepped forward. 'We should tell the police. I can see Sergeant Burrows down the road. I'll fetch him.'

She disappeared and was back a short while later with a tall policeman who, with his grizzled hair and weathered face, looked to be approaching retirement age. 'How can I help, Mrs March? This young lady' – he indicated Pearl – 'said something about your Georgina running off to London. I can't believe that.'

Mrs March, with assistance from Deedee, poured out the whole story. When she had finished, Burrows tugged his moustache. 'So your daughter went to Lincoln this morning? I'll get straight on to the Lincoln police and ask them to check the railway station in case she's still there. There's a chance the trains have been delayed by the snow.'

While Deedee was struggling to organise her thoughts, Pearl spoke up. 'This Mr Mountjoy – didn't you get his card, Deedee?'

The words cut through the tangle of self-recrimination and pictures of Georgie, vulnerable and alone in London.

'Yes, of course.' She opened her handbag and rummaged inside before she remembered. 'Dash it! I gave it to Tom.'

Mrs March leaned over the counter. 'Do you mean to say you know this Mr Mountjoy?'

Deedee nodded. 'Georgie told me he'd approached her after the show, and I admit I was suspicious, so, as she accidentally ended up with two of his business cards, I asked for the spare. Tom – Thomas Haughton of Haughton Newspapers – checked up on him for me and his London contact told him he's a reputable agent.'

'Well, that's something, I suppose,' Mrs March said. 'But Georgie's right in saying I'd never have let her go. She's far too young.'

Deedee was inclined to agree but didn't want to add to Mrs March's worry. 'Do you have a telephone? I can call Mr Haughton and ask him to contact Mr Mountjoy.'

'That would be wonderful. I don't have a telephone, though.'

'Not to worry. There's one at the Gatehouse. I'll phone from there. You're welcome to come with me.'

Mrs March shook her head. 'I need to stay here in case Georgie sends a telegram.'

Pearl stepped in. 'Good idea. I can pop round if we find anything out.' Then a look of dismay crossed her face, and Deedee knew she was thinking that she wanted to be close to a telephone herself in case any news of Greg arrived.

Deedee put a hand on her shoulder. 'Or we could phone through to the police station.'

The sergeant nodded. 'Sounds a sensible plan.' He turned to Mrs March. 'If you'll excuse me, I'll get back to the station and phone through to the Lincoln police. I'll let you know as soon as I hear anything.'

'Thank you, all of you.' Mrs March dabbed her eyes with a handkerchief. 'I can't bear to think of my Georgina all alone on a day like this.'

But as she and Pearl marched through deepening snow towards the Gatehouse, Deedee wondered if Georgie wouldn't be safer alone, for she couldn't rid herself of a niggle of suspicion regarding Mr Mountjoy.

Chapter Twenty

Pearl took charge of calling her grandfather the moment they reached the Gatehouse. Deedee hovered at her shoulder as she asked to be put through. At the sound of his assured yet concerned voice, Pearl felt some of her worry seep away.

'Yes, I still have his business card,' Thomas said once Pearl had explained what had happened. 'I'll ring him straight away.'

Pearl thanked him and hung up, then turned to Deedee. 'I can't tell you how glad I am to have Thomas as my grandpa. I don't know what it is about him, but he always makes me feel as though whatever problem I've got I can get through it, as long as he's around.'

Deedee gave her a faint smile. 'I always felt like that around him. Well' – here she gave a roguish grin that always made Pearl dread what she was about to say next – 'that and other things.'

Pearl gave her a quelling look, feeling not for the first time that there should be a law against grandmothers making those sorts of pronouncements in their grandchildren's hearing. 'Come on. Let's wait in the living room. I don't know about you, but my feet are like blocks of ice and they feel like if I don't get them warm, they're going to drop off. It could be a while before Thomas gets through to London, so we might as well wait in comfort.'

As she held up her stockinged feet to the fire, she reflected that her life seemed reduced to waiting for phone calls or telegrams. The call from Thomas, though, was one she wanted to happen as soon as possible, whereas she was dreading to hear more news about Greg. Despite Jenny's apparently unwavering optimism, Pearl couldn't shake off the conviction that the body found in the crashed Lancaster must be either Greg or Edwin. Either way, confirmation would lead to heartbreak for one of the friends, and Pearl felt guilty for hoping the body wasn't Greg's.

Not wanting to dwell on it, she turned to Deedee. For once she wasn't going to ignore an outrageous remark from her grandmother, not if it could provide her with some distraction, no matter how embarrassing Deedee's reply might be. 'You know, if you still have feelings for Thomas, why are you hesitating about getting back together with him?'

Deedee sighed and took her time adjusting the position of her footstool before answering. 'As I once said to Thea, there has to be more to a relationship than how a man makes you feel in the knicker department.'

Pearl really didn't want to contemplate whatever stirrings Deedee might be feeling in her knickers and was on the verge of suggesting she make tea when it dawned on her that Deedee was being deliberately provocative to deflect the conversation elsewhere. It was high time she beat Deedee at her own game. 'I agree.' She gave her grandmother a calm smile. 'But it's plain that your feelings for Thomas extend beyond your gussets.'

Deedee's lips twitched. 'Maybe you are my grand-daughter after all. Clearly marriage to Greg must have done wonders for you.'

Pearl didn't want to think too much about the wonders Greg did to her, either, because the thought that she might never again wake in his arms sent a wave of misery crashing over her. She drew a shaky breath. 'This isn't about me and Greg, but you and Thomas. You seem to have genuine affection for him, and he clearly adores you. What's stopping you? If it's anything to do with me or Thea, then you mustn't let us hold you back. I love Thomas and nothing would make me happier than to see you together, and I'm sure Thea feels the same.'

Once again, Deedee seemed caught up in trying to place her feet at the optimal distance from the fire. When she finally drew breath to speak, the sound of the telephone made them both jump. As Pearl sprang up to answer it, she could have sworn she heard Deedee mutter, 'Saved by the bell.'

She dashed through the hall, sliding a little on the polished floor in her stockinged feet, and hurried into the study to pick up the receiver. A sudden chill shot through her, accompanied by the dread that this wasn't her grandfather but Fitz with bad news, but then she heard Thomas's reassuring voice and she relaxed. Until she heard what he had to say, at any rate.

'It's most strange,' Thomas said. 'When I spoke to Mr Mountjoy, he confirmed the number on the card was his, but he assured me he'd never been to Lincoln, and certainly not last week.'

A tap on Pearl's shoulder made her spin round. Deedee stood behind her looking strained. 'What's he saying?'

she asked. When Pearl relayed Thomas's news, Deedee snatched the receiver from her hands. 'There has to be some kind of mistake,' she said. 'He personally handed that card to a young friend of mine.' There was a pause while she listened to Thomas at the other end of the line. Pearl could hear the tinny sound of his voice but none of the words. Eventually Deedee spoke again. 'It doesn't make sense. Have you got the number?' There was another pause while she scrabbled to find a pencil, then took down a number on the desk jotter. 'I hope you don't mind me making a long-distance call,' she said finally, 'but I need to speak to Mr Mountjoy myself and give him a piece of my mind.'

Pearl inwardly quailed about what a piece of Deedee's mind might entail, having vivid memories of her marching up to Thea's headmistress and advising her to make school more interesting if she didn't want her students playing truant. She would never want to be on the receiving end of Deedee's blunt observations when she was on the warpath.

–

While Deedee waited to be connected to David Mountjoy, she glanced at Pearl, who had moved aside when Deedee had taken the receiver and now perched on the corner of the desk, fiddling with the blotter. She could tell Pearl wholeheartedly welcomed having Tom in her life, and certainly Tom had shown that he was prepared to move heaven and earth to prove he was an able grandfather. Although neither of her granddaughters had ever shown signs of missing a father figure in their lives, it had been gratifying how easily they had welcomed Tom as their grandfather.

The trouble was, it was getting harder to explain to them why she felt unable to be more than friends with him. And it was becoming ever harder to ignore the old feelings that she now realised had never died, but simply gone into hibernation. Now they were wide awake and screaming for attention. And those feelings included what she had delicately referred to as stirrings in her knicker department. Some people seemed to think women her age were good for nothing apart from knitting and baking, but she could tell them a thing or two about that. If it was only about her libido, she would have said yes to Tom right away.

Then her call came through and she pushed aside all concerns apart from Georgie's wellbeing.

The moment she heard Mr Mountjoy's voice, she knew something was seriously wrong. 'I'm sorry,' she said, 'I think I must have the wrong number. I thought this number was for David Mountjoy the theatrical agent.'

'Yes, that's me,' said the voice that didn't seem to fit with the man she had seen in Lincoln. This voice was low and sounded like the voice of an older man, with gravelly undertones. 'Who is speaking, please? How can I help you?'

Deedee gave her name then, clinging to the hope that he sounded old due to a poor telephone line, said, 'I wanted to know if you spoke to an actress friend of mine in Lincoln the other day.'

The irritated tut sounded clearly over the line. 'Look, as I said to the gentleman who called a few minutes ago, I've never been to Lincoln, and I certainly wouldn't attend a performance by a company of amateurs. This has nothing to do with me.'

After she had hung up, she gazed at Pearl and saw her fear mirrored in her face as she repeated the pertinent details. 'Someone's lying,' Pearl said. 'The question is, who?'

'I know how we can find out.' Deedee picked up the receiver with trembling hands and called Tom. 'I need you to do me another favour,' she told him once she had summarised her brief conversation with the possible Mr Mountjoy. 'Your London friend who vouched for David Mountjoy – I need you to call him again and ask for a description. I need to know for sure which of the two Mountjoys is the real one.' However, she replaced the receiver, feeling almost certain it was the older one.

Far sooner than anticipated, Tom was back on the line with a description. He was so quick Deedee pictured the cables between London and Lincoln catching fire as his urgent calls zipped to and fro along the lines. 'My friend says David Mountjoy is in his late fifties, tall, with greying dark hair.'

Deedee's heart felt like lead. 'That's not the man I saw after the show. He was certainly not in his fifties.' Who had Georgie got herself mixed up with? A strange hissing sound filled her ears and grey dots swirled before her eyes. For a horrible moment she thought she was going to be sick, but Pearl gripped her arm. Gradually her vision and hearing cleared. She gulped and nodded her thanks at Pearl. Belatedly, she realised Tom was speaking. 'Deedee? Are you still there?'

She nodded, then remembered he couldn't see her. 'Yes, but I have to go. I need to call the police.'

'Yes, of course. Shall I come over?'

She didn't need to think about it at all. 'Yes, please.'

'I'll be right there.'

And even though logic told her that he didn't have any more power than her to find Georgie, the knowledge that he would soon be there made her feel better.

Once she had conveyed the worrying news to Pearl, her granddaughter insisted on Deedee returning to the warm living room while she contacted Fenthorpe police. However, she had only just taken her seat by the fire when she was surprised by the ringing of the doorbell. She dashed into the hall, convinced it was dire news concerning either Greg or Georgie, only to see Thea and Jenny troop inside, coated in a layer of snow. As they peeled off their outdoor clothes and brushed themselves down, Deedee explained about Georgie.

'Go through everything you know,' Jenny suggested, once Deedee had ushered them into the warm living room, 'and I'll write it all down. I know when I'm studying, I find writing everything down in a list helps me to clear my mind and look at things in a different way.'

After Deedee had finished, Jenny consulted her list. 'Right,' she said, counting off each point on her fingers. 'One: a man claiming to be David Mountjoy, a theatrical agent from London, introduced himself to Georgie after the pantomime. Two: he gave her his card, plus an extra one that she gave to you. Three: you saw a man talking to her at the church hall, whom you believe to be the same man calling himself David Mountjoy.'

Thea snorted. 'You sound like a detective in a whodunnit.'

Jenny's cheeks turned pink. 'A friend was transferred to another station last month and gave me all her novels before she left. Most of them were detective stories.'

Deedee frowned at Thea before saying to Jenny, 'Don't mind her. I'm finding this helpful. Go on.'

Jenny turned to her list again. 'Four: this belief was backed up when you saw the same man speaking to another actress from Georgie's drama class. Five: Georgie told her mother she was going to Lincoln this morning and hasn't been seen since. Six: you found a letter from Georgie saying she'd been invited to London for an audition by David Mountjoy. Seven: there is an agent called David Mountjoy, but he is not the man seen with Georgie.' Jenny put down her list. 'Have I missed anything?'

Deedee drew a shaky breath. 'I think that sums it up.'

'And eight,' Pearl added from the doorway. 'I've just got off the phone to Sergeant Burrows. There was no sign of Georgie at the station in Lincoln.'

Deedee's heart sank. 'I suppose it was too much to hope for.' She gazed into the fire for a moment, wondering where Georgie was. If she was safe and warm or if she was out in the snow. 'I can't stop thinking about poor Mrs March. She must be frantic.' Then a sickening thought struck. 'Hang on. There have been other reports of missing girls in the papers recently. You don't think they're linked, do you?'

Pearl went pale. 'I hope not. Wasn't one of them found…?' She swallowed, and Deedee knew why she had felt unable to finish the sentence. *Dead.* That was the word that had made her falter. A missing Cambridge girl had been found murdered in London. Deedee remembered seeing the report, which also mentioned other missing girls, when she had been wrapping gifts in newspaper.

'I pray I'm wrong. Her poor mother,' was all she could say.

'That reminds me.' Pearl rose. 'I said I would let her know if we had any news. She ought to be told.'

'True,' Thea said, also rising, 'but let Jenny and me go. You stay with Deedee. By the phone.'

Pearl didn't put up any argument; in fact she looked relieved.

They all trailed into the hall to see Thea and Jenny off, only to meet Tom, brushing the snow from his hat and coat. The sense of relief Deedee felt at seeing him was profound. She knew it was ridiculous, but somehow, now he was there, Deedee could believe things might turn out well after all.

'The snow's really coming down hard now,' Tom said once he was installed in front of the fire. 'I popped in to the railway station before I caught the bus, just in case the snow had delayed Georgie's train and she was still there, but I couldn't see her.'

'That was thoughtful of you,' Deedee said, not having the heart to tell him the Lincoln police had already done the same.

'Wait. How do you know she's travelling from Lincoln?' Pearl asked.

Deedee sat bolt upright, slopping cocoa into her lap. 'That's it. That's what we can do. Why are we assuming Georgie caught the train from Lincoln? She might have told her mother she was going to a class in Lincoln, but that doesn't mean she actually went there. What's the nearest railway station to Fenthorpe?'

'Potterhanworth,' Tom said.

'How far is it?' Deedee's heart was beating hard. If there was any chance Georgie was still there, they had to look.

'A couple of miles. Shorter if we cut off some corners using the footpaths.'

We. Deedee's heart gave a happy skip at Tom's assumption that, whatever they did, it would be together.

Pearl looked horrified. 'You're not seriously thinking of walking all the way to Potterhanworth in this weather?'

'Why not? Georgie's out in it.'

'But you can't know for sure you'll find her at the station.'

'Then we'll come back without her. But at least we'll have tried.'

'Why not call Sergeant Burrows?'

Tom answered. 'He doesn't have a car, and we're closer to the station at the Gatehouse. We'll get there sooner.'

'I'll come with you, then.'

'No, you won't,' said Deedee. 'You need to be by the phone in case there's news of Greg. I'll be fine with Tom.'

Pearl threw up her hands. 'There's no stopping you when you're like this, but why not at least wait until Thea and Jenny get back?'

'Because we can't afford to waste any more time.' Without waiting for Pearl's response, Deedee went to the kitchen to ask Izzy if she had any boots she could borrow, before dashing upstairs to pull on dungarees and her warmest jumper. A matter of minutes later, Deedee bundled up in hat, coat, scarf and gloves and wearing the borrowed boots, they set out. Thankfully Thomas had left his own boots at the Gatehouse when he had moved to Lincoln, so he was able to dress appropriately. Pearl's voice chased them down the lane, urging them to take care.

Chapter Twenty-One

The snow was falling steadily with no sign of stopping. Although it was still light, with another hour before sunset, the slate-blue clouds blotted out the sun, casting the fields and lanes into dim twilight. All around her, Deedee could hear the soft hiss of snowflakes hitting bare branches and hedges, and already there was enough snow lying to crunch underfoot. Deedee silently thanked Izzy for providing sturdy boots with a good grip.

'This way,' Tom said, striding up the lane. 'There's a footpath about a quarter of a mile up here. If the snow's not too deep, we can cut across the fields and take a good ten minutes off our time.'

'We'll go that way then.' Deedee blinked snow from her eyes. 'I don't want to waste a single minute.' If anything happened to Georgie, she knew she'd never forgive herself. She couldn't forget that she was the one who had encouraged the girl to follow her dreams. Georgie would never have been in the pantomime or met Mountjoy if it hadn't been for her.

Tom offered her his arm. 'If she's there, we'll find her.'

She took his arm, once again overcome by a sense that all would be well as long as she was with him. Tom shortened his stride to match hers, and they made good time to the stile where the path across the fields began.

Tom climbed over first, then stood by the fence to help her. Deedee, who would usually have batted away any offer of help, still felt a little stiff after her fall of less than a week ago and so gratefully took his hand and allowed him to help her as she stepped over the fence. He was about the same age as her and she was glad to see he had kept himself fit and active in the years since she had left London. Some people seemed to think anyone over fifty was good for nothing but dozing by the fire until they were summoned to the Pearly Gates, but Deedee was having none of it. As far as she was concerned, in recent years she had tasted her first freedom in a long time. Not that she begrudged the decades spent bringing up her daughter and grandchildren, but she had been enjoying her freedom from childrearing in the past few years, and only the war had prevented her from leaping on a train and exploring all the places she had longed to see. She had taken good care of her health and gone for long walks along the Severn most days and had been rewarded by feeling just as healthy as when she was forty or fifty. It was good to see that Tom was equally spry.

Giving in to impulse, when she was ready to jump down from the stile she placed both hands on Tom's broad shoulders and jumped. Tom grasped her by the waist and swung her to the ground, laughing, making her feel twenty again. She let her hands linger for a while after her feet hit the ground, gazing up at him. Twenty? No, she felt sixteen, giddy with the prospect of a life stretching out ahead of her, full of intriguing possibilities.

Tom didn't seem to be in any hurry to let go of her waist, either, and he stooped over her, smiling. When a fat snowflake landed on her eyelid, he brushed it away with gentle fingers. For a heart-stopping moment she thought he was going to kiss her, but then a buzzard swooped low, its eerie mewling cry making them both jump.

Deedee dropped her hands and stepped back, the brief enchantment swept away. With it gone, the knowledge of why they were out in the first place crashed down on her, and she cursed herself for forgetting. 'Come on,' she said. 'Georgie needs us.'

She took his arm again and they set out at a good pace. The path beneath the snow was firm and, although the snow continued to fall, they made rapid progress. The wide, open space of a Lincolnshire field was alien to Deedee, used to the more hilly country around Shrewsbury. It felt bleaker, unfriendly, and she drew closer to Tom's side. The wind was picking up now, whipping the snow ahead of it, and even in the dull light she could see it building up along the hedgerows. 'I hope we're not going to get cut off by drifts,' she said.

'They shouldn't be a problem.' Tom gave a heap of snow an experimental kick and it exploded in a shower of fine particles. 'See: it's quite powdery, so it shouldn't block our way.'

Deedee was more grateful than ever that Tom had volunteered to come with her. As they marched on, she knew she could no longer deny that she was every bit as in love with him as she had been all those years ago. And if he had kissed her, she wouldn't have pushed him away. In fact, she might have initiated a kiss herself if it hadn't been for that buzzard.

At the thought of kissing him, a delicious thrill trickled down her spine, and she gave an involuntary shiver.

Tom at once pulled her closer and wrapped an arm round her shoulders. 'Are you cold? It's not far now. Just through that gate, then another quarter of a mile along the lane.'

'I'm fine. Not at all cold.' But she made no attempt to pull away from him. Maybe they really could make this work. Maybe he wouldn't mind if she told him everything, the real reason she had gone all the way to Shrewsbury. Maybe she was worried about nothing. The thought kept her warm on the remainder of the walk to Potterhanworth.

'Not far now,' Tom said a few minutes later as they stepped onto a narrow lane. 'The station's outside the village, on this side.'

The words were hardly out of his mouth when a train's whistle rang across the fields. Deedee looked around frantically, trying to see where the line was. 'Which way's it going?'

Tom pointed to a line of trees that Deedee could just make out in the fading light. 'It's the Sleaford train. If Georgie's still there, that's the train she'll be waiting for.' He grabbed her hand and broke into a run. 'We can still make it.'

Deedee, her pulse hammering, kept pace with him. When they reached the end of the narrow lane they turned left onto a broader road in time to see a train crossing a bridge that passed over the road about a hundred yards ahead. 'The station's just on the other side of the bridge,' Tom gasped.

But here they met deep drifts that had blown across the road through a gap in the hedge. Even though the snow was, as Tom had pointed out, fine and powdery, kicking it aside so they could get through took up precious time. 'No, please stay in the station,' Deedee begged the train, once they were clear and jogging under the bridge. There was the station house in front of them. They dashed up the path towards the station entrance but, before they could get there, they heard the guard's shrill whistle.

'No!' Deedee moaned. She quickened her pace, but the sound of the steam engine chugging, gradually building up speed, destroyed her hopes. By the time they burst onto the platform the last carriage had rolled out of reach. All that remained was sooty smoke and the lingering metallic smell of a hot engine. If Georgie had been waiting for the train at Potterhanworth, she would be gone.

–

Pearl paced the living room. Now she had two people to worry about, and she felt helpless in both cases. She was torn between a desire to dash out of the house to accompany Deedee and dread of missing some news about Greg.

When Thea and Jenny returned, they listened in dismay to Pearl's news. 'It's freezing out there,' Thea said. 'We should go after them.'

Pearl shook her head. 'Thomas said something about taking a shortcut across the fields, and I don't know the way, do you?' After Thea admitted she didn't, Pearl continued, 'You'd end up missing them, and then there would be another set of people for me to worry about. We need to trust that Thomas knows what he's doing and will keep Deedee safe.'

A wave of exhaustion swept over her – probably a delayed reaction to all the worry – and she sank into an armchair.

Jenny came to perch on the arm. 'Are you all right? You've gone ever so pale.'

'I'm fine.' Pearl attempted a smile. 'It's ironic, really. I wanted something to take my mind off Greg, and now I've got so many worries they're getting too much for me.'

Thea tossed her a newspaper from the pile next to her own chair. Haughton Newspapers had access to papers from all parts of the country, and Pearl had brought a selection with her. 'Try the crossword. It won't be as good as one of mine, but it'll keep us occupied.'

Pearl opened the paper, seeing that it was from Norfolk. 'I doubt there's a crossword. In case you hadn't noticed, most papers are leaving them out to save space.' She turned a page and paused when her gaze fell on a headline halfway down page two: *STILL NO NEWS OF MISSING KING'S LYNN GIRL*. 'Hang on,' she said. 'Deedee said the cases of missing girls might be related, didn't she? Listen to this: *Police still have no leads in the case of missing seventeen-year-old girl Dawn Harlow and have offered a reward for any information that might lead to her return. She was last seen on 2nd December, celebrating with friends after a performance given by the drama school she attends. She left the theatre at eleven that night and has not been seen since.*'

Pearl dropped the paper and looked at Thea and Jenny, her mind whirring. 'What if acting is the link? What if this imposter David Mountjoy is behind it all?' Refreshed now that she had a new sense of purpose, she rose. 'I need to do some investigation.'

Clutching the newspaper and with Thea and Jenny trailing behind her, she strode into the study. A short while later she was speaking to a member of the King's Lynn police on the number given in the newspaper. When she explained who she was, saying she was attached to the Haughton Newspaper Group in Lincolnshire, she said, 'A girl has just gone missing from Fenthorpe, and I couldn't help noticing similarities between the cases.' She went on to explain about the false Mr Mountjoy.

'That's most interesting,' the constable said. 'As a matter of fact, we have an Inspector Jessop from Scotland Yard here at the moment, and I think he would like to hear your information.'

Her shock must have shown on her face, for Thea whispered, 'What's happened?'

In the pause while the constable was going to fetch the inspector, Pearl covered the telephone receiver with her hand and said, 'They're putting me through to a Scotland Yard inspector.'

Thea's eyes shone. 'They must think you're on to something. Look at you – you're a regular Sherlock Holmes.'

A moment later Pearl heard a gruff male voice down the line, speaking with a Yorkshire accent. 'Inspector Jessop here, Corporal Tallis. I gather you have a girl missing under similar circumstances to the one here in King's Lynn.'

Pearl related the whole tale again. When she had finished, Jessop said, 'It's the mention of the fake theatrical agent that got the constable's attention. You wouldn't happen to have a description of him?'

'I never saw him myself, but my grandmother did.' Pearl repeated the description Deedee had given her.

'That *is* interesting. You see, we've asked the press not to print this, but in four other cases of recent missing girls, including the poor girl from Cambridge, friends have mentioned them being approached by a so-called theatrical agent answering that description. He gives a different name each time, but always uses the name of a genuine agent.'

Pearl gripped the receiver. 'So my grandmother was right. Georgie's disappearance really is related to these other cases.'

'I'm afraid it sounds more than likely.'

The inspector ended the call after assuring Pearl he would visit Mrs March in person to break the news. In her turn, Pearl promised to inform him the moment Deedee returned from the railway station. It was a sombre group who now awaited Deedee's return.

Chapter Twenty-Two

Deedee couldn't give up on Georgie, not when she faced such danger at the end of her journey. Nobody remained on the platform, but she went to the ticket office. 'Is there another train going to Sleaford soon?' she asked.

The man at the desk shook his head. 'I doubt it. The train that just left was the two fifteen to Sleaford, but it got held up by snowdrifts on the line. I'm expecting to hear the later trains have all been cancelled.'

Deedee could have kicked herself for missing the train by such a narrow margin. If it had been due at a quarter past two, then surely it was the one Georgie had intended to catch. 'Did a young girl come in and buy a ticket for London?' she asked. 'About sixteen, a little taller than me. Blond, very pretty.'

The man pursed his lips. 'There was a girl that came in. Very upset by the delay, she was. When I said she'd have to wait, same as everyone else, she said she was going to be a huge star and I'd be sorry for being so rude.'

Deedee stared at him. It had to be Georgie, but it didn't sound like her at all. Had the prospect of fame really turned her head that quickly?

Tom put a hand on her arm. 'I'm sorry,' he said. 'I suppose we could try getting to Lincoln and catching the next express to London. We might still get there before

Georgie, since she'll need to change trains a couple of times.' He turned to the ticket seller. 'Is there a bus that runs from the village to Lincoln?'

The man glanced at the clock. 'There's one leaving in half an hour. The waiting room's still open if you want to wait there.'

Feeling despondent, but heartened by Tom's determination not to give up, Deedee followed him out onto the platform, where the entrance to the waiting room could be found. Before she had even stepped inside, the sound of voices warned her they wouldn't be alone. She could hear a girl's voice speaking over another girl's sobs. Once inside, two faces turned to look at her. One was reddened and tearstained; and the other, sombre face belonged to Georgie.

'Georgie, oh, thank goodness.' Deedee pulled the girl into a hug. 'Your mother's beside herself with worry.'

The other girl said in a quavering voice, 'Don't blame Georgie. This is all my fault.'

Deedee looked at her properly for the first time and recognised her as the girl she had seen in the cafe with the false Mountjoy earlier. She exchanged glances with Tom, then sat beside the girls. 'Why don't you tell me all about it?'

The story poured out. 'After you warned me about that agent,' Georgie explained, 'I got worried. I'd been so excited at first that it hadn't occurred to me to question his sincerity.' She blushed. 'I suppose I wanted so badly for it all to be true. I mean, isn't it the dream of any actress to be discovered like that? But when you told me to be careful, well, it slowly dawned on me that it wasn't very likely for a successful agent to be scouring the provinces. Then I got a letter from him, telling me about a new show in London and how I'd be a dead cert for one of the main roles. And I knew it was too good to be true. Mrs Stokeley – that's our drama teacher – is always saying how difficult it is to get the good parts, so I didn't understand how he could be virtually promising me, an unknown with no experience, the best role. So I decided not to go.'

The other girl started sobbing again. Georgie shot her a sideways glance and chewed her lip.

Deedee thought she could understand what she was thinking and addressed the weeping girl. 'Don't tell me,' she said, concentrating on keeping her tone free from criticism, 'you got the same letter. What's your name, child?'

'Marjorie. I did, yes.' Marjorie drew a deep, shaky breath. 'It's all right,' she said to Georgie, 'I can explain from here.' She turned reddened eyes to Deedee. 'I feel so embarrassed,' she confessed.

'There's nothing to be ashamed of,' Deedee assured her. 'Older and supposedly wiser people than you have made far greater mistakes.'

'But I *am* ashamed. I let that man flatter me and turn my head. I wanted to be a star so badly I forgot my common sense.'

Tom, who had remained in the background until this point, now spoke. 'That's how con artists work. Believe me, the newspapers are full of stories of people from all walks of life being taken in because they heard what they wanted to be true. And many of them compounded their error by refusing to believe they had been taken in.' He looked at Marjorie kindly. 'It takes a lot of courage to admit you've been fooled, not to mention intelligence to understand that it happened at all.'

Marjorie wiped her eyes on a handkerchief that Deedee had handed her and gave a wan smile. 'That was thanks to Georgie. I… I didn't want to leave without telling my mother where I was going, but I knew she wouldn't let me go if I told her. So I sent a note to Georgie, telling her what I was doing, and asked her to pass the message to my mother.'

Deedee's eyes widened in comprehension. 'So the letter we found wasn't from Georgie but you!' That explained why it had seemed out of character.

Marjorie frowned and turned to her friend. 'Didn't you give it to my mum?'

Georgie shook her head. 'I was all in a tizzy when I got your letter. I went straight round to your house, but your mother was out, and I didn't know what to do. I was so worried for you. Then I worked out I could still get to the station before your train left, so I dashed home to put on some warmer clothes. I must have left the letter somewhere.'

'You left it in your bedroom,' Deedee supplied. 'I found it when your mother asked me to leave a dress in your flat. We were getting worried about you because you weren't in Lincoln where you told her you would be.'

Georgie looked embarrassed. 'I made up the first thing I could on the spur of the moment. I hated lying to her, but I was trying not to get Marjorie into trouble. I thought, if I could stop her from taking the train, no one need know what she'd been about to do.'

Marjorie started crying again. 'I'll never be able to face my mum after this. I can't bear for her to think badly of me.'

—

Thea paced to the window, eased the curtains aside and peered out.

'You'll have the ARP warden banging at the door,' Pearl warned. Then: 'Any sign of them?'

Thea shook her head and closed the curtains. 'It's pitch black out there. Can't see a thing. What possessed you to let her go out in this weather?'

'Have *you* ever managed to stop her doing something once she's set her mind on it?'

'Well, no.' Thea glanced at her watch. 'What time did they leave?'

Pearl was saved answering by a commotion at the door. She dashed into the hall to see not only Deedee and her grandfather but also Georgie and a very sorry-looking girl she didn't recognise. 'Thank goodness,' she cried. Then, drawing her grandparents aside while Mrs Stockwell helped the two girls out of their coats, she quietly repeated what she had learned from Inspector Jessop. 'We must phone him right away.'

Pearl dealt with the necessary phone calls, including getting word to both Mrs March and Marjorie's family that the girls had been found safe and well. Inspector Jessop had been delighted and had told Pearl that he would be there as soon as the weather permitted to interview both girls.

Marjorie had burst into tears upon hearing of the narrowness of her escape. 'My mum will never let me leave home again,' she cried, tears dripping into her cocoa. She turned pleading eyes on Pearl. 'I've already told Georgie everything I know. Do I really have to speak to the police? I just want to go home and forget about it all.'

Pearl dropped into a crouch beside Marjorie's armchair and patted her shoulder. 'There are other girls not as lucky as you. You want to help them, don't you?'

Marjorie sniffled and nodded.

'Well, then. There might be something that you haven't thought of that proves to be the key to catching him.'

'I suppose.' Marjorie sobbed a few moments more, then said, 'My mum's never going to forgive me.'

'She'll be relieved to see you safe and well. And you've learned to be careful in future, haven't you?'

'Oh, yes. I don't think I'll ever leave Lincoln again.'

Pearl smiled. 'You will when you're ready.'

It had been arranged that Marjorie would stay with the Marches that night and remain until Inspector Jessop had been able to visit. Thea and Jenny cadged a lift back to RAF Fenthorpe in the truck used to transport the night watch officers to and from Fenthorpe Hall. When the driver learned that Georgie and Marjorie had been stranded by the snow – Thea and Jenny withheld the whole truth – she kindly agreed to drop the girls in the village.

Pearl had a quiet word with Georgie before she climbed into the truck. 'You did well today. You should be proud of yourself.'

'It was really thanks to your grandmother,' Georgie told her. 'If she hadn't warned me to be cautious, I might have been getting on the train with Marjorie instead of persuading her not to go. You're lucky to have a grand-mother like that.'

Pearl smiled. 'I really am.' She resolved always to be grateful for Deedee and never again to be embarrassed by her.

Just as Georgie was climbing aboard the vehicle, Pearl called, 'You'll still be singing at the dance, won't you? It wouldn't be the same without you.'

Georgie waved. 'You bet. Wouldn't miss it for the world.'

Once the truck had rumbled off, its huge wheels making light of the snow, only Pearl, Deedee and Thomas remained, Mrs Stockwell having retired to her room some time earlier. They returned to the living room to finish their cocoa. Eventually Thomas looked at his watch. 'I suppose I'd better go. The last bus will be leaving soon, assuming it's still running.'

'I'm sure it's not,' Deedee remarked. 'I wouldn't feel happy turning you out on a night like this. We can make you a bed on the sofa.'

'If you're sure,' Thomas said. 'I wouldn't want to put you out.'

'Nonsense. This is your house, after all.'

'Then thank you.'

It seemed to Pearl that there was more than simple politeness behind their words, and she suddenly felt as though her presence was unwanted. She gave an exag-gerated yawn. 'I'll fetch some bedding. I saw where Mrs Stockwell keeps it when she made up the camp bed for me. Then I think I'll turn in. It's been a tiring day.'

–

While they waited for Pearl to return with the bedding, Deedee found herself making inane comments to Tom about the weather. All the while, she heard Marjorie's despairing voice over and over again. *I'll never be able to face my mum after this.* The words haunted her because that was how she felt about telling Tom the whole truth about her move to Shrewsbury. There had been something so intimate about their walk to the station, even before the moment she had been tempted to kiss him. It had felt like a homecoming. A return to how it had been between them in London. It had inevitably led to thoughts of agreeing to let him court her again. But when Marjorie had said those words, the dream had shattered. Because once he knew, Tom would never look at her the same way again. He would always remember what she had done.

After Pearl had dropped off the bedding she immediately departed, and Deedee knew she couldn't put off the moment any longer. Tom insisted on helping her to tuck in the sheets. As she wrestled a cushion from the armchair into a pillowcase, Deedee drew a deep breath. 'I'm sorry, Tom, but this isn't going to work.'

'Let me try.' Tom took the cushion and pillowcase from her.

Deedee shook her head. 'I don't mean the bedding. I mean us.'

Tom stood, unmoving, the pillowcase dangling from his hands. 'I see.' He blinked and then gazed at the cushion as though he couldn't work out why he was holding it. 'Is there any chance you might change your mind?'

'No. I'm sorry.' She couldn't disappoint him without providing some explanation, even if it was only a partial truth. 'I have my own life in Shrewsbury now, and you're clearly needed here. It just wouldn't work. I'll keep in touch, though. And you have Pearl and Thea now, of course. They're so happy now they have their grandfather in their life.'

'My life is all the richer now I have them,' Tom said. He dropped the cushion on the sofa, took off his glasses and rubbed his eyes. 'I'll respect your decision, of course, but I'll never feel complete without you.'

Now it was Deedee's turn to blink back tears. In many ways she would have been able to deal with it better if Tom had begged her to reconsider, made wild promises to be exactly who she wanted him to be. This sad acceptance broke her heart. She opened her mouth to speak, found her aching throat too tight for words, and needed to clear her throat before she could manage to say, 'I think it's for the best. Thank you for understanding.'

Then she made her escape before Tom saw her heart was breaking.

Chapter Twenty-Three

Deedee slept badly and rose late, to find Tom had already left.

'He said he needed to arrange for a space to be left in the *Eastern Express* in case we hear more about the missing girls,' Pearl told her. She was sitting at the table in the warm kitchen, with a cup of tea and an open notebook in front of her. She looked at Deedee with glowing eyes. 'He's asked me to write the article. He even thinks there's a good chance of it being picked up by the nationals.'

'That was good of him.' Deedee went to sit opposite Pearl, dropping onto her chair with all the grace of an arthritic buffalo. It didn't exactly soothe her sore heart to know that Tom was proving yet again what a fine man he was by giving Pearl this opportunity. Not to mention that it was another distraction from her worries over Greg.

With Pearl occupied, there was little for Deedee to do. The snow lay deep and, although the lane was clear enough for the occasional bus to get through, she didn't feel like going out. Her fall was still too recent in her memory to risk a repeat experience. In the end she got out her neglected knitting and set to work with a distinct lack of enthusiasm. It was hard to summon up the energy for anything when her low mood was entirely her own fault. There was no one but herself to blame for what she had done over fifty years ago, and now she was suffering the consequences.

The only bright spot in the day was a call from Inspector Jessop. Pearl took the call and Deedee, burning with curiosity, hovered in the doorway, trying to piece together the conversation from Pearl's occasional comments and exclamations. However, they were too disjointed for Deedee to make any sense of what Jessop was saying.

At long last, Pearl replaced the receiver and faced Deedee. 'They've caught him,' she said.

'And the missing girls?'

'Found locked in the basement of a house in Chiswick. Mountjoy confessed to everything,' Pearl replied. 'Or, rather, Slater did. That's his real name, apparently. Police in London freed them late last night.' Pearl grimaced. 'It's horrible. Jessop said that Slater broke down when he was arrested and begged the police not to take his "family" away. He had some twisted notion that the women he'd kidnapped were his family who needed his protection from a corrupt world.'

'He must have been sick in the head.' Deedee shuddered, remembering how he had shoved past her at the pantomime. 'To think I've been in the same room as him. Breathed the same air. I mean, I didn't like him, but I'd never have imagined what he was really like.' Another thought struck. 'But how did he find the girls? They came from all over.'

'Jessop told me that he works in sales, supplying agricultural tools to farms, and his patch just happens to be the east of England.'

'Where all the missing girls came from,' Deedee breathed, light dawning. 'So he could have found out about upcoming performances from local newspapers and arranged his business visits around them.'

Pearl nodded. 'That's what Jessop said. Slater had a supply of real cards from agents that he handed out to potential targets to make himself seem genuine.'

'Marjorie had a lucky escape, thanks to Georgie.' Deedee hated to think what would have happened had Georgie not gone after her.

'She did.' Pearl spoke with feeling. She hesitated before adding, 'He confessed to killing that poor Cambridge girl, although he swears it was an accident. Apparently he caught her trying to break free and decided to punish her.' Pearl drew a deep breath and closed her eyes briefly. When she opened them she looked calmer. 'Anyway, it doesn't do to dwell on such things. They're free now, and will soon be back with their families, and that's the main thing. Too late for the girl he killed, but at least the others are safe.'

Deedee shook her head sadly at the cruelty of the world but consoled herself with the knowledge that her actions had contributed towards their release. 'Thank goodness for Georgie.' She put her hand on Pearl's wrist. 'Please keep Marjorie's name out of this if you can. You saw how ashamed she was; she'd never live it down if what she was about to do became public knowledge.'

'Don't worry about that. I'll make sure no one knows it's her, although it might come out eventually if she's called to give evidence in Slater's trial.'

'And Georgie?'

'She'll be the heroine of the piece. Thanks to you, she wasn't fooled by that man, and she stopped another girl from falling prey to him. If it hadn't been for her, the whole scandal would never have come to light. There's no keeping her out of it, which is probably why Thomas asked me to write the report. He knows I'll show her in the good light she deserves and won't sensationalise the story around the girls who were taken in.'

Pearl went on to give full details around Slater's capture. Jessop had fought through the snow to Fenthorpe to interview Marjorie and Georgie. When Marjorie was asked about travel arrangements, she had remembered that the man calling himself Mountjoy had told her to meet him outside the left luggage office. Jessop had immediately contacted Scotland Yard and, using the detailed description from both girls, police officers had picked the man up.

It was a relief to know that he would never again be able to prey on a young girl's dreams. Deedee also reflected that being the heroine of a news story would probably help Georgie's career if she still wanted to be an actress. She could only hope the experience hadn't put the girl off.

–

The day of the dance dawned clear and bright. No more snow had fallen, and it covered the ground in a crisp, sparkling blanket. Jenny and Thea's leave was due to start that evening, and it should have been a happy festive day, leading up to an event that everyone had eagerly anticipated for weeks if not months. And for many people, Pearl was sure, it still was. For her, though, it was a cruel reminder of all she stood to lose. Today was supposed to be the start of Greg's leave, and she had clung to the hope that by this time he would have been found safe and well. Ever since the news of his crash had arrived, all of Pearl's energy had been devoted towards the arrival of this day. Yet now it was here, nothing had changed, and she didn't know how much longer her resilience could stretch. Not even the sight of her byline in the *Manchester Guardian* and a whole host of London newspapers could raise much of a smile. What was the point when there was no Greg to share her success?

Her worries were brought to the front of her mind when there was a missed phone call. Deedee had pulled on her borrowed boots an hour or so before lunch and tried to persuade Pearl to come for a short walk. However, Pearl was feeling too tired, and in any case didn't have any boots, so she declined, saying she would take a bath instead. She was just getting out when the telephone rang downstairs, setting her nerves jangling. She didn't dash to answer, sure Mrs Stockwell would take the call. She pulled on her dressing gown and strained her ears for Mrs Stockwell's voice, unable to move until she knew the call wasn't for her.

But the telephone rang and rang, and there was no sound of Mrs Stockwell's footsteps hurrying from the kitchen. With dawning dismay, Pearl realised the house-keeper must have stepped outside. Dripping water, she ran barefoot down the stairs and flung herself into the study. She had just reached the desk when the ringing stopped. Shaking, she sank into the desk chair and stared at the telephone, willing the caller to try again.

Mrs Stockwell dashed in, clutching a bundle of letters. 'Did you get it?' When Pearl shook her head, Mrs Stockwell dropped the letters on the desk. 'I'm so sorry. I was out in the lane, talking to the postman. I only heard the telephone when I reached the back door.'

She looked so upset with herself that Pearl couldn't hold it against her. 'I'm sure it was nothing. And if it's anything important' – she couldn't bring herself to say *news of Greg* – 'they're bound to call back.'

But there had been no further calls, and by mid-afternoon Pearl had managed to persuade herself that the missed call had been nothing to do with Greg. She played a listless few hands of rummy with Deedee, until a glance at her watch told her it was time to start getting ready for the dance.

'Are you sure you still want to go?' Deedee asked. 'I'm happy to stay here for a quiet evening in if you don't feel up to it.'

This roused Pearl from her lethargy enough to stare at her grandmother in surprise. No one enjoyed a party more than Deedee. 'You'd do that for me? Even though Thomas will be there?'

'Thomas will understand.' Something about the way Deedee said this made Pearl stare at her in surprise. She had detected a distinct frisson between her grandparents the night they had found Georgie and Marjorie and had rather assumed they would soon be a couple again. The only reason Pearl hadn't asked Deedee about it yesterday was the excitement of having to write her article driving everything else from her mind.

'Is everything all right between the two of you?' she asked.

'Oh yes. It's good to have a friend like him back in my life.'

'A friend?' Pearl examined Deedee's face for any sign of a blush. Not that she could imagine Deedee ever being embarrassed by anything. 'Nothing more? I thought you were considering getting back together.'

Deedee made a dismissive gesture. 'I was for a while, but we decided too much water had gone under the bridge since we were together. It just wouldn't be practical, either, what with me being all the way on the other side of the country.'

Pearl could hardly believe what she was hearing. 'When did you ever object to something because it wasn't practical?' It sounded more like an excuse *she* would make.

Deedee shrugged. 'It wasn't meant to be. Anyway, we were talking about you. There's no need to go to the dance if you don't want to.'

Pearl sighed. 'A part of me would like nothing better than to curl up by the fireside with a good book. But I'm supposed to be writing a report of the dance for the *Bombshell*. Anyway, I don't want to spoil Thea and Jenny's night. They might feel obliged to keep us company if we stay here, and they've been looking forward to this for ages.' She rose, wishing she didn't feel so tired. Making a conscious effort, she squared her shoulders and offered Deedee a hand to help her out of her armchair. 'Come on. Let's make ourselves look beautiful. As beautiful as I can be in uniform, anyway.' Although she was on leave and so, strictly speaking, permitted to wear civvies, she didn't feel comfortable attending an RAF event out of uniform. Besides, she didn't possess a dress suitable for a dance, so she would have to wear her best blues.

As they mounted the stairs, she said, 'There's another reason why it's good for me to go tonight.'

'Because you want to jitterbug until you drop?'

Pearl gave a grim laugh. 'Believe me, the way I feel at the moment, it wouldn't take more than a single slow waltz. No, it's because I need to keep working. If I'd curled up by the fire feeling sorry for myself the other night instead of picking up the phone and investigating when I saw that article in the paper, the police might never have caught Slater.'

Deedee opened the bedroom door but, instead of going in, she turned to face Pearl with an impish grin, the first genuine smile Pearl had seen on her grandmother's face all day. 'So you expect excitement and intrigue at the dance?'

'Maybe not, but the point is, I need to keep doing my job. It's given me purpose through all this. And I won't find a good story shut in the house.'

'That's a good way of looking at things.'

Pearl followed Deedee into the room, then pulled off her jumper and unbuttoned her blouse before taking her uniform shirt off the hanger in the wardrobe and digging in her suitcase for her freshly starched collar. Before putting on the shirt, though, she fiddled with her bra. 'This always used to be my most comfortable bra, but it's really digging in,' she complained. 'It feels like it's shrunk two sizes.'

Glancing up, she caught Deedee's face in the wardrobe mirror, wearing the most peculiar expression. 'Why are you looking at me like that? What's the matter?'

'Pearl,' Deedee said, speaking like a patient teacher to a slow child, 'when did you last have your monthlies?'

Pearl gazed at her, uncomprehending. 'I'm not sure. I mean, with all that's happened I suppose I've forgotten about it.'

'Before or after you last saw Greg?'

'I— oh!' Pearl dropped with a bump onto the bed, still holding the shirt. 'I mean, I've been tired all the time and off my food, but I put it down to the worry. You think I'm expecting!'

–

Deedee sat beside Pearl, amused that her granddaughter, who was usually so quick on the uptake, had not worked it out before. 'I think it's a possibility.'

'But it was the one thing Greg and I actually talked about. We weren't going to start a family until we were out of the services.'

Deedee couldn't resist. 'Then you should probably have spent more of your time in Ludlow seeing the sights and less of it in bed.'

'But it wasn't part of the plan.' Pearl's words ended in a wail.

Deedee patted Pearl's hand. 'These things rarely are.' She gave a crooked smile. 'I should know. But if you are pregnant – and remember, nothing's certain yet – how do you feel about it?'

Pearl's eyes opened wide, and she clutched Deedee's arm. 'I'd have to leave the WAAF.'

'Not just yet. You're not even showing. Now forget about your work and the WAAF. How do you feel about bringing a baby into the world?'

Deedee saw the moment when the reality sank in; Pearl released her grip on Deedee's arm and let her hand drift to her stomach. Her expression softened. 'A baby. Greg's baby. It would be wonderful.'

'Then there's nothing to worry about, is there? You just focus on this and everything else will sort itself out.'

Although she prayed with all her heart that Pearl wouldn't be forced, like her, to bring her baby up without its father. It had all worked out well in the end, but there had been times in the early years when Deedee had come close to despair. The memory made her wrap a reassuring arm round Pearl's shoulders. 'And remember. Whatever happens, you won't have to do this alone. You've got me and Thea, and Tom, of course. And Jenny. She's part of the family too.'

'And Greg.' Pearl's face was determined. 'He's got to come home now, because there's no way he'd want to miss this.'

Deedee felt she had to ask a question that had been on the tip of her tongue ever since Greg's crash. 'Do you regret getting married so fast? I hate to see you like this, facing life without him, and now with the possibility of a baby. Do you regret not waiting?'

The question seemed to rouse Pearl from her shock. 'No,' she said, her voice definite. 'Whatever happens, I'd never want things to be otherwise. When we married I knew that' – her voice wobbled – ''till death do us part might only be a short time ahead. I accepted it at the time, and I'd never want things to be otherwise. I will always cherish the time we had together; if we hadn't married when we did, I would have always regretted that. I know it was taking a risk, but you can't go through life playing it safe all the time.'

Deedee laughed. 'I'd love to see Thea's face if she heard you saying that.'

But as she dressed in her favourite gown – a low-waisted midnight-blue lace dress she'd had since the Twenties – she couldn't shake Pearl's words from her mind. *You can't go through life playing it safe all the time.* If Deedee had been asked which of the three women in the family would be most likely to say that line, she would have put Pearl at the bottom of the list, with Thea and herself tied at the top. When had she stopped taking chances?

When had she let fear take control of her life?

As the realisation sank in, she couldn't suppress a sob.

Instantly Pearl was at her side. 'What's the matter? Don't you feel well?'

'I'm fine. I just… oh, Pearl, I think I've made the biggest mistake of my life.'

'What have you done?'

'I told Tom I didn't love him any more, but that's not true.'

'Then tell him tonight that you love him. It's not too late.'

'I know. But there's more. I knew that, if we were a couple again, I would have to tell him the whole truth about why I moved to Shrewsbury.'

'You mean there's more? You haven't told me or Thea either?'

Deedee shook her head. 'I'm sorry. But I was so ashamed. I'm afraid that once Tom knows, once you and Thea know, you'll lose all respect for me, and I couldn't bear it. I couldn't bear to see the love fade in Tom's eyes if I told him.'

Pearl handed Deedee a handkerchief and put an arm round her shoulders. 'I could never stop loving you. Nothing you could tell me about your past would make me forget what a wonderful grandmother you are, and what you sacrificed for me, Thea and our mother. I'm sure Thomas would feel the same way.' She paused, then said, 'Can you tell me what it is?'

'I will.' Deedee wiped away her tears. 'I want to tell you. You and Thea. But I need to tell Tom first. Do you mind?'

'Of course not. When are you going to tell him?'

'Tonight.' Deedee folded away the hanky and pulled out her face powder. 'I'm not going to let fear destroy my happiness a moment longer.'

Chapter Twenty-Four

Thea and Jenny turned up at the Gatehouse a little before eight. Their faces were pink from the cold.

'You didn't walk all the way here?' Deedee asked, ushering them into the hall.

Thea, rubbing her hands, shook her head. 'They've put on buses to get everyone to and from the dance, but the windows on ours were jammed open.'

Pearl, who had been pinning up her hair, came down the stairs at this point. 'I thought I heard voices.' Then she frowned, looking at Thea. 'No Fitz?'

'His train must be delayed. We arranged to meet at the dance if he was late.'

Deedee could tell Thea was feeling down, despite trying to put on a cheerful face. 'He'll be here soon, I'm sure. Anyway, we'd better get over there if that's where you're meeting him.' She didn't add that she was anxious to meet Tom.

Even though she had helped with the decorations, Deedee still gasped with delight when she saw the ballroom in all its glory. The fairy lights on the Christmas tree had been switched on, and they gleamed like stars in the corner of the room, if stars were coloured like jewels. The sprigs of mistletoe Jenny and Thea had collected and arranged now dangled from every doorway. Most wonderful of all, though, was the series of painted panels everyone had worked so hard on. The Christmas trees, against their starry backgrounds, looked cheerful and festive, and the central panel, now revealed, was a masterful example of trompe l'oeil. Or 'trompy loyal' as Jenny called it. It showed a pair of French windows, opening onto a starlit, snow-covered garden, where a path led the eye to a floodlit fountain. It was so lifelike Deedee could hardly believe she couldn't walk through the doorway. Even as she watched, she saw one man surreptitiously touch the panel and then laugh self-consciously when his friends teased him.

Marvellous as the sight was, however, it couldn't long distract her from her purpose, and Deedee cast her gaze over the heads of the revellers already crowded into the room, looking for Tom. She couldn't see him anywhere, and her stomach twisted into knots. What if he had decided not to come?

'Are you all right, Deedee?'

She dragged her gaze from the crowd and saw Thea watching her with an anxious frown. 'Never better!' She drew a deep breath and forced a smile. 'Doesn't this all look lovely?' She had to raise her voice to be heard over the buzz of conversation and laughter. 'First things first, let's find the drinks. Mine's a double whisky,' she added, not altogether joking.

The drinks table was along a wall near the band, who were placing sheet music on their stands. Deedee was pleased to see Georgie there, dressed in a stunning scarlet gown that made her look even more like a film star. Then she ruined her sophisticated act by waving enthusiastically when she saw Deedee.

Deedee waved back, pleased to see Georgie didn't seem to be suffering any ill effects from her experience. Seeing that the band was about to strike up, she resisted the temptation to go and talk to her and instead went to inspect the drinks available. Sadly there was no whisky on offer, or any other spirits, so she risked a glass of what was described as Christmas punch. A tentative sip reassured her that it was nothing worse than orange squash mixed with ginger beer. She drained her glass and left it on the table, then resumed her search for Tom while Pearl, Jenny and Thea were still trying to decide on their drinks.

She found him just as the band started playing. He was standing by the painted window panels, examining the artwork, and her heart gave a little thump when he turned his head and their eyes met. *Courage, Deedee*, she muttered behind her smile. It was now or never. On the stage, Georgie started singing 'A Nightingale Sang in Berkeley Square'. Deedee stretched her hand out towards him. 'Dance with me?'

Tom looked surprised and delighted. 'Are you sure?'

'Never more so.'

As Deedee stepped out in Tom's arms, the years fell away, and she could almost believe she was twenty again and in love for the first time.

'After what you said the other night, I thought we'd never dance together again,' Tom said.

'I thought so too.' She leaned back a little so she could see his face while she made her confession. 'Then I had a conversation with Pearl earlier about cherishing every

283

moment with those you love, and I knew I'd made a terrible mistake.'

Hope and uncertainty mingled in Tom's expression. 'You mean—?'

'I mean that I love you. I only said I didn't because I was afraid.'

'Afraid of what?'

She drew a deep breath. 'Afraid that, when you heard the whole truth about why I left you, you would never want to see me again.'

'That could never happen.'

'Don't say that yet. Wait until you've heard my confession.' The trouble was, now it was time to speak she couldn't get the words out. She opened and closed her mouth a few times, then stepped on Tom's foot and stumbled. 'It's no good. I can't dance and hold an important conversation at the same time. Is there somewhere quiet we can go?'

'I know the perfect place. Come with me.'

He led her out of the ballroom into the grand entrance hall, where he fetched their coats. Then he offered her his arm and they went outside. The moon hung high in the sky and was more than half full, casting enough light to illuminate the paths. They walked in silence, Deedee's mind churning with too much anxiety for light conversation, until she saw the direction they were headed. 'Oh, you're taking us to the rose garden.'

'It seems appropriate,' Tom replied. 'We can sit by the Heart of Hope rose and you can tell me what's on your mind. Just promise me we can finish our dance once you've had your say, because I was enjoying it.'

'I promise. If you still want to.'

'I can't imagine ever changing my mind.'

They were by the bench where Deedee had first seen Tom at the start of her visit. She sat down and patted the seat beside her, praying he still felt the same way when she had finished. Staring out across the garden, the pruned rose bushes dimly visible in the cold light, she began her tale. 'I've already told you that I left because I thought you never wanted to marry me.' She hurried on before he could reply, knowing that if she didn't say what needed to be said, she might lose the nerve to get it into the open. 'I know now that was a terrible mistake, that your father deceived me. Deceived us both. But your father did something else before he left London.' She drew a gulping breath. 'You see, he wanted me out of your life so badly that he offered to buy me a cottage and set me up with enough money that I wouldn't need to work to support my child and myself. His only condition was that I would make no further attempt to contact you.'

Tom twisted in his seat until he was facing her, and when he spoke his voice was thin with anger. 'He forced you to do that?'

'Yes.' Deedee gazed down at her hands, not wanting to look at him any more and see his love fade and turn to disgust. Her fingers were cold, and she rubbed them together to try to warm them. 'I'm sorry.'

She jumped when Tom covered her chilled hands with his warm ones. 'Sorry for what – for doing what you felt necessary to keep our daughter fed and clothed? For accepting a house so that you knew you would never struggle to put a roof over her head?'

She dared to look up and meet his gaze. She searched his face for any sign of revulsion but saw only love. Hope flared in her heart. 'You're not angry?'

'Oh, I'm angry but not with you. I can't believe my father would go to those lengths to keep me away from the woman I loved and my child. His own grandchild.' Then he frowned. 'You thought I would be angry at you? Why?'

'Maybe because I've been so ashamed of myself all these years. I took money from a man I despised and allowed him to bribe me to cut off all contact with the man I loved. You never got to know Clara, because of me. I put money over my family.' She was breathing hard now, trying to force back her sobs. She ended in a rush, 'I'm no better than your father!'

'Deedee!' Tom was still squeezing her hands and, as it filtered through her consciousness that he was neither running away nor regarding her with disgust, she relaxed and drew several deep breaths.

'You're really not angry with me?'

He shook his head. 'Why would I be? You were put in an impossible situation. It would have been different if you'd thought I'd be there for you but, as far as you knew, I was on my way back to Lincolnshire to marry another woman.' He squeezed her hands. 'Knowing you, you really struggled with the decision.'

'I did!' Tears filled her eyes, but this time they were tears of relief and gratitude. 'All these years, I've dreaded anyone learning the truth. I hate lying, but I let everyone believe I was a widow and the money came from my late husband. I couldn't bear for anyone to find out the mercenary reality.'

'There's nothing mercenary about the way you cared for our daughter. Anyway, if we'd married, as we would have if my father hadn't intervened, the family money would have been yours. You deserve every penny of what he gave you.' He rose and pulled her up after him. 'Now, you promised that, once you'd told me everything, we could finish our dance. Let's go back to the ballroom.'

'Wait. There's one more thing I have to ask.' Deedee gripped his hand to stop him moving away. 'You asked before if you could court me, and I don't want that.'

His face fell. 'You don't? Well, of course I—'

'I want to marry you.'

Tom's transformation from dejected to joyful was miraculous. 'You do?'

She raised herself onto tiptoe and kissed him. She wanted to linger there for ever. This time she wasn't transported back to the past; she remained in the present, brimful of joy and eagerly anticipating the future, when they would be together at last. When she finally drew back, she grinned. 'I think the correct response is *I do*. That's what you'll be saying at the ceremony, assuming you want to marry me.' She had no doubt, though, not if his beaming smile was anything to go by.

'I do. I very much do!' He pulled her close and kissed her again. When he broke the kiss, he didn't release her but hugged her even tighter. 'I'm not dreaming, am I? After all this time, we're actually going to get married?' He gave a breathless laugh. 'I get to spend the rest of my life with the first love of my life?'

'You're not dreaming. Now, I suggest we get out of this freezing cold and warm up with a dance.'

'Your wish is my command!' He let her go and offered her his arm. 'I feel like I could dance all night. I want to finish our waltz, then maybe we could try a foxtrot? The way I feel, I could even attempt a jitterbug.'

Deedee pulled him close to her side. 'As the youngsters say, okay, bring it on!'

–

Pearl had never felt less like celebrating. Although the initial shock at the discovery of her possible pregnancy had quickly led to excitement, all she could think now was how painful it would be to watch her child grow if she couldn't share the joys of each new discovery with Greg. When she, Jenny and Thea took a seat at one of the tables arranged around the walls, she contemplated telling her sister and friend about the baby, yet she couldn't bring herself to do it. For one thing, it was very early days, and she didn't want to say anything until she was sure; for another, if there was any chance of Greg returning, she wanted him to be the first to know.

They hadn't been at the table for more than a minute before one of the male Met Officers approached Jenny and asked her to dance. After a brief hesitation, she rose and allowed him to lead her onto the dance floor. Pearl idly followed their progress, but her attention sharpened when she saw Deedee and Tom leave the ballroom. She nudged Thea and pointed. 'Look! I think Deedee's about to confess this terrible thing she says she did.'

'What terrible thing?'

'I forgot I hadn't told you yet. Deedee and I had a bit of a talk earlier.' Pearl hesitated, trying to work out how to give the gist of their conversation without revealing her pregnancy. 'Deedee asked me if I regretted marrying Greg so quickly,' she settled on finally. 'I told her I didn't. That I would always cherish every moment we had together, whatever happens. It set her thinking about Tom, and she said she regretted turning him down.'

'Then she's going to get back together with him?' Thea's eyes were shining.

'I hope so, but she was worried because she said she'd done something awful and needed to confess first. I've no idea what,' she said quickly, before Thea could ask. 'She said she'd tell us but wanted to tell Tom first.'

'Well, it looks like she's telling him now. I wonder where they've gone?'

Pearl shrugged, distracted by a sudden thought. 'Actually, thinking about cherishing every moment has made me realise something.'

'What?'

'I owe you an apology.'

Thea's eyes opened wide. 'Whatever for?'

'Because I've been so busy mourning what I might have lost I forgot to appreciate what I still have.' Pearl drew a deep breath. 'I'm sure you noticed I've been jealous that you still have Fitz.'

'I might have.' Thea's voice was dry.

'Well, I feel awful. I knew I was being mean and crabby, but I couldn't seem to stop myself.'

Thea leaned across the table. 'I understand, Pearl, I really do. And if it makes you feel any better, had our positions been reversed, and I had to watch you getting all lovey-dovey with Greg while Fitz was missing… well, I think you'd have been lucky to have come out of it alive.'

Some of the weight that had been lodged in Pearl's chest lifted. 'For what it's worth, I'm really sorry, and grateful for the way you've stood by me even when I've snapped at you.'

Thea grinned. 'What are sisters for?'

'And I also wanted to tell you to have fun and dance all night with Fitz once he gets here. You should cherish your time with him, too.'

Thea suddenly sat bolt upright, her gaze fixed on a point past Pearl's right shoulder. 'Oh, I intend to.' A beaming smile made her face grow brighter than the Christmas tree. 'But somehow I don't think you'll mind at all.' She gripped Pearl's arm and pointed. 'Look!'

Bewildered, Pearl turned. Then shot to her feet when she saw who was standing in the doorway.

Greg.

There were other men beside him, she couldn't see who. Greg's was the only face in clear focus. She could see it all the way across the room, clear as a beacon.

'Greg!' Even she was shocked by the scream that tore from her throat. Then people were hastily springing aside to get out of the way as she raced across the ballroom. Dimly she was aware that the music had drifted to a stop, and all she could hear was the pounding of her feet on the wooden floor and the voices of the partygoers raised in a hum. Greg, too, was pushing his way through the crowd, his gaze fixed on hers.

Then she was folded in his arms, engulfed in the familiar scent of coal tar soap, engine oil and cigarette smoke. He murmured in her ear, sounding like a man waking from a dream. 'Pearl!'

'It's really you,' was all she could say, her voice muffled against his shoulder.

Feeling him wasn't enough, and she leaned back to drink in the sight of him, running her hands up his lapels and touching his face, reassuring herself of his presence, afraid that at any moment he would melt into mist. At the same time, Greg reached up to wipe the tears from her cheeks. Until then, she hadn't even known she was crying.

Gradually, reality seeped into her consciousness, and she saw that, although it was assuredly Greg standing there, he didn't look the same as the last time she had seen him. He was pale, with new hollows in his cheeks and beneath his eyes. And when she put her hands on his shoulders, they met less muscle than she was accustomed to, and the bones felt sharper, somehow.

'What happened to you?' she asked, flooded with sudden dread. 'Were you hurt? Have you been ill?' She had so many questions her words came tumbling out. Then memory of the last report she'd had from Fitz came crashing back, and she said, 'Edwin – is he…?' She couldn't bring herself to say *dead*.

Greg shook his head. 'Edwin's fine. He's here. Fitz too.' He pointed to Fitz and Thea, who stood with their arms wrapped round each other a few paces away, grinning at them, clearly enjoying the spectacle. Edwin was also nearby, obviously feeling a gooseberry, although Pearl could see Jenny making her way towards him. Edwin looked as gaunt as Greg, and Pearl turned back to her husband, her worries not relieved.

'What happened to the two of you? You look as though you haven't eaten for weeks.'

'That's because we haven't.' Greg grimaced. 'Let's find somewhere quiet to sit, and I'll tell you all about it.'

Chapter Twenty-Five

They found a seat in the deserted lounge, which currently served as the anteroom to the officers' mess. Greg sank onto a leather sofa and pulled Pearl down to snuggle beside him. For some minutes she was content to sit in silence with her head on his chest, her fingers entwined with his, listening to his steady heartbeat. Finally, though, she needed answers to her questions.

'How did you escape the crash?' she asked. 'Fitz told me your Lancaster had been found with a body inside. We all thought it was either you or Edwin. I've heard the report from the crew who baled out,' she added, to save him explaining the things she already knew.

Greg released a long, shaky breath. 'That's something I don't think I'll ever forget. Edwin and I struggled to keep the Lanc flying level for long enough to miss the houses. It took two of us at the controls. I'll never know how we managed it, but somehow we kept it in the air long enough to pancake onto the trees. It was still pretty hairy, but at least the branches broke our fall.' He gave a crooked grin. 'You know the saying: any landing you can walk away from is a good one.'

'Then it was your best landing ever,' Pearl said with fervour.

'I couldn't have done it without Edwin.'

'Remind me to thank him.'

'I will. He's going to need some gentle handling for a while.' He released a shaky breath before adding, 'You asked about the body.'

Pearl sat up, feeling sick, suddenly sure she knew what Greg was about to say. 'Oh no. *Edwin* killed him?'

Greg gave a single, curt nod. 'It was a German soldier, come to investigate the crash. We were still dazed but knew we were in occupied territory and needed to get away before we were found. But we had to collect our emergency ration packs first. Well, I don't know how this soldier had got ahead of his troop, but he stumbled upon us just as we were climbing out of the wreckage. He pulled his gun on me.' Greg shuddered and Pearl gripped his hand in her own. He squeezed her fingers and smiled. 'I'm fine, really. But it was clear the soldier was going to shoot and not attempt to take us prisoner. Edwin... I think he acted on instinct. He pulled his revolver and got his shot off first. Killed the man. Just like that.' Greg gazed into the distance and Pearl knew he was picturing the dead soldier. A moment later, he gave another little shake of the head, as though trying to dispel the image. 'Edwin saved my life. He hasn't said anything, but I can tell he's pretty cut up about killing a man face to face.'

'I can imagine,' Pearl murmured, her heart full of sorrow for the man who had studied astronomy before joining the RAF. Although she didn't know him that well, she thought that taking a life must be hard for someone who had devoted his life before the war to contemplating the mysteries of the universe. 'What happened next?'

'Well, we knew there must be more troops on the way, so we dragged the body into the Lanc and set fire to it, hoping to fool any soldiers into thinking there were no survivors. Then we legged it, as fast as we could seeing how shocked and bruised we were.'

'How come you're so thin?'

It was as though the light faded from Greg's face. 'There was no food. The Dutch people are starving. We couldn't get far that first night, and it was bitterly cold – the ground was frozen solid – but we daren't go to any of the houses for shelter in case they turned us in. We were desperate for a rest, though, and broke into an outhouse to take shelter. The owner found us and insisted on taking us into their house.' Greg gazed at Pearl, his face drawn as though he was in pain. 'There was a whole family there – parents, children, grandparents. And they were all starving. Can you guess what they had to eat?'

Pearl could only shake her head, dreading to hear yet knowing that Greg needed to talk about his experiences.

'Tulip bulbs. That's all they had. Yet they insisted on helping us and sharing their food.'

To Pearl's horror, tears started to drip down his face. She had never seen Greg cry before; he had always seemed to shrug off tragedy and positively revel in danger. She could only imagine what a terrible case the Dutch family must have been in to bring him to this state. Feeling helpless, all she could do was pull him close. 'I had no idea things were so bad over there,' she said after a while.

'Nor me.' He heaved another breath. 'I'll never complain about our rations again, that's for sure. Assuming I make it through this war, that's what I'll carry with me, and what will make me fight tooth and nail to prevent another one. The fact that little children can be starving to death while the troops who are tearing a country apart are getting fed.'

She kissed him, the only comfort she could offer, and Greg clung to her for long minutes before he resumed his tale. 'Well, we shared our rations with the family, not that we had much, but it beat tulip bulbs. The family insisted that we stay with them a few days until we'd fully recovered. We lay low in their attic to prevent any of their neighbours knowing we were there. But as soon as we could, we left to try and make it to Allied territory.' He gave a little laugh, and Pearl was relieved to see he was looking more like himself. 'If you're ever going to get lost in a strange land, make sure you've got a navigator with you who's an expert in astronomy. Edwin used the stars to lead us in the right direction. It was slow going, though, because we had to keep hiding up to avoid German troops. The whole region's in chaos, and we were afraid if any German soldiers saw us, they would shoot on sight rather than be lumbered with a couple of prisoners.'

'But you got here in the end, and that's all that mattered.'

'Exactly. It's a good thing the Allies managed to advance, or I doubt we'd have made it. We stumbled into a camp of Americans, and after a few days they were able to provide us with transport back to England.' He snorted. 'Probably glad to get rid of us before we ate all their food.'

'When did you get back?' Then another thought occurred to her. 'And why didn't you contact me? Do you know how worried I've been?'

He held up his hands in mock surrender. 'We only got to Market Harborough this morning and they wouldn't let us speak to anyone until we'd been debriefed and then

seen the MO. As soon as I could, I tried to telephone –
Fitz told me you were staying at the Gatehouse – but no
one answered.'

'That was you?' Pearl explained how the call had been
missed. 'I was terrified for ages afterwards. Why didn't you
call back?'

'Because I had to dash to catch the train. I didn't want
to miss a single moment with you.'

'I suppose I might forgive you, then.'

He leaned closer. 'And how would you feel if I told
you the MO has signed me off for at least a week?'

Pearl raised her eyebrows. 'I'd say you'd better be nice
to Deedee, because I'm sharing her room at the moment.
I mean, she's broad-minded, but even she has her limits.'

Greg murmured in her ear. 'We could always get a
room in a hotel. Just the two of us. Pick up where we
left off in Ludlow.'

Pearl opened her mouth to break the news of just what
she had been left with after Ludlow. Unfortunately the
moment was ruined when his stomach gave a loud gurgle.
Pearl was instantly concerned. 'When did you last eat? We
should find you something.'

Greg grimaced. 'I'm under strict orders to eat little and
often. I don't suppose there's any food in the ballroom?'

Pearl shook her head and scrambled to her feet, then
gave him a hand and helped haul him up. 'I'm sure they'll
have something in the kitchen, though. I've no idea where
it is, but we can explore.'

They wandered into the entrance hall, hand in hand,
only to meet Deedee and Thomas, who had evidently just
come in from the grounds. Before Pearl could comment
on their bright eyes or the fact that the pair were holding

hands, Deedee gave a cry and threw herself at Greg. 'I can't tell what a relief— but look at you, you're skin and bones.' She stepped back and took Thomas's hand again.

'We were just on our way to find food,' Pearl told her.

'Well, off you go. But don't be long. I'm dying to find out what happened to you.'

Greg was gazing at Deedee and Thomas's joined hands. 'I won't be long. And it looks like I'm not the only one with news.'

It only struck Pearl then how much Greg had missed in a relatively short time. 'You're not wrong.' She pointed at Thomas. 'Greg, I'd like you to meet my grandfather.'

Greg gave a start and said to the couple, 'You mean you got married? Congratulations!'

'No, I mean he's my actual grandfather. My mother's father.'

Greg looked stunned. 'I'm starting to wonder if this is all a mad dream.'

'Not at all,' said Deedee with a laugh. 'But your congratulations aren't far wrong. We are getting married.'

Now it was Pearl's turn to stare. 'When did that happen?'

Deedee gave a vague gesture in the direction of the grounds. 'Just now.'

Pearl had thought her happiness couldn't be any greater when she'd realised Greg was safe. Now she knew she'd been wrong. She thought her smile might split her face in two. 'That's wonderful news!' She kissed Deedee on the cheek, then turned to Thomas. 'I'm so happy for you, Thom—' She bit her lip. 'I really am going to have to start getting used to calling you Grandpa.' She kissed him on the cheek too.

Greg was looking completely baffled. Thomas – her *grandpa*, she corrected herself – stepped in to his rescue. 'I'm sure we've all got a lot of news to share, but you look like you need feeding up. I'll show you to the kitchen.'

Pearl, wishing she'd had the chance to tell Greg about the baby, called after him, 'Don't be long. I'll see you back in the anteroom. There's something important I need to tell you.'

Greg paused. 'Me too.' His face was suddenly serious. 'Oh, can you find Edwin and send him to the kitchen? He needs to eat too.'

On her way to find Edwin, Pearl waited long enough to say to Deedee, 'I really am so happy for you and Thomas.'

'And I can't tell you how relieved I am to see Greg safe and well. Or well as can be expected. What does he think about the baby?'

'I haven't told him yet. That's what I need to speak to him about. Look, I really want to celebrate his home-coming and your engagement, but I have to tell him first. Can you keep Thomas occupied without us for a while?'

Deedee gave a wicked grin. 'I think I can manage that. Oh, and don't worry about sleeping arrangements. Tom and I will be going back to his apartment.'

'Really? I didn't think he had a spare— oh.' Pearl felt her face burn. 'Really, Deedee, are you sure that's wise? You know how people like to gossip.'

Deedee put her hands on her hips. 'Considering we've already had a child together, I think we're way beyond worrying about decorum. Anyway, we're going to get married as soon as possible, so I don't see how a few days is going to matter. Wasn't it you who said we should cherish every moment together?'

Pearl shook her head, marvelling at how she was related to Deedee. 'Well, I won't try and stop you. I'm just surprised Thomas would suggest such a thing. I always thought of him as very proper.'

'Oh, I haven't told him yet. He won't argue, though.'

Pearl was sure he wouldn't. Trying not to think too much about her grandparents' love life, she went to find Edwin.

She saw him just inside the ballroom and quickened her pace. Then she skidded to a halt when she noticed Jenny beside him, her hand on his arm. Only then did Pearl spot the mistletoe dangling overhead. They would definitely not welcome an interruption now. She tried to back away unobtrusively but, before she'd taken two steps, Jenny raised herself on tiptoe and kissed Edwin on the lips. He made a reflexive move as though to put his arms round her waist, but then, to Pearl's surprise and dismay, he put his hands on her shoulders and gently pushed her away. 'I'm sorry,' he said. 'I can't do this. We can still be friends, though?'

Jenny smiled, although to Pearl's eyes it looked forced. 'Of course. I was just' – she pointed at the mistletoe – 'I'm sure it would have been bad luck not to kiss.'

'Oh. Yes. I didn't see it. Sorry.' Edwin shuffled his feet.

Taking pity on the pair of them, Pearl hastened forward. 'Oh, there you are, Edwin. Greg wanted me to remind you to eat. He's just gone to the kitchen.' She pointed out the direction where Greg and Thomas had gone.

'Thanks, yes.' Edwin patted his stomach. 'I ought to eat. Doctor's orders.' He bolted.

The moment he was out of sight, Pearl put an arm round Jenny's shoulders. 'I'm sorry. I was trying not to intrude, but I saw what happened.'

Jenny gave another strained smile. 'It's fine. Really. I just misunderstood his feelings. We're still friends, and that's the main thing.' Pearl gave her a searching look, but Jenny insisted, 'Honestly. I'm fine. Anyway, I don't want to spoil your reunion.'

In other words, Jenny was hurting but was hiding it so as not to spoil anyone else's evening. At any other time, Pearl would have tried to get her friend to share her feelings, but she was aware that it wouldn't be long before Greg returned, and she had to tell him about the baby. Promising herself to give Jenny all the attention she needed as soon as Greg's leave was over, she said, 'If you're sure,' feeling like the worst friend ever. Then, in two minds as to whether it would cheer Jenny up or make her feel left out, she said, 'There's good news about Deedee. She and Thomas got engaged.'

Jenny smiled, a genuine smile this time. 'Oh, that is good news. Where is she?'

'Out in the hall.'

Another round of congratulations later, Pearl and Greg managed to separate themselves from the group and slip unseen back into the anteroom.

Pearl decided to get the difficult conversation over with first. Well, after indulging in a spate of kisses. Pulling away reluctantly, she said, 'I was upset after our Ludlow break, because of what you said about volunteering for another tour.' He nodded but, before he could say his piece, she

301

went on, 'It made me realise how much we haven't really discussed. Like where we're going to live after the war, what we do for a living. All the important things we should have talked about before we got married.'

'I know.' Greg looked shamefaced. 'I know that's my fault, because of my reluctance to think too much about the future.'

'It's both of our faults. I didn't want to spoil our precious time together and, I admit, I was scared in case it turned out we disagree on something fundamental. But we can't go on like that. Of course we can't talk about everything right now, but promise me we'll have made a start on each topic before the end of your leave.'

'I promise. You're right, we can't avoid it any more. In fact...'

He paused to draw breath, and she leapt in before he could continue. 'I think I can make this easier for you. You've decided to volunteer for another tour.'

'I have. I know I said I wouldn't make any decision until after we'd discussed it properly, but ever since I met that starving family I haven't been able to get them out of my mind. Our advance seems to have ground to a halt and it's the civilians like that poor family who are suffering. I'm desperate to help, and the only thing I can do is go back to active service and try to finish the war as soon as possible. I owe it to them. Please don't try and talk me out of it.'

'I won't.' That was one of the most difficult things she'd ever said, but she knew it was the right thing to do. 'I've been selfish, trying to keep you safe when you knew your duty was elsewhere. And anyway, events have proved you weren't even safe as an instructor. No one will be safe until the war is over and, if you flying bombers again helps, then it would be wrong to stop you.'

Greg's tense features relaxed, and he pulled her close. 'I don't know what I did to deserve you.' They shared a lingering kiss. When they reluctantly broke apart, he said, 'I wish there was another way, I truly do, because I don't want to leave you.'

She forced a smile. 'Look on the bright side. You might be posted back here. Then we can finally live together, even if it is in RAF married quarters.'

'Now if that's not an encouragement to get back safely from each op, I don't know what is. Just think of all the time we can spend together when I'm not flying ops, just the two of us.'

'Three of us.'

She felt his arms stiffen round her waist. 'What?'

She leaned back in his embrace so she could study his face while she broke the news. 'That's the important thing I had to tell you. I know we agreed we wouldn't start a family yet, but—'

The rest of her words were smothered by a kiss. It was some time before they came up for air, Pearl laughing, giddy with relief. 'You don't mind?'

'Mind? I'm over the moon!' Greg pressed his hand over her still-flat stomach. 'There's really a little Pearl or Greg in there?'

'It's early days, but I'm pretty sure.'

'And how do you feel? This means you'll have to leave the WAAF. That's why I agreed we shouldn't start a family. I know how important your work is to you.'

The tears that never seemed far away reappeared in her eyes, only this time they were tears of happiness. She knew she was lucky to have a husband who cared for her the way he did and positively encouraged her in her work. 'I won't deny I'm going to miss the WAAF. That's why I'm going to keep quiet about the baby for now and work as long as I can. And after I leave… well, I've got time to think about it.' The events of recent weeks had taught her that carefully made plans could be shattered with no warning and that, while it was sensible not to rush blindly through life, she also needed to learn to be more flexible and bend with the prevailing wind.

'If there's one thing I know about you, it's that, whatever you put your hand to, you'll be a success. And you have my support, whatever you choose to do.'

She kissed him again. 'I knew there was a good reason why I married you,' she said with a happy sigh a while later.

The opening notes of 'Moonlight Serenade' drifted into the room, and Pearl grabbed Greg's hand. 'Come on. I love this number and I promised Deedee we'd join the dance and celebrate her engagement.'

And so the day that had begun with Pearl so miserable ended with her in Greg's arms, and as they swayed in time to the music, locked in an embrace, she revelled in a sense of homecoming.

Chapter Twenty-Six

Christmas Day was so joyful Deedee could almost forget there was a war on, if it hadn't been for the somewhat meagre amount of goose on their plates. Looking around the table, she couldn't believe how much her family had grown. Not only had Greg and Tom recently joined the ranks, plus the new addition that Pearl and Greg were keeping secret for now, but Fitz and Jenny were as good as family, as was Izzy. And if Edwin came to his senses and declared his obvious love for Jenny, then that would increase their number again. All in all, despite the worry of recent weeks the year had ended well, and Deedee refused to let the news that both Greg and Fitz were volunteering for another tour spoil the day.

When they had all eaten their fill, Tom rose and tapped his glass. 'If you'd have told me a few weeks ago that I'd be celebrating Christmas round a full table, I wouldn't have believed you. I'm sure Mrs Stockwell will forgive me for saying Christmas has been a lonely time these past few years. However, this year has shown me how quickly life can change. I was expecting no presents, yet I got the three greatest gifts anyone could hope for. I now have two remarkable granddaughters and will soon be married to the woman I thought I'd lost years ago. I don't have any gifts to give that can match such a treasure trove, but I have a few to hand out nonetheless.'

Deedee saw Thea and Pearl exchange curious glances. Tom had already presented Thea with a pocket watch that had belonged to his son, saying he knew she would be able to keep it in working order, and Pearl with her very own typewriter. He'd also managed to find gifts for everyone else, including a beautiful tortoiseshell hair comb for herself, that he said he had bought in Lincoln soon after she'd arrived in the hope that she'd accept it. Jenny had been particularly grateful for the little collection of books he'd given her. So what could he have left to give?

He drew two small jewel boxes from his pocket. 'When my late wife died, I gave away all her jewellery, as I had no children to pass them to. But I couldn't bring myself to give these away, for they had originally belonged to my mother.' He addressed Pearl and Thea. 'That's your great-grandmother, of course.' He handed one box to Pearl and the other to Thea. 'Go on. Open them,' he urged with a smile.

Thea opened hers first and lifted out a beautiful amethyst and diamond pendant on a fine gold chain. The pendant was crafted in a delicate flower shape, with long, oval amethysts set into each petal and a cluster of tiny diamonds making the centre. 'That's gorgeous,' she said. 'I don't know what to say. Thank you!'

For Pearl there was a heart-shaped gold locket, set with a circle of seed pearls surrounding a bright sapphire in the centre. 'Thank you so much,' she said huskily, and Deedee could tell she was fighting tears. She immediately turned to Greg and asked him to fasten it round her neck.

Deedee had expected that to be all and picked up her glass, expecting Tom to make his toast now, but instead he produced one last box. He looked at her and, when their gazes met, she felt a jolt of pleasure. 'Last but not least,' he began. 'This didn't come from my mother – I didn't think you'd want anything from my family after what they did to you – this is something I bought for you in 1893 and never got the chance to give to you.' This box was smaller than the others, and Deedee's heart sped up as she guessed what it must contain. 'You've already made me the happiest man in the world by agreeing to marry me, so I hope you'll now accept this.'

Deedee held her breath as she opened the box and caught a glint like firelight. Inside was the most beautiful ring she had ever seen. It was set with a brilliant topaz that gleamed first gold then amber then deep red as the candlelight caught different facets. The ring itself was platinum. 'I've never seen anything so beautiful,' she breathed. She didn't dare try squeezing it onto her ring finger – she knew she'd never fit it over her knuckle – but was gratified when she found it fitted her little finger.

'I'll get it resized,' he promised. 'I chose it because it's the perfect match for your rose: Heart of Hope. And now it's even more appropriate, because you've brought love and hope back into my life.'

Deedee couldn't answer that, her throat being too tight. Instead, she rose and kissed him, eliciting cheers from most and protests from their granddaughters.

Finally Tom raised his glass. 'A toast – Happy Christmas to one and all. May this be the last Christmas of the war and the first of many that we all celebrate as a family.'

Everyone clinked their glasses. Then Deedee saw Pearl murmur something in Greg's ear and he nodded.

Pearl rose. 'I think now's the right time to mention one more gift, although it isn't quite ready.' She smiled at her grandfather. 'You say you can't give anything to match the gift of your new family, but I want to say first of all that having you as my grandfather is one of the best things that's ever happened to me.'

'Hear, hear,' chimed in Thea.

'My only regret,' Pearl continued, 'is that we never knew you when we were children. So I've got a gift that I hope you'll be able to enjoy to the full.'

Thea must have cottoned on to what Pearl was referring to, for she gasped, 'You're up the duff!'

Pearl turned an icy glare on her sister. 'I wouldn't put it quite like that.' Then her lips twitched. 'But, yes, Greg and I are going to have a baby.' She pointed at Tom. 'And you're going to be a great-grandfather.'

'That's the best present of all!' Tom raised his glass again. 'To baby Tallis.'

'Baby Tallis!' the others chorused.

'May she be every bit as courageous, strong and independent as her mother, auntie and great-grandmother,' Tom finished.

'She?' Pearl asked, brows raised.

'Seeing the remarkable women this family turns out, I wouldn't want it any other way.'

Once everyone had drifted away from the table and the younger ones had started a boisterous game of charades, Tom turned to Deedee. 'You know, we haven't talked about where we'll live once we're married, but I do hope you'll come and live with me here. The Shrewsbury cottage is yours, of course, but we could rent it out.'

Deedee looked at her granddaughters, at Pearl, so soon to become a mother, and Thea who still faced an uncertain future while the man she loved remained in Bomber Command. 'Yes, we'll stay here,' she said. 'I want to keep an eye on this lot. Someone's got to keep them out of trouble and, whatever they get up to next, I wouldn't miss it for the world.' And she marvelled at the fate that had reunited her with the only man she had ever loved, and wondered what other adventures the Gatehouse would witness before the war was over.

Acknowledgements

I'm incredibly grateful to my editor, Emily Bedford, and agent, Lina Langlee, for encouraging me to try something different with this book. When I tentatively proposed giving Deedee and Thomas the central romance and putting Pearl through the wringer, I wasn't sure they would approve. However, their enthusiasm and belief in me gave me the confidence I needed, and I had so much fun in the process.

Thanks also to the whole team at Canelo for all their hard work, and I must give a special thank-you to the cover designer, Becky Glibbery, for producing what has to be my favourite cover ever.

Finally, to all the wonderful readers who have taken the time to leave reviews – thank you for giving me the encouragement to keep writing!